The Rancher's Lost Bride

THE RANCHER'S LOST BRIDE

A Malones of Grand, Montana Romance

Roxanne Snopek

TULE
PUBLISHING

Dedication

I have many loyal readers whose support has touched me deeply over the years. But my number one fan, for whom all books are dedicated, remains my husband, Ray. He believed in me long before I believed in myself, and that means everything.

PROLOGUE

J OSEPH PATRICK MALONE stood just outside the gate to the arena, sweating. The building had been built in the '50s and nothing about it, the ventilation especially, had improved in the ensuing the three decades. Hot summer dust rose around him, and the air was filled with the earthy odors of livestock and sawdust, and the cheers of rodeo fans.

He was having an excellent season. The last bull he'd drawn had been a high scorer, a real live one with some big moves, and JP had stuck it out. The sound of the buzzer as he leaped to safety, followed by screaming applause, still rang in his ears as he walked through the arena to the sea of trailers out back. Maybe he'd go out with some of the guys, to celebrate.

"Nice ride," said a voice behind him.

He turned to see a cute, curvy blonde in snug jeans and a Western shirt. Smooth, tanned skin glowed at her neckline and enough snaps were undone to reveal a hint of creamy cleavage.

"Thanks. I got lucky."

"You've got skill," she corrected. "You been doing this

long?"

He shrugged and continued toward the exit. She had an eager gleam in her pretty eyes, but he wasn't interested in starting a conversation with a buckle bunny too young to know better.

"I'm Heather," she said, keeping pace with him.

"I've got to feed my horse, Heather."

"I'll help you. He's beautiful. I watched you ride. He's got a great eye."

JP glanced at her in surprise. "You know cutting horses?"

"Everyone around here knows cutting horses."

He'd learned late and fast; no one, where he came from, knew anything about horses. Imagine if he'd have been brought up in this world. He could have been a star.

The outdoor air was cool and fresh, touched by the scent of approaching autumn. The crowds had begun to drift out of the building now that the main events were over. It was quiet on this side of the building, just tired competitors tending to their animals before they went out to find whatever they needed to ready them for tomorrow's events.

"What does JP stand for?" Heather asked.

He kept walking.

"Don't you have a last name? Or is it a stage name, like Cher?"

He turned. "Won't your parents be wondering where you are?"

Her smile faded. "I'm nineteen."

"Bullshit."

"What do you care?"

He rolled his eyes. "You're coming on like a freight train, Heather. You think that's smart? It's not. It's goddamn stupid. You're lucky I don't haul you into my trailer and—"

"Why don't you?"

He gaped at her. Part of him was kicking himself. She was here, who knew why, as ready and waiting as any girl he'd ever seen, and he couldn't let himself partake.

"I don't know you."

"I'm Heather Hudson. My mom always called me Honey, but she's gone now. I'm from Sweetheart. I live with my dad, but I'm saving up for a place of my own, somewhere with good light and space, where I could have a cat. I work in a diner, but I'm really an artist. Or, I'm trying to be, at least. Is that better?"

Something about her intrigued him. He hadn't seen her flirting with anybody else. Maybe she really did like him, in particular. For some reason.

"No. What do you see happening here, Heather?"

She tipped one shoulder. "We're getting to know each other. That's nice, isn't it? I don't know a lot of nice guys."

"I'm not a nice guy."

"I think you are. I've watched you. You're polite. You don't lose your temper. You're good to your horse. That means something."

They'd reached the trailer. Aramis gave a low whuffle, nudging Malone for his oats. JP stepped away from Heather, secured the horse in the shade, made sure his water was fresh

3

and cold, and tossed him a flake of alfalfa. This girl reminded him of Lizzie, but the feelings she stirred in him were in no way brotherly.

"It means nothing."

It had been too long since he'd been in the company of anyone other than men and boys like himself, rough, gruff, grubby cowboys not given to conversation. They weren't friends; they exchanged information, brief words of commiseration or briefer congratulations. They were competitors in the saddle, at work or at play, and they never forgot it. There was no room for softness.

She stepped closer to him and ran a finger down the placket of his shirt. "You're a good guy, aren't you, JP?"

He grasped her hand, tight enough to make her eyes flicker. "I'm not. You need to leave. Now."

CHAPTER ONE

"I NEED TO get away," Leila Monahan announced as her friend sidled up to her end of the bar. "Forever, if possible. Mexico would work. I could use my Spanish."

She'd closed at the gallery in Forsyth last night, then opened the pub this morning, so she was tired and cranky. She was behind on her research project, but she had such a bad case of writer's block she wished she'd never embarked on her art history degree in the first place. And she was still adjusting to no longer having a fiancé.

As usual, Kendall McKinley was decked out like a tropical bird in vibrant colors and windblown hair. While Leila's life was swirling the toilet bowl, Kendall's was on an upswing. Her SOS for a brief girls' night was about the only thing that could pull Leila away from sinking into a bowl of popcorn and *The Bachelorette*.

"*¿Cómo estás?* to you too. Is your father aware of your desire to flee the country? He's right behind you." Kendall used a low voice and screened her face with her blond mane, as if that would stop anyone from overhearing.

"I don't care." Leila sent him a glare.

Lou, the father in question, and owner of the pub, eyed

Kendall. "She's on a tear, my dear. Use caution."

"Or," Leila said, handing Kendall her wine, "accept the fact that I'm tired of pussyfooting around people who disagree with me. It's not always my problem. Sometimes I'm right and men are wrong."

"Cheers to that," Kendall said, lifting her glass. "I'm guessing we're still hating Gary. Congratulations."

"No Diana tonight?"

"Couldn't get away."

Diana Scott O'Sullivan, the third side of their triumvirate, had three small children. Time was fluid in her life.

Leila slipped off her Lou's Pub apron, gave her father a rough kiss on the cheek, poured herself a small mango wheat ale, and walked around the bar to give her friend a hug. The lunch rush had been more intense than usual, which was good for business, but hard on the back. The sting of her breakup had moved into the anger stage, mostly at herself for not seeing what was in front of her. But after years of refusing to set a date, her fiancé had sidestepped the conversation for the last time.

She'd met his *Why fix it if it ain't broke?* with *Don't let the door hit you on the ass.* And that was that. Goodbye. Forever.

Just another man with commitment issues.

Her father, for some reason, liked Gary and thought she should give him another chance.

"Let's take that four-top by the window," she said, leading the way through the tables. You'd think she'd prefer going someplace other than her father's pub, but given that

Lou might need her to step in if things got busy, this seemed easier.

"I hope you've got some crazy client story for me because I need a laugh," she said. "Dad's sad because he misses Gary. Gary, who probably wanted to wait for a senior discount on a wedding. And you know that old guy who delivers our liquor? He winked at me today. Winked!" She shuddered. "You got the last good man in the universe, I think. Come on, my friend. Distract me. What's up?"

Kendall glanced at her watch, then took a seat. "Don't be mad at me. I wanted to tell you sooner."

Her tone of voice, Leila noticed belatedly, was serious.

"What is it, Kenny? Are you okay? Are you—" she gasped, gripping Kendall's elbow "—pregnant?"

"Very funny." Kendall yanked her arm away and smiled apologetically at a table of older women who were listening avidly. "This is a one-hundred-percent baby-free zone, thank you very much."

They got settled at their seats and Kendall continued. "It's about a client of mine, but this will affect you."

"You're making me nervous, Kendall. Get to the point."

Kendall could always be trusted to know the comings and goings of Grand. She worked in real estate, so she knew it in a literal sense.

"I've been talking with him for a few weeks," she began. "He's looking for a place here." She took a sip of wine. Irish pubs weren't typically known for their wine lists, but Lou kept a stock of what his favorite customers preferred. Leila might be his best girl, but Kendall was his next best girl, so there was always a nice unoaked Chardonnay chilling for her.

"Yes?" Leila said. "It's your job, after all. So?"

"I wanted to warn you, but you know. Ethics." Kendall fingered the stem of her glass.

The sounds around them faded, drowned out by the sound of her pulse in her ears. She'd seen this kind of body language before. It never ended well.

Leila, your mom is sick . . . Leila, we have to sell the house . . . Leila, I love you but . . .

"Kendall." Her voice was hoarse. "You're scaring me."

Her friend reached out and gripped her hand. "Oh, honey, I'm sorry. It's nothing really. It's just . . ."

"What? For God's sake—"

"Leila." Kendall swallowed. "My client. It's Sawyer."

A beat passed. So many things had already flashed through her mind . . . but she hadn't been expecting this.

Sawyer.

Even now, his name had the power to both lift her heart and send it skidding into a tailspin.

But she'd had a lot of time and practice dealing with this, so she forced a laugh. "This is the worst joke ever, Kenny."

"I'm serious."

"Right," she snapped. Hurt was dangerous, but anger was powerful. "Like he'd show his face in this town again."

Kendall's expression didn't change.

That wasn't good.

"And he's just moving back? As if nothing ever happened?" Leila's voice had gotten high and a wee bit too loud, if the heads turned in her direction were any indication.

"So it seems."

"Sawyer Lafferty." Like there was another one.

"Yes."

"The same *cabrón* who dumped me because I wanted to get married and have kids, and then immediately got married and had a kid with someone else?"

"No one's arguing that he was a bas—" Kendall cut herself off with a grimace. "What you said. But I'm sure there's more to the story, Leila."

"Of course. There must be. Sawyer couldn't be the villain, could he? No, he's such a great guy. Whatever. I don't care." She was such a liar. "But that doesn't mean I want to see him and his happy family gadding around town together while I—"

She stopped abruptly.

While she what?

While she languished in a never-never land of broken dreams, her life on perpetual hold?

"I think he's single, Leila," Kendall said. "He's coming back alone."

She looked up at that. Sawyer, married, would be impossible. But Sawyer, single, could destroy her.

"What do you mean? Divorced? Widowed? Abandoned and brokenhearted?" A girl could hope, right?

"I mean," Kendall said, lowering her voice again. "He spoke in terms of 'I'm looking to buy a place,' not 'We're looking to buy a place.'"

Leila blew a raspberry. "Means nothing."

"Okay," Kendall said. "But when I asked what he and his wife do for work, he said, 'It's just me and I'll be managing Belle Vista.' You know, that new riding stable northeast of town."

Leila took a shaky sip of her beer. She'd heard that someone was setting up an equine therapy center about thirty minutes outside Grand. No one had mentioned that Sawyer Lafferty was involved.

"He's coming back, and he's alone." It was a surprise, but still nothing to her. She just needed to process it, that's all.

No man had ever made her feel the way Sawyer had. She knew now, in the cool aftermath of breaking her engagement, that she'd never loved Gary with anything like the kind of passion she'd once felt for Sawyer. She'd done him a favor in ending it. Even he, the skunk, the chicken, the relationship sloth, deserved someone who loved him fully.

She cleared her throat. "When?"

"Well," Kendall said, "I found him a nice little bungalow close to where his mom lives. He's put in an offer. Financing is in place, inspections are completed and the seller is motivated. Closing date, next month."

Next month.

Sawyer Lafferty was coming back into her life. Alone. Next month.

Suddenly, she felt faint. "I'm not ready," she whispered.

Kendall shifted around so that she was next to Leila. "I know, honey. It's a lot to take in. But you don't have to do a thing about this, okay? I just wanted you to know."

"Why now?" Leila said. "Why here?"

"Maybe his mom needs him," Kendall said. "Maybe he feels bad about how things ended with you and—"

"Don't say it!" Leila said with a hiss. She couldn't bear the thought. Sure, she'd fantasized for years that Sawyer would come back, that the wife and baby would magically (but harmlessly, she wasn't a psycho) disappear, that she and Sawyer could go back to where they'd been before she'd been so epically stupid and immature and stubborn and . . . young.

There's nothing to say that even if they hadn't had their awful breakup that their relationship would have survived them being parted for college. How many high school sweethearts end up together, after all?

Not many.

But now, her fantasy was coming true. Maybe. He was a father now, and even if his ex had the child, they would always be connected. His life was complicated, and Leila was dumb enough to fall back in love with him before they'd finished saying hello. And if that happened, and something went wrong again, how would she ever survive a second breakup with him? She wouldn't. That's how that would go.

CHAPTER TWO

P IPER LAFFERTY WAS overtired, overstimulated, probably hungry, and about to have a meltdown in the middle of the sidewalk. Sawyer picked her up and settled her on his hip, smoothing the tangled caramel curls off her sweaty neck. She was almost eight, chronologically, but petite for her age, a featherweight in his arms. Her emotional development was a little behind, however, despite the "old-soul" gaze he glimpsed on her occasionally. An eight-year-old who looked like six, with behavior that alternated between tired four-year-old and heart-sick forty-year-old. He pressed a kiss to her damp forehead.

It had been a rough week for him, a grown man, moving from Nevada to Montana, sleep disrupted by strange sounds and strange beds. They could have done it in three leisurely days, but he'd added a livestock delivery onto the first day, and then stopped at several ranches to look at horses over the next days. It was supposed to be a two-birds-one-stone situation, but he hadn't counted on a child's travel tolerance.

Or lack thereof. Any kid would be upset with so much change in such a short time. A kid who was missing her mother had license to lose her little mind, and it seemed like this might be the case.

"Daddy!" she cried, kicking his thighs. "Put me down! I'm not a baby."

"I know, Pipes." He tightened his grip. "But I can't have you running off on me."

"I won't! I promise."

Yeah, that's what she'd said ten minutes ago when he was checking them into the Yellowstone Hotel, just before she'd bolted out the door straight into the street. He'd nearly had a heart attack.

He needed his mother. Hopefully, she could handle Piper better than he could. A month in a hotel wasn't going to be easy, but the sooner Piper started acclimatizing, the better, with school around the corner. Secretly, he hoped his mom would invite them to stay with her while he waited to take ownership of the new house, but while she'd been enthusiastic about her only son moving back to town, she'd made it clear that part-time childcare was on offer, but not extended tenancy.

He didn't blame her. She had a good life now, with friends, hobbies, peace and, after so many years of struggle and sacrifice, she deserved it. Grandparents should be for short, fun-filled, happy stints. They weren't a replacement for parents.

Grandma wasn't a replacement for Mom.

But poor Pipes.

He felt like such a failure. What kind of husband drives his wife away? What kind of father doesn't know how to talk to his own daughter?

"Daddy!" Piper squirmed. "I want to walk!"

He put her down, but kept a tight hold on her hand. "There's a pretty park across the street," he told his daughter. "We've been cooped up in the truck for so long, right? Let's go stretch our legs for a few minutes."

Some fresh air, a chance to unwind. That's what they needed. He'd get some sandwiches, maybe some fruit and yogurt, and they'd eat them in front of the TV. Tomorrow, once they were rested, they'd head over to his mom's place.

Trees, shrubs, and a few picnic tables dotted the banks of the Yellowstone River. The soft rushing sound of the water and the warm, late afternoon sunshine began loosening the knots in his shoulders. Small groups of people moved to and fro, their conversation and laughter drifting over the breeze. He hoped they'd find friends here. He needed to settle, to give Piper some stability.

"Ducks!" Piper cried in delight.

He let her chase them, the birds quick to scatter or take to the wing. They were clearly used to humans, probably wanted to be fed. He found a picnic table and sat down, grateful to see his daughter running and laughing.

The stress of the past few months began to shift, but in its place came a crushing fatigue. Finalizing the divorce, selling the house in Spring Creek, the battle for custody—which shouldn't have been a battle at all, given Miranda's history—switching jobs . . . it felt like he'd been lurching from one crisis to the next for far too long.

He did not want to be here. Sooner or later, he'd have to face Leila Monahan, to congratulate her and wish her well. It hadn't been easy to hear that she was getting married, but he had no right to feel anything. She'd always believed in happily-ever-after. He hoped she'd found it.

Lou's Pub was still in business, he saw, though the owner and proprietor might not be thrilled to see him. After he and Leila broke up, well, he was pretty sure his name was mud for a long time. But if Lou was the man Sawyer remembered, maybe he'd have a little compassion, single dad to single dad.

If not, there were other places in town to get a beer. The Wayside Cafe, with its pretty awning and outdoor tables, probably wasn't licensed, but it looked like a good place for takeout. He'd give Piper another minute or two before heading over.

He sighed and some of the tension in his chest eased. Blue sky peeked through leafy branches and, for a moment, he just let himself be still.

They would be okay.

He would be okay.

Happily-ever-after wasn't for everyone. For him, happiness arrived unexpectedly, in small, electric moments, usually in the aftermath of panic.

Piper was the joy of his life, but there was so little time, and those moments flashed by so quickly. Maybe here, he'd be able to find more of those moments.

A squeal of tires jolted him upright, as if conjured by his thoughts.

"Piper?" He scanned the grass. She'd been there just a moment ago. "Piper!"

There, half a block away and, horrifyingly, already halfway across the street.

He raced across the grass and darted into traffic. Vehicles swerved and horns blared, and in the chaos, he lost sight of his daughter. Once on the sidewalk, he stopped and stood, turning in circles.

"Piper?" he shouted. He turned to passersby. "Have you seen a little girl? About this high, light brown hair, wearing . . . a red ball cap and . . ."

He couldn't remember what she was wearing.

Strangers gaped at him as he whirled this way and that, scanning the business fronts. Where would she go?

"Lose something?" someone said.

It was Lou Monahan. A little older, but otherwise the same friendly, implacable Irishman he'd always been.

"My daughter," Sawyer gasped. "Have you seen her?"

Lou tipped his head toward the heavy doors of the pub. "She has excellent taste, your lass. I saw her sneak in when the door was open."

"Piper!" He ran after her, but after the bright summer sunshine, the dim indoor lighting left him half-blind.

All eyes turned to him, and conversation lowered as it always does when you want the earth to open up and swallow you whole. He scanned the room frantically, but no wispy-haired demon-child appeared anywhere.

How much trouble could she get into inside a place like

this? At least there was no traffic to run her down.

Then he heard a surprised shout in a young female voice, followed by a crash.

Sawyer sighed. All he had to do was follow the trail of destruction and he'd find his daughter, the one creature on earth who held his heart in her antsy little hands and threatened every day to crush it to smithereens.

✪

LEILA SAW DIANA making her way to their table and lifted her hand, but before they made eye contact, she heard a whoop. She looked up just in time to see Sam, one of their servers, windmill her arms, which were unfortunately laden with a tray of clean glasses. Leila leaped to her feet, all thoughts of Sawyer gone, instantly guilt ridden about all her self-centered complaints. She should have made sure the floors were mopped properly, shouldn't have left Sam and Lou carrying the post-lunch load alone, should have made sure her father took a break before she met her friends.

He wasn't a young man anymore. What if he slipped on broken glass? He could break a hip . . .

All this flashed through her mind in a split second, as a lifetime of fear came home to her. If something happened to her father, who did she have?

No one.

If she turned her back on her father, who did *he* have?

No one.

A cheer went up from the patrons as Sam raised both hands in the air and then took a bow.

She was okay, thank goodness, but where was Lou?

Before Leila took two steps, something careened into them. A small, warm package of young human.

"Oof," said the package, which then sank to the floor and burst into tears.

A little girl.

"Hey, *niña pequeña*," she said, squatting next to the child. "Where'd you come from?"

"Good thing this landed in your lap." Kendall leaned away as if the child had scabies. "I petitioned to get my tubes tied at sixteen."

Diana reached them then and slung her bag over the back of her chair. "So much for my kid-free evening."

The child sat huddled between the table legs, sniffling.

"The view's better up here," Leila said.

The kid kicked a leg out at her.

Leila ducked. "I hate to break it to you, *chica*, but we have a strict no-fighting rule here."

"I don't care! I have to go pee! And I want to go home!" The last word ended on a wail.

"And I," Leila replied calmly, "would dearly like to see that as well. But I can escort you to the washroom. How about we start with your name?"

"No!"

"Okay, Ms. No," Leila said without missing a beat. "I'm Leila. Upsy-daisy. Where're your parents?"

Under a faded ball cap, the kid had gossamer caramel-colored hair that curled in wisps around her face. There were circles under her eyes that suggested she was badly sleep-deprived. Something twisted deep in Leila's belly.

"I don't know-oh-oh!" cried the waif. She wore a pink T-shirt with little ruffled cap sleeves and denim shorts, both of which could have used a laundering. The faint evidence of some snack or meal clung to her cherubic cheeks. There was a linear scab from a scratch on her thin, tanned forearm, and this mark, accompanied by the wrenching wails, touched something in Leila's heart.

To a little one like this, being temporarily misplaced carried the same level of panic as losing a parent permanently. Whichever it was, this kid was spiraling into a dark place.

She sat on the floor next to the weeping child and put her arm around her. "Hey, hey, it's okay. Let's go to the bathroom and then I'll help you find them, okay? Do you want some pizza after? We have great pizza here."

The child glared at her. "Pineapple pizza?"

She pronounced it PINE-uh-pull. So cute.

"We do. Is that what you like?"

The kid gave a decisive nod. "Daddy hates it."

"My dad, too, and that makes them weirdos, doesn't it? Ham and pineapple is the best pizza combo ever."

So what if she never got married and had a family of her own? She'd look after her dear old dad, get a couple of nice cats, maybe an orange one named Simon and a silver tabby named Tabitha. They'd be fine.

She didn't need a husband to keep her company, especially one that spent half his life on the road. Lou had spoiled her for all other men, trained her to have high standards that apparently no one else could meet.

Almost no one, anyway.

Her mind skittered away from that thought. Later. Not now.

The little girl squirmed.

Leila held out her hand. "Bathroom?"

The child nodded.

The small hand felt warm and sticky in her own, and it triggered a flush of yearning in her. The trust and responsibility that went along with caring for a child—what a beautiful, terrifying, wonderful gift.

She waited for the child outside the stall and then helped her wash up because the little thing couldn't quite reach the sink.

"I'm tired," whispered the girl.

Leila hesitated. "Do you want me to carry you?"

The child nodded, not meeting her eyes, and Leila hiked her up onto her hip. Instinctively, the girl wrapped her little legs around her waist and tucked her head onto Leila's shoulder.

Oh, dear. This felt . . . tremendously good. Too good, given that she'd just ditched the front-runner for baby-daddy. Maybe it was time to reconsider going solo.

As she exited the washroom, a voice come from the area of the front entrance and carried across the crowded bar.

"Piper!"

Immediately, the hairs on the back of her neck lifted.

She knew that voice.

The little girl lifted her head. "Daddy," she said in a small, hitching voice.

Leila froze. Daddy?

She wasn't ready. He wasn't supposed to be here for a month!

She pulled back and looked at the child. She was about the same size as Diana's son, who was entering kindergarten shortly, but the gamine features on this tyke suggested she was older than she looked. For some reason, in Leila's mind, Sawyer's baby had remained a baby.

Nine years ago, he'd smashed her heart by marrying someone else, and then ground it into the dust by immediately starting a family.

Everything Leila had ever wanted with him, he'd gone and done with some other woman.

Piper squirmed away from Leila and allowed herself to be scooped up into a pair of strong arms that swooped in front of them.

"You scared the crap out of me, Pipes," the man said, and the voice was as strangely different as it was horribly familiar.

"Oh!" he added, suddenly noticing Leila. "Oh."

Leila backed away from them, bumped her hip on the corner of a table, jostling a couple of beer bottles that, thankfully, remained upright. She could feel the blood pounding in her cheeks. Years ago, she'd have given anything to have this man walk into her pub. Now, she'd give anything for him not to be here.

"Hey, Sawyer," Leila said, aiming for a casual tone. As if that were remotely possible.

"Leila."

Sawyer's voice was low and rough, just like she remembered, and a rush of heat flooded the skin on her throat. She gripped the edge of the table.

"This is yours, I take it?" she said, nodding to the child nestled under his chin.

He nodded slowly. "Her name is Piper."

"So I gathered. I think she wants her mom. Your wife, I guess that would be, correct?"

Sawyer blinked, those dark eyes holding hers, full of meaning but nothing she could determine. "Thanks for helping. She's fast and very determined." He looked at Lou, who was back at Leila's side, a guardian angel in a pub apron. "Let me know the damage and I'll Venmo you the amount."

Lou waved away the offer. "Did you and the sprite need refreshment? A ham and pineapple pizza is about to come out of the oven. I understand the sprite has a fondness for this abomination."

"What's a bomb nation?" Piper asked. "What's a sprite?"

"You're the sprite," Sawyer said, "and Mr. Monahan here agrees with me about pineapple on pizza."

"Because you're weirdos," Piper said. At Sawyer's expression, she added, "The nice lady said! Right?"

"One hundred percent," Leila replied, biting back a smile.

Sawyer gave a little huff which might have been laughter, might have been exhaustion. It was hard to tell. "The nice lady is named Leila. Can you thank Leila for keeping you company?"

"Thank you, Leila, for taking me to the bathroom," Piper said promptly. "I like you because you're not a weirdo about pineapple."

"That's debatable." Sawyer turned to Lou. "Would it be possible to get that pizza to go? This one has had a long day and I need to get her back to the Yellowstone. Sorry again about the mess."

"You go ahead," Lou said with a wave. "I'll have someone run it up to you once it's ready."

Sawyer turned to go, then paused to look at Leila. "Thank you. I really appreciate it."

She looked into those fathomless eyes, the ones that once held the world in them for her, the ones that had turned away from her and made a new life without her.

"You have a lovely daughter," she said. "Congratulations."

Then she softened her voice and looked at the little girl. Whatever failings of the man she'd been dealt, the child didn't deserve to be punished for them. "Nice to meet you, Piper. Thanks for running into me. Most fun I've had all day. Get some sleep, okay, kiddo?"

The little girl gave her the ghost of a smile, and something turned over inside Leila. She was a sweet kid.

A sweet kid that Sawyer had immediately fathered after breaking Leila's heart.

★

SAWYER WAS RUNNING water in the hotel bathtub when a knock came at the door. Piper was on the bed, watching cartoons. She was fighting sleep but her eyes kept drifting shut. He hoped she'd be awake long enough to get a piece of pizza into her. They hadn't been eating particularly well while on the road. Not that pizza was much of an improvement.

He opened the door to find Leila Monahan, in ripped jeans, a white sweater, and a silver chain around her neck. He'd barely had time to look at her earlier; now, he couldn't stop. Her dark hair was a little shorter than he remembered, though it still waved down around her shoulders in a way that begged him to touch it. Her eyes were as bright and wide and honest as ever, though there was a faint line between her eyebrows that was new. She held herself bowstring tight and had spots of color high on her cheekbones. She had a pizza box in one hand and two plastic bags in the other, one of which appeared to hold a four-pack of craft beer.

"Lou made me do it. I didn't want to interrupt your evening. There were other servers, but . . . anyway." She held out the bags. "He said you'd need it. There's macaroni and cheese, carrot sticks, and chicken fingers too. We don't really have a kids menu, but he likes to have stuff on hand for when families come in."

She was nervous.

He'd been nervous about seeing her again for the first time, too, but Piper had taken care of that nicely. Now that they were talking in relative privacy, however, it all came back.

It made him feel better to see that she felt the same way.

"Thanks," he said, taking the bags. "Do you, uh, want to come in?"

Her life had gone on, just as his had. He'd always hoped she was happy. He hoped he'd imagined how intensely they'd loved each other. He hoped she'd found someone better than him.

"Me? No! I mean, I'm just the delivery girl." But she bit her lip and didn't move to leave. "Kendall told me earlier this evening that you were moving here, but she said next month. I guess I'm the last to know. When did you, uh, get into town?"

He took pity on her. "Yeah, I wanted to get settled as soon as possible, so we came early. Arrived a couple of hours ago. In that time, Piper's run off twice. She's pretty mad at me. Thanks for catching her. She can be a handful."

He felt a little traitorous saying that about his daughter, but there was also relief. There was a lot about Piper's behavior that worried him; bolting was just one, but it was the one that scared him the most.

"Um," Leila looked over his shoulder. "Where's . . . where's . . . her mother?"

Right. He'd been on his own for so long, he tended to forget that not everyone knew it.

"Piper's mom isn't with us."

"Oh." Her eyes widened. "I'm so sorry."

He was such an idiot. "She's alive, I don't mean that. But she's not . . . in our life. In Piper's life. She's not . . . we're not together anymore."

"Oh!" Her voice softened. "Well, I'm still sorry. That must be tough."

"Tub's running," he said. "I've got to turn off the tap. Come in, just for a minute, okay?"

He wanted to tell her everything that had happened to him over the years, how he was a single father now and how he'd never stopped loving her, how maybe now that he was in Grand again, they could see if there was anything left between them.

"I don't think so, Sawyer," she said quietly. "I don't know you anymore, and I don't want to start any gossip."

"Right," he said, remembering the fiancé he'd heard about. "I heard you're getting married. Congratulations."

A pained expression flickered across her features. "Enjoy the pizza. Tell Piper good night for me."

And she left, taking the little brightness of the day with her. Just as well. She was promised to another.

Karma was a bitch, as they said.

CHAPTER THREE

Billings, Montana

T HE GREEN OF spring came not a moment too soon for humans and livestock alike. The frostbite JP had suffered on his right hand made him clumsy with the lasso. He hoped the numbness would resolve. Team roping was his best hope of making money this weekend. And he needed the money.

He was bent over, checking his horse's feet, when the girl found him. Again.

"I knew we'd see each other again."

Heather. She looked just as good as she did a year ago. Better, maybe.

"You stalking me?" he asked, keeping Aramis's back hoof braced on his leg.

"I like rodeo."

"You like cowboys."

"Just one."

He set the horse's leg down and straightened. She was smiling, like she'd come to invite him to dinner at her grandmother's house. She had on the same outfit that everyone did: jeans, boots, a Western shirt with pearl snaps.

Many girls wore more makeup, tighter jeans, and showed more skin than Heather did.

The girl-next-door thing was incredibly appealing. He wished he knew if it was real or engineered for effect.

"What do you want from me, Heather?"

"I told you last year. I like you."

He exhaled, frustrated and flattered equally. "You don't know me."

"Don't you like being liked?"

She asked it so innocently, but he didn't trust her. He'd heard of girls who found the raw testosterone irresistible, who sought out cowboys, thinking they could tame them, fix them, turn them into respectable family men.

He would never be a respectable family man. Shame trailed him like smoke. If she couldn't see it, then he was grateful, but it didn't mean he'd let her throw herself away on him.

"I'm pretty busy here."

He went to put the hoof pick away and when he turned, she was right behind him, pushing him against the door of the trailer.

"You want to show me your trailer?"

For a moment, he felt the warmth of her body, mere inches from his. He backed up, tripped on the step and before he knew it, he was on his back in the straw, with Heather on top of him. Her eyes were so blue, her mouth a pink O of surprise. His breath was coming faster, and the warmth and softness of her skin was spreading through his callus-roughened fingers, infusing him with the desire to lose himself in something warm and sweet, kind and gentle.

Then she smiled. "Can I kiss you?"

He slid out from beneath her, though his body was aching to keep her there, to slam the door shut and take what she was offering.

"Go away, Heather."

Her face fell. She swallowed, and when she spoke, her voice was husky. "I'm not a bad girl, JP."

"I'm sure you're not, but whatever you think this is"—he gestured between them—"you're wrong. I'm leaving tomorrow morning. Might never see you again."

"I found you. I'll find you again."

There it was, that determination, for no apparent reason. He couldn't understand it.

"Why?" he demanded. "Why me?"

"I told you," she said patiently. "I've been watching you. I have a good sense about people. I like you. You're a good man. I want to know you more."

"Wherever you think this is headed, it's not. I go from job to job, living out of my truck. I've got no money, no house. I don't just sleep with random women and disappear."

Her smile returned. "You see? This is why I like you. You are a good man. We could write to each other. You could tell me when you'll be around again, so we can meet up."

She liked him.

It had been a long time since he'd heard that from anyone.

CHAPTER FOUR

Twelve years earlier

LEILA WAS IN high school when she first laid eyes on Sawyer Lafferty. Grand Secondary didn't get a lot of new students; most kids had been together since kindergarten, so seeing an unfamiliar face was a big deal. And this particular student was something different, especially to the female population. When Mrs. Higgins entered her homeroom that day, she said, "Class, we have a new student. He and his family have just moved here from California. Please give him a warm welcome!"

Leila had been chatting with a couple of friends about the upcoming English exam, but one look at Sawyer gave *The Catcher in the Rye* a whole new meaning.

Sawyer, with his lean slouching beauty, had a tragic air that made her want to take him in her arms. When he tossed that long fall of dirty-blond hair, revealing intense, observant, unsmiling eyes, she knew she was in trouble. She'd never dated much, with the awkwardness of boy-girl dances in middle school triggering more laughter than lust, as far as Leila was concerned.

But this boy was different.

For the first few weeks after his arrival, she watched him. They shared several classes, and she quickly saw that he was a good student, smart and diligent. Math and accounting were his strong suits. Leila was aiming for a career in the arts and had no use for calculus, but she appreciated a mind that did.

She wanted him. Being inexperienced in love, she had no idea what to do about this and got horribly, ridiculously tongue-tied around him. Leila made friends easily, so this awkwardness mystified her. She could be joking around with a group of pals, her usual self, but when Sawyer appeared, she froze. Her throat thickened and her thoughts scrambled, and the air didn't seem to make its way to her lungs. It didn't help that he rarely spoke and never looked directly at her. She was aware of him down to the skin of her fingertips but wasn't even sure he knew she existed.

It was a problem.

WHEN HIS MOTHER told him they had to move to Grand for a few months so she could look after her sick sister, Sawyer had been dead set against it. He was heading into senior year. All his courses were chosen. His top-pick college applications were ready to go.

But Aunt Lindsay needed her.

"Just for the summer," Mom said. "Just while she's going through chemo."

Shortly after they arrived, however, they learned that

Aunt Lindsay had maybe eighteen months to live. Mom wasn't going to leave her, so Sawyer had to make a choice. Stay with his mother in Grand and fight like hell to get all his credits transferred or return to California and live with his father.

Unfortunately, Sawyer's father wasn't any more interested in welcoming his teenage son than Sawyer was in joining his dad's second family. It had been only three years and one month since Steve Lafferty had been caught in a "moral failing," when his latest long-legged, much younger girlfriend Mia Tornado—yes, that was her name—got pregnant for the first time. Sawyer now had three half brothers, one-and-a-half, two-and-a-half, and three-and-a-half years of age.

The kids were the only part of the whole thing that he didn't wholeheartedly despise. He'd always wanted siblings. These were so much younger than him, they almost didn't count, but they looked up to him with enough adoration that it was hard to resist. They were pretty cute, actually. Mia didn't trust him to babysit, thank the Lord, so when he came for mandatory visitation time with his father, he spent it mostly playing with the rug rats in the vast room over the garage that had been converted to a children's paradise.

He'd never had anything like that when he was little. Guess the insurance business had blossomed since he'd been that age.

He'd miss the brats while he was here, and Dad was pissed about it. Probably not because he'd miss seeing Sawyer, but because Mom had done something on her own initiative. Dad didn't like not getting his way, and he was completely unprepared for Wife of Years Past to do something unexpected.

That part made Sawyer happy to be in Grand. The cheating bastard had had everything his way for far too long. Mom refused to believe that her handsome, charming husband was gone for good. She, in good Christian tradition, was willing to forgive him and welcome him back. What she intended to do about the three musketeers, Sawyer wasn't entirely sure. Dad wasn't leaving Wife 2.0 to go back to Mom, no matter how much she prayed, and why she even wanted him back was a mystery to Sawyer. The man was a snake.

Sawyer hoped getting out of California might help his mom accept the divorce, but, while he knew his dad had court-ordered obligations to look after her, he didn't trust that Steve wouldn't find a way to weasel out of them. So, he intended to graduate high school, go to college, get a good job, buy a house, and make sure neither he nor Mom ever had to beg Dad for a single red cent ever again.

That had been his plan for the past three years.

Grand, Montana, was a major glitch.

But he forced the anger into a tight little ball deep in his stomach and adjusted his plan. He'd study his ass off, get his college applications in, and count the days until he left this sleepy little hick town.

Then, on the first day of school, full of nerves about breaking into long-established social circles, he followed Mrs.

Higgins to his new homeroom . . . and he got his first sight of Leila Monahan.

She had a quick laugh that sounded like music, and graceful hand movements that looked like dancing. Dark-eyed, dark-haired, with dark expressive brows that could convey so much with one quirk, yet she seemed somehow lighter and softer than the tough, tanned, toned girls of Monterey. Snow White, ranch version.

There was no point in making friends or getting involved in anything. There was certainly no point in getting involved with a girl. His mom needed him, his aunt was getting sicker, and juggling college prep with a full course load took up most of his spare time.

So, the things he felt for Leila Monahan were completely, one-hundred-percent unwelcome.

★

A FEW DAYS after Sawyer and Piper returned to Grand, he walked out of Styles Realty with the keys to his new house in hand. Less than a decade ago, he'd arrived here a resentful, self-centered little prick. Now, bludgeoned into humility by life, he recognized the beauty of the community and hoped whoever remembered him might be generous enough to welcome him back.

He recalled his real estate agent Kendall McKinley from high school, though he hadn't known her well. She'd been a friend of Leila's and therefore had reason to hate him, but she'd kept things completely professional and found him the perfect house, for which he was grateful.

Piper was at his mom's, so he drove out to take another walk-through by himself. The little bungalow was on the northeast side of town, convenient for dropping Piper off at his mom's house on the way to work. Knowing he was anxious to get settled, Kendall had unexpectedly managed to get the possession date moved up. The moving company, however, couldn't adjust their schedule to deliver any earlier than next week. Hurry up and wait, that's what moving was about. Lurching from crisis to crisis, that was his life.

As he parked in the concrete carport, he felt a moment of anticipation that maybe now things would become smoother. A new home for him and Piper, a fresh start, with no bad memories permeating the walls. He got out and admired the little house before walking through the gate into the back. His mom wanted him back for lunch, so he wouldn't stay long; she was loving time with Piper, but she was scheduled for a new knee and the activity wasn't doing the old knee any good.

The yard, fully fenced, was small but had enough space for a play structure, maybe a sandbox or a little experimental garden where Pipes and her friends could grow radishes or sweet peas. He could put a swing on the big shade tree on the west side. The room overlooking the yard had twin dormer windows; Piper would love that. He would build bunk beds so she could have sleepovers.

He turned the key in the back door and stepped inside

just as his cell phone vibrated with an incoming call.

Miranda.

He leaned against the wall, preparing himself for a conversation that he'd been dreading.

She dove right in, without greeting. "You can't take her so far away from me, Sawyer. How am I supposed to see her?"

"Hi, Miranda." He kept his voice calm. "I see you finally contacted your attorney."

"Sawyer!"

"I don't even know where you are right now! You could be couch-surfing again. You could be living with some guy you met last weekend. You could be back with Travis."

"I'm not."

"How do I know?" He paced to the kitchen and stared, unseeing, out the window to the backyard. "The only reason I knew about Travis is because Piper told me when she woke up from a nightmare. What happened, Miranda? She won't talk about it."

His pulse was pounding, as it always did when he thought about all the things that could have traumatized his little girl.

"That was months ago. It was just a fight. Nothing happened."

True, Piper had no physical marks from the event, but whatever she'd witnessed had been enough to get her wetting the bed again. He'd refused to let Piper visit after that, and now he had enough ammunition to win the battle permanently. He hoped.

"Since then, you've had two DUIs. You got picked up for drugs—"

"Marijuana is legal now."

"Cocaine isn't. You've been pumped full of Narcan once that I know of."

She snorted into the phone. "Paramedics overreacted."

He took a deep breath and played his ace. "How about the 5150 hold?"

California law enforcement could commit someone into psychiatric care for up to seventy-two hours if they believed that person was a danger to herself or others.

Silence.

"Miranda," he said, softer now, "you must have known I'd find out."

He could hear her breathing shakily on the other end, but she didn't reply.

"Miranda, you know that I can take Piper wherever I want, as long as I inform your attorney. Which I did." He rubbed a familiar ache at the base of his skull. "Why don't you sign away your parental rights so we can stop this charade? It's no good for Piper and it's killing you. Please, Miranda."

"And let my daughter believe I've abandoned her?" Miranda's voice was thick with tears. "I love her."

"You're not well."

"I'll get better. And when I do, I'll be a mom again and she'll be happy about it. You'll see."

The words sent a shiver of icy dread down his spine because that was the shit of it. Piper missed her mother. When Miranda was okay, she did love Piper. But her periods of being okay were unpredictable. When Piper was with her, he couldn't sleep for fear that Miranda would simply refuse to bring her back or, worse, take her and disappear.

It was a risk he couldn't take.

But for all his fear, Piper still wanted her mother.

"I don't owe you anything," he said, squeezing his eyes shut. "But, if you come to Grand, I'll let you see her. Under my supervision."

"Like I'm a distant relative."

"You said it, not me."

"Whatever."

"If you come, let me know first, okay? No surprises."

"Fine."

She hung up.

He slipped the phone into his pocket and walked back out to his truck. In the waning light, shadows shifted over his pretty little house, revealing warped siding and shutters that needed repainting. The big shade tree stood still, like a sentry.

CHAPTER FIVE

"*MIERDA*," LEILA MUTTERED to herself. They didn't teach curse words in Spanish class, but everyone learned them anyway. Her concentration, after discovering that Sawyer Lafferty was back in town, was shot. She closed her laptop with a snap and tossed it onto the bed near her feet. "Some mysteries aren't meant to be solved."

The mystery she was trying to solve: the cultural significance of intentional mimicry in eighteenth-century oils and whether it should be considered copyright infringement by current standards.

The real mystery: who cared?

She leaned back against the pillows and squeezed her eyes shut and tried not to think about what might have happened with the mother of Sawyer's child and how long he'd be around.

Why had she ever wanted a degree in art history in the first place? The only people more boring than artists were art historians, and she was both. Or at least, she might be if she ever finished this project. Right now, the most useful thing she'd gained from her lengthy studies was an expensive arsenal of Spanish swear words.

"Here's another mystery, Mom," she said out loud. "If an aspiring artist waits tables for a living while being a perpetual student, what's her true occupation?"

"Your mother," Lou said from her bedroom door, making her jump, "would answer same as me, darlin'. You're an artist. No 'aspiring' about it and no starvin', either, if I have anything to say about it. Diana and Kendall just walked in downstairs. Go have a bite to eat with them. The dinner rush will be upon us soon enough."

"See?" she said, sliding off the bed. "I'm a waitress."

"Only because you take pity on your dear old dad."

She gave him a kiss. "You'd scare away all our customers, and then where would we be?"

Lou's Pub was an icon of the Grand community, largely because Lou Monahan knew everyone, loved most of them, and didn't hesitate to boot out those who deserved it. He was almost as protective of his town and his bar as he was his daughter, and he'd earned his reputation as an honorable man.

Leila was lucky. She'd never questioned her father's love or his support. Not everyone had that, and she didn't take it for granted.

"Boyd's making fish tacos for today's special." Lou's expression darkened. "Try them out, will you, love? I don't want him poisoning our friends."

"I'm sure they'll be great, Dad. It's nice to change things up now and then."

Lou made an Irish sound deep in the back of his throat

and went back down to the bar. He wasn't a fan of change, especially when it involved food. Or the pub. Or Leila.

She packed up her study material and slipped on a sweater. She and Lou lived in the apartment above the pub. They'd had a house back when Mom was alive, but Lou had sold it to pay her medical bills.

She hurried down the narrow staircase, running her hand along the polished wooden handrail. Even though architecture wasn't her focus, she knew enough to appreciate the beauty of their building and had played an instrumental role in getting it added to the historic society's list of protected heritage buildings.

When she rounded the corner that led to the pub, Diana was waving at her.

"Leila!"

Despite having a house, a husband, and three small children, Diana Scott O'Sullivan looked like a rosy-cheeked schoolgirl ready to break into song. If Leila didn't love her so much, it would be easy to hate her. Diana had ended up with the life that Leila had once expected for herself. Some high school sweethearts, at least, could make it work.

Leila greeted her with a hug. "How are the munchkins?"

"Just before I left, I caught Marcus entertaining Olivia and Reese by shooting ear plugs out of his nose," she said. "I swear, I'll count my life a success if I can channel that boy's power for good and not evil. His current obsession is to get a ride in an ambulance. He's going to be the death of me."

Kendall's fiancé, Dr. Brade Oliver, had developed a close

relationship with Diana's family by being their favorite emergency room physician, but also by discovering, while searching for his biological roots, that he and Diana shared a mother, Heather Hudson Scott. Together, they'd learned that Weldon Scott, Diana's father, had let everyone believe his wife was dead rather than admit that she'd abandoned them when Diana was a toddler. Whether she was still alive remained a mystery, as did the identity of Brade's biological father.

Unlike Brade's parents, Leila's had always been open about her adoption. They didn't have much information for her about her birth parents, but she'd never felt the need to search for more. Brade's journey, however, had piqued her interest. That, and the idea of conceiving a child with donor sperm, was making her think she ought to piece together her own genetic heritage.

"Parenting. You love it," Leila said, pouring them each a glass of low-alcohol cider.

"I'd love it more if Rand didn't egg him on quite so much." Diana narrowed her eyes. "I think the next time that kid needs something pulled out an orifice using guided imagery, it'll be Daddy's job to hold him down. Let's see how much he laughs, then."

It was good to see Diana enjoying her life again. Her third pregnancy had been complicated and no one had fully realized the extent to which it had affected her mental health as well as her physical health. But once little Reese was safely, if dramatically, delivered, and Diana got the support she'd needed, she'd returned to the happy, sassy friend they all knew and loved.

Leila put their order for the fish tacos in with the cook. "Where's Kendall? And how'd you score a night off?"

"She's running late. Said to go ahead without her." Diana made a face. "I think Rand would rather feed the horde himself than listen to me anymore."

Leila understood Rand's position. "The search for your mom."

"Yes!" Diana reached across and took Leila's hand. "Brade's added the new information to all his adoptees-seeking-birth-parents databases, and he's hoping something will hit. I'm placing ads in various print publications, as well as online, looking for anyone who knows something about my mom from that time. Checking missing persons reports. I feel it in my bones that she's still alive, Leila." She shivered. "All those years I thought my mom was dead and now I find out she's alive!"

Maybe, thought Leila. Maybe not. That was a lot to hope for, given the time she'd been gone.

"She's out there somewhere," Diana continued, "and we're going to find her. I could have my mom back, Leila!"

Yes. Leila understood how exciting this must be. But did Diana not see how this might be hard for Leila to listen to? Diana had been too young to remember when her mother disappeared, but Leila had watched her own mother wither away before she died. There would always be an ache, an empty space in her heart for Mom.

"Of course, you're excited," Leila said patiently. "But you and Brade have already done a lot of searching without any luck. You might have a long wait in front of you."

Or they both might get an ending they weren't expecting.

"I know, I know," Diana said. "But I'm choosing to think positively."

Sam arrived with their meals, handing the plates around with her long, elegant fingers. She was a classically trained pianist, and one of Leila's favorite servers.

Around a mouthful of cod and coleslaw, Diana continued. "Are you going to send off a DNA test kit for yourself? Wouldn't that be cool if you ended up having relatives around here, too?"

In Diana's world, everything had a happy ending, but Leila believed that if they did, they were the result of hard work, combined with a fair bit of luck. You did your best and then hoped to be at the right place at the right time for luck to strike. She thought she'd been lucky with Sawyer, but mostly, she'd been young, starry-eyed, and blind to reality. Then, she'd tried her best with Gary, but in the end, he wasn't the person she'd thought he was. Now, she understood that it was easier if you kept your eyes open, your heart protected, and your expectations low. Even the happiest of stories, like that of her parents, ended in grief.

"It would crush my dad," Leila said. The creamy dressing was delicious, the slaw fresh and crunchy, the cod perfectly crisp on the edges. She'd have to make sure to let Lou know that Boyd was doing a good job. Lou didn't share kitchen privileges easily.

"But surely he'd support you," Diana insisted. "You two are so close."

"That's part of the problem," Leila said. "I'm all he has. I'm really glad you and Brade have discovered each other. I hope you find your mother. I'm interested in finding my biological parents, for sure, but I don't want to hurt him. And, with my luck, any blood family I'd find would be in prison or want money from me."

Diana chattered easily for another twenty minutes, telling Leila all about her family, how much the kids liked their new uncle Brade and how much Brade enjoyed them. Leila had to admit it sounded idyllic. Even if they never got a satisfactory answer about their missing mother, their lives were richer for finding each other.

What would it be like to find people out there in the world who looked like her or acted like her? Then again, whoever had given her up had done it for a reason. What if a search only resulted in more rejection?

"Oh!" Diana said suddenly. "What about you and Sawyer? What's happening? Have you guys talked?"

Leila's stomach plummeted. "Not really. Dad made me deliver his meal that first night, I think to make me face him. But he's busy with his daughter and . . . I-I have nothing to say to him. Have you seen him?"

"No. Should I punch him for you if I do?"

She reached across to squeeze Diana's hand. "Yes. Right

in the throat."

Diana's smile faded. "Seriously. Are you okay with this?"

Leila shrugged. "I don't have much choice, do I? But we're grown-ups now. It'll be fine. We can be . . . friends. I hope."

"I hear he's divorced."

"Yes, Diana, I'm aware."

"Leila. He hurt you. Remember that."

"How can I forget?" She dropped her face into her hand and gave an anguished little laugh. "Am I that transparent?"

"I know you, that's all. Whatever happens, I'm here for you, okay? Throat punches or rah-rahs. Just be careful."

"Believe me," Leila said fervently, "I will try."

LEILA'S HIGH SCHOOL crush on the new boy had been well under control. She tried to avoid him, though it seemed they often ended up in the same classroom or hallway or bus. When that happened, she felt his presence in the little tingling hairs on her arms and in the suddenly starving cells of her lungs. Her feet turned to cement, and she forgot what she was doing.

She wanted to be near him and desperately wanted him not to see the misfit social disaster that she was.

Then came the day of the white-water rafting trip. Though not an official school event—liability was a bear for stuff like this, apparently—it had become something of a tradition, with parents providing oversight. They'd all been looking forward to it for months, a six-mile thrill ride down the Yellowstone, where they were guaranteed to be soaked with icy spring runoff, cold and delicious.

Leila sat with Kendall on the winding bus ride up and was slightly motion sick by the time they arrived. She was a little nervous too. Lou hadn't been thrilled with her going and couldn't leave the bar to join the parents who'd volunteered to supervise, so he'd run through a list of the ways she could die or get hurt.

"Don't let go of the ropes," he cautioned. "Even if they're telling you to paddle, you hang on."

"Yes, Dad," she promised. They'd had a preliminary training session, in which she'd learned that paddling was necessary to get out of the rough spots. Those who didn't paddle were considered deadweight, worse if they screamed. "I'll try."

"Watch everyone else's paddles. You're all inexperienced and you're likely to get whacked in the head."

Not if we're all hanging on to the ropes and the guide is the only one paddling, she considered telling him. But best to just listen.

"Okay, Dad."

"Hypothermia is real. That is ice water you'll be rafting through. Get your suit wet first. You need to get used to the cold before you get started or you'll seize up when you fall in."

"I might not fall in," she argued.

"You'll fall in," he said, darkly. "Make sure you go down the river feetfirst. If you get stuck on a snag headfirst, you'll drown for sure."

"Dad," she said, putting a hand on his arm. "There will be parents in every raft. The guides have done this thousands of times. I'll be okay."

"Grab the nearest rock and climb out," he said, ignoring her. "And then sit there and wait for rescue. No hiking out by yourself, do you understand?" He glared at her. "They'll be coming back to get you. But only if you stay where they last saw you."

"We'll all be wearing helmets and personal flotation devices," she assured him. "I'll hang on, I won't get brained by a paddle, I won't fall out, and if I do, I'll float feetfirst downstream until I can climb out and wait for the cavalry. It's going to be okay, Daddy."

He softened his gaze at that. "You're my best girl," he said. "I can't lose you."

Her parents had been nearing forty when they'd adopted her. Her mother had been unable to have children due to chronic kidney disease and passed away when Leila was twelve. Lou had never recovered from the loss of his wife, nor had he ever dated anyone since then. "I had the one love of my life," he was fond of saying. "And now I have my best girl."

Or, if Kendall was around, which she usually was, his two best girls. Kendall was also parent-compromised, her mom having made bad choices in the two men who had fathered her three children. Lou had a soft spot for his daughter's young friend, a girl who had been forced to take on too much responsibility at too young an age.

So Leila understood that his overprotectiveness came from a place of love and vulnerability. But, nevertheless, it chafed. She even kind of wished sometimes that he'd find a girlfriend. It was hard being everything to him, and she felt guilty every time she did something that annoyed him or disappointed him.

So, mostly, she didn't.

He had high hopes for her, wanted the best for her, and was always thinking of her future. She'd stay in Grand, of course. She'd graduate high school, paint, study art history, and build her portfolio. Then, she'd marry a good man, someone from Grand, preferably, and settle near Lou, so she could keep an eye on him as he aged.

She was a good girl, a good daughter, a good student, a good friend, and one day, she'd be a good wife and a good mother. Hopefully, she'd also be a successful artist, but she had her whole life to build that side of her. For now, this is who she had to be.

That's what she'd always thought about her life. Until she nearly drowned in the Yellowstone and Sawyer Lafferty made her wonder if there was more to Leila Monahan, a side of her that no one, not even her father, knew about.

CHAPTER SIX

SAWYER DROPPED PIPER off at his mother's place first thing the next morning and went straight to Belle Vista. He wasn't officially starting for two weeks, but he was eager to meet his new boss in person and get a feel for the place. He wouldn't stay long; he also had an appointment with the principal of Piper's new school and then needed to be back to Mom's for lunch.

The drive gave him time to think, uninterrupted, a rare treat for a single parent. He hadn't spoken to Leila since that first evening when she delivered the meal to the Yellowstone Hotel. He wanted to explain himself to her, to tell her that he'd made a mistake, that losing her was the biggest regret of his life and that he wished her well and hoped she'd be happy.

She wasn't married yet, he mused. If he got a chance to talk to her, he'd be able to see if the memories he had were accurate or if comparison to his marriage had made them seem sweeter than reality.

As Belle Vista came into view, he sighed and turned his thoughts to the new job. This, finally, was a career move for him, something that could have him and Piper settled and secure. The ranch wasn't a big spread, by Grand standards. Four hundred acres of mostly dry grassland, with mountains in the background and a few feeder streams to the river. But it was perfectly set up for the owner's purpose.

Over several video chats and many email conversations, Sawyer had come to the opinion that Bayleigh Sutherland, the owner, was an articulate, intelligent woman who knew what she wanted and didn't allow anyone to waste her time. She'd lost her husband a few years back and had used some of the life insurance proceeds to purchase the land.

He'd stopped in to drop off his own horse, Turtle, on the way to Grand, but hadn't taken time for a proper tour, so he surveyed the place with interest now as he drove down the long driveway. If anything, it looked even better than the photos on Bayleigh's website.

A small house came into view, set back from the road and bordered by a windbreak of cottonwoods. Behind the house was a line of six cabins, all needing a little love, but well-suited for what Bayleigh intended as retreat lodging or private horseback riding vacations.

He parked the truck near the outbuildings, then walked out to check on Turtle. The barns were set up with comfortable box stalls, a couple of decent-sized corrals and two large riding rings, one covered and one uncovered. Once they were up and running, Belle Vista could provide services year-round, though, even under cover, winter riding would be chilly.

Ted Sutherland, Bayleigh's son and ranch hand, was in

the first barn, cleaning stalls.

"Hey there, Mr. Lafferty," Ted said. He was tall and rangy, with sun-bleached hair and a lot of teeth. "Turtle is doing just fine today. I just put him out into the north corral. He'll sure be happy to see you. No Piper today?"

Piper was the only reason Turtle, Sawyer's swaybacked, platter-jawed chestnut gelding, still walked the earth. The creature had been abandoned, tied to the old hitching post outside the feedstore where Sawyer had gotten his first job after leaving college to support his young family. The hitching post was a branding detail, perfect for a livestock supply company, but every now and then, some yokel decided to ride up the side roads and play cowboy.

That day, the rider had come bareback and left his mount behind.

Ezra Johnson, his boss, had been ready to send the animal to auction, which would have almost certainly spelled its end, when he saw Sawyer outside with him.

"You look like you're remembering a horse of your own, son," he said.

In fact, Sawyer had never had a horse of his own. They'd been on the move too much. His stay in Grand had been the longest time he'd spent around horses, and the most time spent riding, of his life. It was just another reason he'd loved it there.

"No, sir," Sawyer replied. "But he's a sweet fellow. I'm guessing no one has given him any affection for some time."

He understood that feeling.

Stroking the bony animal's soft muzzle and breathing his horsey scent had been a tiny respite that day, a moment of calm in a world in which, after long hours at work, he was greeted by a hungry daughter, dirty laundry, and Miranda's empty eyes.

So, Ezra let him bring the horse to the back of the building where they loaded and unloaded feed. There was a grassy fenced area and, of course, plenty of feed. They found a bucket for water and let the animal stay for a few days while they decided what to do with him. He was unkempt and underweight but had good feet and a nice temperament.

The next day, Sawyer brought Piper to see him. With typical two-year-old logic, she named him Turtle, demanded to ride him, and that was that.

Sawyer could no more afford a horse than he could afford a trip to Aruba, but Ezra told him of a place that kept horses for therapy animals and might board Turtle for free if they could use him in their program.

And that's how Sawyer found the lifeline that now, he hoped, would carry him to smoother waters.

"Piper's with her grandmother," he told Ted. "And call me Sawyer."

"Sure thing, Mr. Lafferty," Ted said. "We've got a couple of new boarders coming in tomorrow, did you hear? Some guy in Forsyth, kid wants to do dressage. I tried to tell him she ought to learn barrel racing, but he just laughed at me. I didn't much like him." He frowned, then brightened. "But he wants special care for the horses and is willing to pay top dollar, so Mom says let's treat him like gold."

Sawyer waved at him and headed over to the corral. Ted was a good worker and, if his interactions with Piper and Turtle were any indication, he loved animals and kids, so it seemed like a good fit. Sawyer hoped that was the case. At Ted's age, no amount of money could have kept Sawyer with either of his parents, but to each his own.

Turtle nuzzled his hand for the alfalfa treat he'd brought.

"Hey, old buddy. How are you doing?"

The horse had to be at least twenty, but recovery and rehabilitation had resulted in him being extraordinarily fit for his age. Proper health care, a good diet, and lots of love did wonders.

Footsteps sounded behind him, and he turned to see Bayleigh Sutherland approaching.

"Sawyer Lafferty," she said, smiling and holding out her hand. "You're eager to get started."

"I am," he said. "Happy to see how well this old boy is settling in."

"He's a sweetheart." Turtle nudged her inquisitively and she laughed, pulling a carrot out of her pocket. "You've met Ted, I see?"

Sawyer's heart warmed at the easy affection she bestowed on the horse. "I have. Seems like a nice kid."

She rubbed the spot between Turtle's eyes. "If he's ever not, you need to tell me immediately, okay? Just because he's my son doesn't mean he gets special treatment."

Sawyer nodded, glad to hear it. "It's a beautiful place

you've got here, Ms. Sutherland. You're starting something good and I'm happy to be part of it."

"Bayleigh, please," she said, giving him a mildly scolding look. "Or you'll make me feel old."

She showed him through the barns and riding rings, the tack rooms, the storage facilities, and the cabins. They discussed which horses were ready for clients, which ones needed training, and whether they needed to purchase more animals.

In the viewing room overlooking the covered riding ring, she got them coffee and waved him to a seat. The furniture was mismatched and shabby, but riders often came upstairs a little grubby and smelling of horse, so it worked.

"How are you finding Grand?" she asked.

"It's familiar territory," he said. "I used to live here. My mom and I moved here my senior year in high school."

"Oh," she said, surprised. "Then you probably know it better than me. The only place I've been to, besides the bank, the grocery store, and the gas station, is Lou's Pub. And that was just for takeout, but it made a good first impression."

"Yeah, Lou's is great. The owner's daughter was," Sawyer said a little hesitantly, "a high school friend."

Bayleigh leaned forward, her expression bright. "Dark hair, artsy clothes, very friendly? I think that's the woman who served me. Lisa? Laura? A lovely girl, so welcoming. She said my bill was taken care of, thanks to her ex-fiancé. I don't know what he did to annoy her, but I got the feeling he paid for a few meals that evening."

Sawyer's brain snagged and faltered. "Leila," he said, finally.

Bayleigh's eyebrows lifted. "Yes, yes, that was her name. Did she make up with the guy?"

"I have no idea. When was this?"

She frowned. "Three months ago, maybe four. Why? Sawyer? Are you okay?"

"Yeah," he said, glancing at his watch. "Sorry, I just realized I'm late for a meeting. Thanks for the coffee."

Three or four months ago. Leila's engagement was off before he'd even arrived in town. But when he'd congratulated her, she hadn't corrected him. Why? She had to know he'd find out.

Then again, he was lucky she was speaking to him at all, after what he'd done. God only knew what she thought of him.

✪

THE MEETING AT Piper's school went well enough, Sawyer thought. He explained that Piper's mother was not authorized to see her, on the off chance she should make an appearance. They discussed if and when speech therapy might be warranted and whether Sawyer should be worried that Piper wasn't reading yet. The teacher was warm, friendly, and unfazed by his worries. Kids were resilient, she reminded him, especially at this age. Piper was a sweet, articulate child. She'd quickly make friends. If her style of learning required extra resources, they would make sure she got them. Piper would be fine. Sawyer could come by at any time if he had specific concerns. Then, another set of parents arrived, and he was kindly but firmly dismissed.

He glanced at his watch again as he pulled out of the school parking lot. He had just enough time to stop in at Lou's before he went to pick up Piper at his mom's place. Leila owed him nothing, but he felt the same old pull that had drawn him in back in high school, when it seemed the more he tried to ignore her, the more she seemed to appear in his peripheral vision. He'd heard her tinkling voice around every corner, saw those red lips and white teeth when she lifted her head in laughter. Saw her dark hair flashing across creamy skin.

And he'd seen it all close down when she realized he was in the room. Flash forward and it was the same damn thing. Is that why she hadn't told him she was single? Did she feel it again, too? Despite everything?

There was some kind of force field between them, like two magnets on the same side, dancing around each other, unable to connect until one of them flips.

Back then, the flip happened on the day of the whitewater rafting trip. Sawyer had almost not gone. And if he hadn't, his life would have been forever changed.

And Leila's might have ended.

★

WHEN THE BUS carrying Sawyer and his classmates reached the place where the rafts would put in, the head guide hopped out and distributed wet suits to the group.

"Where are we supposed to change?" asked one girl, looking worriedly at the vast wilderness around her.

"Girls behind the bus," the guide instructed. "Boys on this side."

"Does this make my ass look fat?" A girl named Courtney twisted to see her backside. She'd have fit right in back in Monterey.

A wiseacre named Other Other Mike (there were three Mikes in the class . . . did their parents have no creativity?) yelled back happily, "No, your *ass* makes your ass look fat."

The guide put them into groups of eight and led them to a small pool above the river. Sawyer was in the same group as Leila, who looked like she wanted to throw up.

"We're starting up here," the guide, Robby, called. "Come on."

They climbed into the black rubber vessel, and then, one by one, the guide had them jump into the water. When it was Leila's turn, she hesitated, sending Kendall a pleading look.

"Jump," said Robby.

"I'm not—" she was saying, when Robby picked her up and tossed her in.

He saw the moment her face hit the water, saw her hands slapping ineffectually, knew that, with her small body mass, the cold would be slicing through her like a hot knife, tearing the breath from her lungs, making her chest seize up. She flailed up through the surface, her eyes wide, her face white.

"You look like a harpooned seal," laughed one jackass.

"Shut up, idiot," Sawyer said.

She couldn't climb back in by herself if her limbs were numb. How long were they going to leave her floundering there?

"Get in, Monahan," yelled one of the other Mikes.

"Come on," Robby said, reaching down for her. "You can do it."

Finally, the guide grabbed the back of her wet suit. Sawyer reached down for her arm and together they tugged her over the inflated edge. She landed, gasping, on the bottom of the craft, and the guide began getting the rest of the students into the water.

Sawyer knelt at her side and put his hand on her forehead. "Leila? Open your eyes."

She was shivering and her lips were white.

"W-w-watch out." She swallowed, then inhaled raggedly. "You're in the s-s-splash zone."

"You're not gonna puke." He took both her hands in his, looked steadily into those beautiful eyes, and breathed slowly and deeply. "Follow my breath."

She mimicked him, her rib cage stuttering. He hoped she wouldn't start crying.

"I d-d-don't think I'm made for this." Her lips wobbled in an attempt to smile, but the color was returning to her lips.

"You'll be fine," he said. "It's just a little shock."

"H-h-how do you know?"

"First aid class." Mom had made him take it, and it was all worth it now. "It'll fade in a minute, but you'll be shaky for a bit."

"Why on earth would they make us do that?" She looked at the icy lake. "Is this to thin the herd or something? Scare some of us into staying on dry land?"

"Nah." Even freaked out as she was, she had a sense of humor. "Acclimation. Once you have a layer of body-temperature water in your wet suit, the cold river water won't feel as bad." He examined her face again. "Better now?"

"Have you done this before?" She pulled her hands away and smoothed her hair.

He grinned. "Used my first aid training? White-water rafting? Or rescuing a girl?"

She sat up straighter and narrowed her eyes, all threat of tears gone. "You didn't rescue me."

"Okay, tough girl," he said with a laugh. He slid onto the seat beside her. "I've rafted once before," he added. "Used my first aid a couple of times. But it's my first time rescuing a girl."

CHAPTER SEVEN

S AWYER HESITATED OUTSIDE the door of Lou's Pub. What was he hoping to accomplish by talking to Leila? He'd changed so much since they were together; no doubt she had too. She'd been such a spitfire then, so passionate, so determined. Being loved by Leila was . . .

He shook his head.

Don't go there, man.

She'd moved on. Someone else had earned that love, and if he hadn't managed to keep it, well, Leila was better off without him. She knew her own mind.

But his disaster of a marriage aside, he'd never gotten over Leila. He tried. He had to. In fairness to Miranda, it wasn't all bad, at first. But they'd never really had a chance, not with Sawyer's heart aching for someone else. Maybe if he'd been a better husband, Miranda wouldn't have gone off the rails so badly.

"Excuse me, son," said a man wearing a clerical collar. "I'm headed inside, and you look like you might be as well. I'm Father Patrick Keane."

He stepped away from the door, then shook the proffered hand. "Sawyer Lafferty. I was, but now I'm not sure."

"Let me encourage you, in that case." He pulled open the heavy door and waved Sawyer ahead of him. "After you."

The priest tipped his head and joined his friends. Sawyer took a seat at the bar and scanned the room for her familiar figure. All he wanted was a chance to explain. To apologize. To set things right so that maybe they could exist in Grand together without this awful weight between them. He craved her forgiveness, he realized. He'd made such a mess of things, broken her heart. But if she'd really moved on, would she appreciate him bringing up the past like this? Maybe she wanted to forget all about him.

Maybe talking about it was for his sake, not hers.

That was just selfish.

"You here looking to bother my best girl?"

Lou's voice was calm, but his eyes were cold, and his jaw looked like it was made of granite.

"No, sir," Sawyer replied, meeting his gaze. "But she and I have things to discuss."

"You in town to stay?" Lou asked.

Sawyer nodded. "I hope so."

"Just you and the sprite?"

"My mom will be helping with Piper. You know as well as anyone, being a single dad is no picnic."

Lou tilted his head in acknowledgment. "You've parted ways from the sprite's mam, then?"

Sawyer hesitated. How did you explain a woman who up and left her family? What was to him a personal tragedy was also a cliché, banal. Embarrassing.

"We're divorced, yes," he said, finally. "She's, uh, not in the picture."

But Lou surprised him. "Not all women are meant for motherhood. You hope that the ones that aren't don't end up with any, but that's not how life works, is it?"

The irony was painful. Leila Monahan was one who was meant, without a doubt, for motherhood. She'd always known it. If he'd have gotten her pregnant, they'd have managed, just like she'd told him they would. But nope, like the man said, that's not how life worked.

THAT SUNNY DAY on the icy river, Sawyer hadn't expected to fall in love. After Leila's freak-out getting dunked in the lake, he expected her to bail from the whole event, or sit there glued to the ropes, but instead, she threw herself into it with a frenzy.

"Kitchen Sink Swirly," yelled their other guide. "Paddle!"

This one's name was Tate. He was from Australia or New Zealand or possibly South Africa and wore a curly blond ponytail under his helmet. Sawyer wondered if Leila was trying to impress him. Girls loved accents.

There were names for the different parts of the river, they learned, as Tate explained on the calmer parts. Or maybe he was just making shit up. But every time they hit rapids, and there were a lot of them—who planned a Class IV ride for a bunch of novices?—he hollered at them to kill it, rip it, paddle, paddle, paddle.

The class had been divided into four groups, and their raft was the last. Each raft had two guides, and three men in kayaks escorted them down the river, the agile little water-craft able to slide in and around the rafts in case of emergency. What they could do, Sawyer wasn't sure. He suspected there would be parental complaints once the kids got home. Then again, he didn't know this crowd. Maybe people were tougher in Montana than they were in California.

The water got rougher. Leila's face, when he had a split second to look at her, was ferocious. She gripped her paddle like she intended to pummel the river to death. She had no idea what she was doing, of course, like most of the class, but she threw herself into it with a vengeance.

"Here comes the Mother-in-law of Death," yelled Tate. "Kill it, guys!"

"Keeling the Muvver-in-low of Deef," the kids yelled back. "Grip it and rip it!"

Their grotesque mimicry of his down-under accent made Tate howl with laughter. Screams came from the girls and probably the guys, too, as they rounded the bed of white water. Vicious rocks jutted every which way, but somehow, the buoyant raft danced its way through it. Spray shot at them from every direction, like someone was standing there with buckets, waiting for them. Sawyer was soaked, but his adrenalin was so high, he barely felt it.

The front of the raft lifted, and his stomach lurched as

they slipped and flew through a small canyon, before landing like a breaching humpback.

More shrieks and yells. This was insane.

Then Sawyer saw Tate turn. His eyes widened and he shoved his paddle into the water hard, but there was no stopping the raft.

Kendall screamed, "Leila!"

Sawyer turned to where Leila should have been sitting and saw only the wet black rubber of the raft.

"She fell out!" Kendall was leaning over the side, reaching and pointing.

But the raft kept hurtling down the river.

"The kayakers will get her," Tate yelled. "I'll put in at the next slow spot. She'll be okay."

Thoughts sparked through Sawyer's head like lightning, outrunning logic or conscious decision-making. Two rafts floated downriver, ahead of them, accompanied by two kayaks. The first raft was out of sight. No kayak visible behind them.

Sawyer gripped his paddle and jumped into the water.

"YOU AND MY girl made your peace?" Lou asked, drawing Sawyer back to the present.

"I don't know," he said. "She's not too keen on talking with me."

"You broke her heart, you know," Lou spoke mildly. "I

wanted to shoot you for a while there, for the pain you caused her."

"I'm sure you did," Sawyer said. "I'd have handed you the gun, for a while there."

"Things happen for a reason. I don't know what it is in this case, but I'm sure the good Lord will reveal it in time."

"I heard she was engaged. Is that true?"

Lou looked at him for a long moment, his gaze unreadable. "You'll have to ask her. But not today. She's got a class. Good chat."

Sawyer set his business card on the bar and pushed it toward Lou. "Ask her to call me, will you?"

Then he left, unsure if he was angry with Lou, the good Lord, the universe, destiny, or the Flying Spaghetti Monster. But really, what had he expected?

CHAPTER EIGHT

Just outside Custer, Montana

J P MALONE NEVER expected Heather Hudson would actually write him. There was no shortage of cowboys ready and willing to take his place. He just hoped that whoever she went to next was decent because this was one girl who was setting herself up to be taken advantage of.

He kept a post office box in Billings for things like license renewal forms and so forth, but he only checked it twice a year. He could count on one birthday card and one Christmas card each year from Lizzie.

To Heather, he'd given the address of a feed supplier named Waylon Cooper, a long-time circuit sponsor who attended rodeos throughout Montana and even farther afield. Even if Coop couldn't go himself, he sent someone else to make sure the livestock handlers knew Cooper Feeds was always looking out for them. He was a jovial man who ran a solid business and was well liked, though his memory for anything unrelated to rodeo was spotty. Coop would pass on any letters JP might receive. Eventually.

But as summer turned to autumn, after a grueling six weeks competing at Big Fork, Rosebud, Fergus, Big Sky, and

Richland, there hadn't been a single envelope for JP Malone, care of Cooper Feeds.

He was relieved, he told himself. His situation was hardly conducive to relationships. He barely knew this girl and even if it did turn into something, what kind of thing could it be? Long-distance pen pals? Or would she follow him to every event? Visit him in the tiny cab of his horse trailer? Have dinner with him at whatever restaurant he could afford in whatever town he was in?

There was romance about the life, no one could deny it, and it wasn't just the thrill of competition. It was the work the competition celebrated. It was the west itself: mountains and sunsets to bring a city boy to his knees, with wild, wide-open land as far as the eye could see. Bands of horses that had never been touched by humans, racing in vast clouds of dust to disappear into the distance. The slide of rope through callused palms, the zing of the lasso when it was ready to fly, the satisfying snap when it hit the target. Bringing herds of cattle, shaggy and suspicious, down from summer grazing, watching those huge heads and long, lethal horns swing back and forth, eyeing your horse, knowing that a single animal bolting could lead to thousands of hooves thundering around you in a stampede that would end you, knowing you had to trust your horse to outsmart the cattle and keep you alive.

Then, sleeping under the stars next to a campfire, listening to the cries of owl and wolf, the occasional far-off scream of a big cat, the sweat of man and beast mingling with sweet smoke as sparks flew into the black night, your crew scattered nearby, all exhausted and exhilarated, ready to rise at dawn and begin again.

What were blisters and scrapes, the occasional broken bone or dislocated joint compared to all this? It was a big life, so big it obliterated anything else outside of it. Out there, beyond telephones, traffic, and TV news, stress was limited to the elemental: food, shelter, safety. You took care of that, and you were fine. Only on the thin bedroll just before sleep hit might you remember disappointment, heartbreak, grief, or shame, and even then, it felt far away, as if it had happened to someone else. On the range, you weren't the person who'd suffered those things. You were someone stronger, better, truer.

But the cowboy life wasn't permanent. It wasn't . . . real. It was a thrilling chance at fame and fortune that usually ended after a few short years, and even the best day on the range was tinged with this sorrowful knowledge. Most cowboys walked away with some great stories, a few impressive scars, and a credit score worse than when they started.

The romance was that of history, place, and time. Not of hearts and flowers.

So, when JP stopped by the Cooper Feeds booth again, he knew not to get his hopes up.

Then Waylon Cooper waved him over.

"Your girl's got a lot to say," he said.

And handed him a stack of twelve envelopes.

Chapter Nine

"YOU THINK MAYBE you could have told me?" Sawyer said in a low voice to his mother.

Faith Lafferty looked out to the sandbox where Piper was making mud pies and singing to herself. "Told you what, son? You came home to be near your mother, not to have an affair with a childhood sweetheart."

She hadn't disliked Leila, exactly, but she'd been preoccupied and exhausted by Aunt Lindsay's care and perhaps a little resentful of her son's youthful joy. Maybe anyone's joy, given the whirlwind family her ex-husband was enjoying with Mia Tornado.

"Mother," he said patiently, "I'm divorced and free to pursue other relationships, should I so choose. You know this."

"And does your wife agree with you on that?"

"Ex-wife."

"You don't think she'd prefer to be with the father of her child?"

He exhaled sharply, then sucked back the annoyance as he saw Piper look over at them.

"Looking good, sweetie," he said, forcing a smile.

She grinned back and tossed a shovelful of sand over her head. He'd have to scrub her hair tonight.

Sawyer's mother had chosen to stay in Grand after Aunt Lindsay's death, to his relief. But she still preached the sanctity of marriage whenever possible and clung to her belief in "'til death do us part."

"Mom, Miranda and I are over. I tried. She tried. It was never going to work, but may I remind you that she's the one who left?"

Maybe he should have explained the grimmer details of their relationship to his mother, but it didn't feel right to publicize whatever personal demons Miranda was battling. She wasn't bad; she was sick. He still didn't know exactly what was wrong with her, but she'd been deeply unhappy long before he came along, he guessed. Protecting Piper was his first priority, of course, but as long as Miranda didn't hurt their daughter, Sawyer would keep things civil.

SAWYER HAD KNOWN from the start that the marriage was a mistake. He couldn't believe that the one time he'd gotten careless—the one, single time he'd let his guard down—he'd been caught.

Yes, the marriage was a mistake.

But the baby was not. How could a baby be a mistake? He and Miranda had created this child, and they would raise it and love it. They would do their best to be good partners and maybe, if they were very lucky, love would grow between them.

It might not be the family he'd imagined building, but it was the family he'd been given, and he would not abandon them.

Miranda was apologetic, teary, even. She'd had a hectic quarter, had broken up with what she'd thought was a casual boyfriend, then spent three months on a student exchange program in Sweden. It had been a good experience, but she'd been terribly homesick. The old boyfriend met her at the airport on her return, to her shock, but the familiarity had been so comforting that she'd allowed him to think they might get back together. Which she did not want.

Hence, the stalking behavior and her sudden interest in Sawyer.

She was vulnerable and had made some very poor choices, but who was he to judge? He, too, was vulnerable and had chosen to take comfort in her body, even though he ached for Leila with every breath.

They'd both made mistakes, but they were both committed to this baby.

He finished out the year, then took a job at a feed distributor and registered for night classes at community college. He wanted Miranda to finish school, but it turned out she wasn't that interested, anyway.

The pregnancy did not go entirely according to plan. Miranda's placenta was lying low, they said, and if it didn't move up with her uterus as the baby grew, she'd have to have a Caesarean section.

Miranda had horrible morning sickness, right from the beginning. The kind that lasted all day and well past the first trimester. From the moment Sawyer knew about the baby, it seemed, Miranda was either puking, had just puked, or was about to puke. She had to take special supplements because she couldn't keep enough food down to gain weight and they were worried about the baby's growth rate.

And she was miserable. That was evident from the beginning too. This wasn't her plan and though she'd intended to be a good sport about it, the catastrophic effect on her entire life had thrown her for a real loop.

So, none of the things that normally happened during the early stages of a relationship—dinners out, doing things together, long lovemaking sessions—occurred. Instead, he held her hair back while she retched, he accompanied her to doctor's appointments, he rubbed her feet, which was all the touching she could tolerate, brought her ice water and crackers, and watched endless TV with her.

He missed Leila constantly, but he forced himself not to think of her. He didn't deserve to miss her. He'd done this. The very thing Leila had wanted most from him, he'd denied her, and done it with another woman instead. He was the biggest idiot in the universe, and if he had a chance in hell of happiness on this earth, it was only if he put Leila out of his mind entirely and focused on the here and now.

The here and now was currently a version of hell, but that was no one's fault but his, so he had to suck it up and be a man. No use whining for what could have been. What was here now, that's what was important.

Married student housing had been a lateral step from his life with his adenoidal roommate, Buckley, at best. They had to do their own cooking, which meant they had to buy their own groceries, which ate into what little spare time he had. And cooking smells made Miranda feel sick, so he mostly ate prepared foods, frozen or canned. And he ate them in another room, so she couldn't see or smell them. Or even hear him chew.

It was pretty extreme.

But everything would change once the baby was born, he told himself. The baby would make it all worthwhile.

And as the day approached, things did improve slightly. The nausea improved enough that she could eat. The baby's development appeared to be fine. The placenta had done whatever placentas were supposed to do, so she would be allowed to deliver naturally.

But then, a month before her due date, her water broke.

Miranda panicked, which Sawyer had learned was generally how she reacted to the unexpected.

"It's too early!" she'd shrieked, looking down at the puddle at her feet. "This isn't right! It's not supposed to happen for five more weeks."

"Four weeks," Sawyer corrected. Attention to detail wasn't her strong suit.

"Whatever!" she snapped. "What do we do now?"

"We call the doctor and let them know." He was already

dialing.

They were instructed to come to the hospital for assessment. Labor pains would almost certainly start soon, and if they didn't, they might need to induce.

Contractions began almost immediately, and the pain was more than Miranda could tolerate. After a blur of activity in which Sawyer felt clumsy, stupid, and in the way, the awful night ended with a rush to the operating room for an emergency Caesarean section. The baby, thank God, had no serious issues, despite being a month early.

After two days in the hospital, they were sent home, but if Sawyer hoped that their relationship, maybe even their sex life, might improve once the baby was born and Miranda had a chance to recover, it seemed that fate was cackling with glee at his optimism.

She could barely sit and only wanted to sleep. She was on strong pain medication, and her milk didn't come in, so Sawyer learned to mix formula and feed. And rock, and walk, and do all the things that he'd expected to learn . . . but he hadn't expected to learn them alone.

Yet the baby was amazing. Piper Rain Lafferty.

He had a daughter.

A LIFETIME LATER, he and Miranda were done, but he loved his daughter more than he thought possible.

"Mom," he repeated, "I just want to know. Is Leila engaged or not?"

He couldn't help but feel responsible for ruining Miranda's life; he hoped that Leila, at least, had found her way to happiness.

His mother pursed her lips and looked away. "It's a bad time for you to be getting involved with somebody new, you know. New job, new house, Piper all disrupted. It's hard on a child. She misses her mother. It would be confusing to her."

She looked back at him and for a moment, Sawyer could see that she was truly concerned for them. The unraveling of her own marriage had broken something inside her, and in her heart of hearts, she feared her son and granddaughter would also be ruined by love.

"I'm not getting involved with Leila again, Mom. I'm probably the last person she wants to see in Grand, in fact. I just . . ." He sighed. "I just want to know that she's okay."

"Oh, Sawyer," his mother said.

"What?"

She shook her head. "Nothing, son. I'm just happy you're here."

He leaned over and kissed her cheek. "Thanks, Mom," he said softly. "It's good to be home."

SAWYER HEADED OUT the door to go for an evening walk with Piper. She had energy to burn off before bedtime, and he could use the fresh air. They'd finally moved into the little bungalow, but their things were still all over the place, with boxes and bags sitting haphazardly, spilling this way and that. Looking at it all exhausted him, but unpacking with Piper underfoot would take as long as it took, and in the meantime, he needed to see something pretty.

Seeing someone pretty would be even better, but he hadn't had a chance to engineer a meeting with Leila yet.

"Let's go to the boardwalk," Piper said, tugging on his hand. "We can get ice cream, okay, Daddy? I ate all my supper."

They negotiated a deal as they walked the few blocks from their house to the riverfront park in the center of town. It was a gorgeous end to a midsummer day, with the air scented with fresh-cut grass and the sky lightly streaked with clouds. Piper was settling into school okay, Faith was enjoying the before- and after-school care, and he was pleased with how the Belle Vista program was shaping up.

As they rounded a corner, Piper jumped, yanking his arm. "Let's find the nice lady!"

"What nice lady, Pipes?"

"You know." She stopped in her tracks, planted her small fists on her hips and glared at him. "The PINE-uh-pull lady."

His pulse jumped and he glanced around. No Leila that he could see.

"Daddy!" She peered up at him from beneath the baseball hat clamped over her silky hair.

Sawyer sighed. "Do you mean Leila?"

"Yeah!" Piper jumped up and down and clapped her hands. "Leila! I really like her. Let's find her. We go to that rest-ront where she works to see her and have more pizza?"

"What happened to ice cream?"

She grinned. "We can have that, too, silly. I like her. She's not . . ." She hesitated, her eyebrows furrowed. "What's that word when big people use squeaky voices and talk to me like I'm a baby?"

"Condescending?"

Piper's intellect was above average, but she had some delays in language processing. Sawyer guessed that adverse early childhood experiences played a role. Just another thing for him to feel guilty about.

"Yeah! Con-dense-ating! She's not like that. She used a normal voice. So I like her."

Exactly the sort of thing Leila would know, instinctively.

Piper squealed, pointing. "There she is!"

And before he could do anything, she slipped her little hand out of his and dashed across the street.

"Piper!"

Brakes squealed, and Sawyer thought his heart would explode. He raced after her, holding his hands out, apologizing and thanking drivers. Leila, who'd been sitting at a picnic table with her laptop, leaped to her feet, alarm on her face.

"Leila, Leila," Piper yelled. "We're going for a walk. Want to come with us?"

Leila bent down and caught the child just before she barreled into her, and Sawyer was relieved to see her features soft_immediately. She lifted the little girl onto her hip, looked up, and met his eyes.

"Piper!" He skidded to a stop in front of them. Blood pounded in his ears. "How many times do I have to tell you? You can't run out into traffic. You could have been killed!"

He watched the smile slip off his little girl's face and hated making that happen. But she had to learn. He was just trying to keep her alive. Of all the people who had to witness his parental failure, why did it have to be Leila? Why now?

"Sorry about that," he muttered, reaching for his daughter.

But Piper turned her face into Leila's shoulder and clung tighter.

"Piper," he said warningly. "That's enough."

A muffled sob sounded.

"Hey, there," Leila said. She lowered herself to the picnic table bench, closed her laptop, and motioned for Sawyer to sit beside her. "That was scary, wasn't it, Piper? You must have been so excited, you forgot the rules, huh?"

"Yuh-uh-uh," Piper cried. "You're not con-dense-ating, and we were going to have ice cream and walk by the river with you."

Leila looked over Piper's ball cap and gave him a wry smile. "You were, were you?"

"Her idea," Sawyer said.

"You objected?" The gentle humor in her tone eased his embarrassment a little.

He sighed. "I wanted to talk. This wasn't how I intended to do it."

"Daddy?" Piper peered out from beneath the oversized brim of her hat, sniffling. "Are you done being mad?"

"Oh, baby." This time, when he reached for her, she jumped into his arms. He buried his face in her sweet hair. "I'm not mad. You scared the poop out of me. And remember when we talked about how being scared and being mad sometimes looks the same?"

She nodded solemnly. "You must have been really, really scared."

"I was." He glanced at Leila. "I think Leila was too."

She had her arms crossed over her chest as if she was cold, and her eyes were shining. "I was. Nobody wants to see you get hurt, honey."

Piper looked between them. "How come Leila's scared look isn't a mad look, Daddy?"

If only he could soften his reactions. He hated scaring Piper, but some days . . .

"Because I'm not your daddy," Leila said quickly. "It's a daddy thing. Kind of like the pizza thing. Remember?"

"PINE-uh-pull," Piper yelled, squirming with joy, her ever-changing mood shifting back to calmer waters.

"Now, did someone say something about ice cream?" Leila stood up and smoothed her hands down the sides of her jeans. "I know just the place."

★

IF THERE WAS one thing everyone knew about kids, it's that ice cream solved everything. It certainly seemed so to Piper, Leila thought.

They walked to the crosswalk, where Sawyer had Piper press the button, then look both ways before they stepped into the street.

"Good job, Pipes," he praised.

While Piper jumped at his side, Leila said quietly, "Good job, Dad."

She loved his explanation to Piper. His daughter's dash through traffic had shaken him badly; he was probably embarrassed too. Anger was much more comfortable than fear or shame, but few people recognized this. How many would know to help a child understand it?

He had the look of a man who suspected he was constantly screwing up the job of parenting, despite his best efforts. Whatever had happened in the past few years had left him with deep wounds.

It was an odd thought, and not entirely welcome. Hurt had fueled her healing journey for a long time, but it hadn't taken her all the way. Perhaps, to move forward from the damage he'd inflicted on her, she had to recognize that he'd been damaged too.

They got ice cream and then wandered over to the school playground, where Piper immediately joined a couple of other children on the climbing equipment.

"Thanks for coming along," Sawyer said quietly. "I've been hoping to talk to you but didn't think you wanted to . . . hang out with me. With us."

"I'm not sure I do." She sighed. "But we can't avoid each other forever. We ought to figure out a way to interact that doesn't end up awkward. Now's as good a time as any."

She joined him on a bench, keeping a safe two-foot distance away.

"I never forgot about you." His voice was low, and he faced straight ahead, not looking at her.

She swallowed hard and tried for a light tone. "Yeah, the marriage announcement said it all."

Oh dear. Was she really as bitter as she sounded?

"Sorry, didn't mean it to come out that way." She leaned forward, braced her elbows on her knees, and took a deep breath. "I broke up with you, Sawyer. I can hardly be mad that you believed me."

Only she was.

She hadn't meant to break up with him permanently. He should have known that.

CHAPTER TEN

LEILA AWOKE AFTER a restless night with a heavy feeling of something important left undone, of forgetting something important. She got dressed, had some coffee, and tried to shake it off, but it wouldn't leave.

Classic student anxiety dream, she told herself as she waited on the boardwalk for Diana's SUV. They were going to Running River, Diana's childhood home, to remove junk from the basement. Time with her friend would help clear her head. She had plenty going on, but this time, she wasn't stressing about Sawyer or Gary or adoption agencies or DNA test kits.

It was all about this stupid project.

Her studies had saved her in those dark days after she'd ruined things with Sawyer, when she needed something to lose herself in. It wasn't working anymore, though. His return to Grand brought her back to a time she wished she could forget even as she treasured the exhilaration of those heady, innocent first days in love.

After the white-water rafting trip, she and Sawyer were together almost constantly. Their love grew with a speed and intensity that was shocking to them both. Between summer jobs—him at a local riding stable, her at her father's pub—they spent every waking moment together.

Somehow, they'd held off sleeping together until after prom. Sawyer borrowed a tent, and they drove to the lake and spent two glorious days and a night alone together. It was the first time for them both, and it was clumsy, funny, and magical all at once. She'd never felt like this before, and the knowledge that they'd soon be parted added a bittersweet urgency to their time together.

When they parted in September, he to study agriculture and business at Montana State University, she for the art program at U of M in Missoula, she wept on his neck, begging him not to go, even though she knew he felt the same anguish she did.

But Missoula was a long way away from Grand, and between missing her home and missing Sawyer, Leila was miserable. She tried to adjust. She and Sawyer called each other every couple of days, long, tear-filled conversations whispered around huddled fists as there was always someone else waiting to use the phone. She lived for those conversations, but long distance was expensive, so they were never long enough.

They always ended with *I love you.*

Because they did. There was never any doubt about it. Maybe most high school romances didn't last, but theirs was the one that would. They'd be the exception to the rule.

One weekend each month, Leila caught a bus to Bozeman, and sometimes, he was able to get out to visit her.

And they both came home to Grand for Christmas, of course.

But as the second semester dragged on, it wasn't enough. Leila missed Sawyer so much. She wasn't enjoying college as much as she'd hoped. She missed her dad. She missed her old dog, Benji. She missed the customers at the pub, the routine of sending a foamy pint of oatmeal stout sliding down the bar to Father Patrick's waiting hands on Fridays, or serving Prosecco and artisan chips to Sue Anne Nylund and her gossipy lady friends on Thursday afternoons. She was a homebody. Always had been. She didn't want travel or adventure. She wanted a home, a family, people to care for, people who cared for her.

She wanted Sawyer.

She even knew which house she wanted to buy for them. It was just a little wartime bungalow, but the owners, an old couple who would surely be selling in a few years, had painted it a beautiful deep turquoise and added gingerbread accents in cream. Yellow roses climbed up the sunny south wall in summer, and the backyard was edged with an undulating bed of ferns and hostas. Benji would love playing on that lush grass. It was a comfortable walk from the elementary school, perfect for when they had kids.

But this sort of talk seemed to annoy Sawyer. How would they buy a house, he wanted to know. They had no money and would never qualify for a mortgage. Did she even know how much property taxes were?

And that response annoyed Leila. How would they get

what they wanted if they didn't dream? They would manifest their true desires, but first they had to articulate them, see them clearly. "Leap and the net will appear," she told him.

"I thought the saying was *look before you leap*," he'd replied.

As spring approached, she began wondering if they still wanted the same things. She hadn't changed. Her dream had always been a quiet life with the man she loved. He used to share that dream. Now, she wasn't sure.

✪

DIANA PULLED UP in a cloud of dust and waved Leila into the passenger seat. They were on their way to Running River, Diana's childhood home. "Why so glum, sunshine? A few hours sorting junk at my dad's house isn't the high point of your week?"

Diana hadn't yet convinced Weldon Scott that it was time to sell, but given his heart condition and their recent, tentative reconciliation, she felt sure she'd get there soon.

Leila laughed, relieved to get her mind off Sawyer. "Actually, it might be."

"Yikes." Diana shoulder-checked and pulled onto the road. "That's rough."

"It's my final project," Leila explained. It wasn't the full truth, but it wasn't a lie, either. "My proposal's been rejected. Not original enough, according to my advisor. Dig deeper, he says. Why did I start my art history degree in the first place? I should have studied marketing. Communications. Something with a future."

"You're doing what you love," Diana reminded her. "You're an artist. It makes sense. Plus, you love showing off your knowledge to gallery customers."

"I do like feeling like an expert." Leila smiled, then shook her head. "It's my last credit, so I can't quit now, but I'm burned out, scraping the bottom of my brain for fresh ideas and coming up blank."

"I know you, Leila." Diana shot her a sharp glance. "I think that if you were just stressed about your project, you'd be up in your pretty little garret, wearing a beret, drinking absinthe, and making it happen."

Leila looked out the window. "I love that you think that's an artist's life."

"I love that you think motherhood is all cherubic smiles and coos. So, your chosen life has shit in it too. That's how it goes, right? I love that you're here with me, but can you afford the time today?"

"Absolutely," Leila assured her. "If I spend another hour staring at my computer screen or going through reference books, I'll lose my mind. Cleaning out a few junk drawers will be a day at the circus."

"Well, maybe a change of scenery will jump-start those ideas," Diana said. "I'm hoping that going through all this stuff might trigger some stories about my mom, now that Dad's finally talking about her. But are you sure it's just school that's got you down? I mean, it's only been a few months since you and Gary broke up."

"It's not Gary."

"Good. To be honest, I never understood what you saw in him," Diana said. "I know you loved him and all—"

"I didn't," Leila interrupted.

"Oh?" Diana glanced over at her.

"I mean . . ." She hesitated. She still hadn't sorted it all out in her head, but having Sawyer reenter her life so soon after Gary departed it had thrown the two relationships into sharp contrast. She'd thought she loved Gary. She'd wanted to love Gary. She'd tried to love Gary. But mostly, she'd wanted *him* to love *her*, to commit to her, to give her the life she'd dreamed of, a sunset-wedding-cake-topper kind of fantasy.

"Gary is a good man and he treated me well," she said finally.

Diana snorted. "Be still, my heart."

"I know you and Kendall couldn't see it, but there was a long time when I was happy with him."

"Were you, though?" Diana asked. "Or were you happy not to be alone anymore?"

She'd had this conversation, or a version of it, with Kendall too. Many times. Even before she'd ended her engagement. That was the thing about good friends. They saw the real you, even when you were hiding from that reality yourself.

"You have the least experience of all of us," Leila said peevishly, "yet you come up with these pithy truths that we can't help but accept. You're lucky we stay friends with you."

Diana reached over and swatted her shoulder. "You guys deserve me. Take that however you like. Anyway, if it's not Gary, maybe it's Sawyer. He's got to be affecting you."

Diana turned down the secondary road leading to Running River, which meant they had ten minutes.

"It's weird," Leila admitted. "He's different."

"So are you. You've grown up. That's a good thing."

"Yeah. It's funny. I thought I'd feel angry, like I'd want to hurt him the way he hurt me. But it seems like maybe he's already been hurt. He seems . . . weathered. Like he's waiting for a hammer to fall, like maybe he's already been hit, but he'll tough it out because that's who he is."

"Uh-oh," Diana said. "You sound sympathetic. He's divorced, right? Even if he's been put through the wringer, it doesn't change what he did to you."

"I know."

Diana was quiet for a while. Then she sighed. "I saw his face. When you were carrying the little girl out of the bathroom. Before you knew he was there."

Leila squeezed her eyes shut. She lived in a fishbowl. Yes, people cared about her, but she was so tired of being the one everyone was worried about.

"He lit up," Diana added softly. "You should have seen it. I mean, I hate him for what he did to you. But maybe he's sorry. Maybe there's more to the story."

Leila's throat tightened. She had seen it. Once, that's how he'd always looked at her, like she was the only girl in the world, and he was the only boy. He'd made her light up too.

But that was then.

"Things are different now," she said. "He'll always be connected to Piper's mother, and that's messy. I want clean. Simple. I used to joke about it, but I'm really considering having a child on my own. I can't wait around forever, and I won't settle for a mediocre relationship."

She'd wanted children with Sawyer, once. He was a good dad, and Piper was adorable. She was also a living reminder of the worst heartbreak Leila had ever experienced, and an ever-present link to the woman who'd ruined the love she and Sawyer had shared.

Diana cleared her throat. "If you're serious, then do the DNA test. Contact the adoption agency. Take it from me ... once you become a mother, your background becomes way more important. You love history, Leila. So, find your own."

IT HAD BEEN a long time since Leila had visited the ranch where Diana had grown up. Kendall boarded her horse at Running River, and while Leila had occasionally explored the river hills on horseback with her and Diana, she hadn't been inside the house for years.

It was a mess.

Kendall had warned her that Weldon's housekeeping had

taken a turn for the worse, despite Gloria, who kept the place as clean as she could and made sure the old man didn't die of starvation. But he wasn't an easy employer, and probably for self-preservation, Gloria had elected to stick to the areas where she was least likely to encounter him and vice versa.

"Hey, Dad," Diana called out as she entered the creaky side door. "We're here. We brought bagels and cream cheese." She lowered her voice in an aside to Leila. "He's not allowed cream cheese anymore, so this is vegan. Do not tell him."

"Awesome," Leila said.

Weldon entered the room, his former barrel-chested, chin-up swagger now a shuffle. He'd lost weight since his heart attack and the skin on his face was sagging. It had been hard on him to admit that the wife he'd adored had wanted out of their marriage so badly that she'd left her baby girl, rather than stay with him.

"You're going to feed me some healthy shit, aren't you?" he said, scowling. "Just like Gloria. Can't get a decent meal anymore and what's the point? I could drop dead any day now, so why can't I eat what I want?"

"Lovely to see you, too, Dad." Diana went over to him and kissed his withered cheek. "You remember Leila?"

"Hi, Mr. Scott," she said.

"Nothing wrong with my mind," he grumbled. "Tell Lou I say hi. I miss lifting a pint with him."

"You're welcome anytime," Leila said. "I think people would be happy to see you."

Weldon snorted. "Happy to gloat, you mean. Well, well, no point wasting time."

He gestured for them to follow him, then ushered them down the stairs into what might have been a game room, if someone had used it as such. Instead, it was like an enormous closet, with boxes lining the walls, black garbage bags bulging beside them, stacks of dusty books, piles and piles of wire hangers spilling everywhere, an old fan, various kitchen appliances and dishes, a chrome dinette suite with matching chairs, and, peeking out from beneath a pile of winter jackets, what appeared to be photo albums.

"Take whatever you want. Use it, sell it, give it away. Dump it, burn it . . . I don't care. I can't be bothered."

They'd be here forever, Leila thought. They ought to have arranged for a dumpster. Even cramming Diana's SUV full would barely make a dent. They'd have to come back with Rand's truck.

She waded into the room, pushing things aside with her foot. "We're not going to find any . . . you know . . . rodents or anything, are we?"

Diana sniffed the air. "All I smell is dust. Gloria assured me that she'd made sure everything was clean before it was stored in here. We should be okay on that score."

They got to work hauling the bags out first. Most of them contained clothing, and regardless of style, they were of decent quality and would be appreciated at the local thrift store, especially the heavier garments. Montana winters were not for the faint of heart.

Behind a collection of bags, Leila found a stack of picture frames, mostly cheap or cracked, but a few were sturdy and worth taking to the thrift shop. Then at the back, she saw what appeared to be an old painting, unframed, about eighteen by twenty-four inches, its front against the wall.

"Hey, Diana, look at this." She moved the other frames aside. "If these are kiln-dried stretcher bars, I could recover it and use it myself. Would you mind if I kept it?"

"Fill your boots, pal." She came over to help Leila free it from the other items. "Unless you've just unearthed a lost Van Gogh. Then I want in."

Leila shuddered as cobwebs drifted from between the wall and the canvas. "Something tells me your dad wasn't a big art collector."

Diana laughed. "It'll be a paint-by-number, probably of a mountain, a horse, or a grizzly bear."

But when they got it out, to Leila's surprise, it was an acrylic landscape on gallery-wrapped, heavy-duty canvas. It wasn't very old, but it wasn't fresh, either. The artist had a unique style that reminded her of something she couldn't quite place, realistic but with a particular flair, almost as if the painter had been looking through a funhouse lens. Interesting. She looked for a signature, but all she could make out were some faint scratchings in the bottom right. If they were initials, she couldn't read them.

Turning it over, she saw a torn scrap of paper attached by a single staple. A handwritten label read *For J*—but the rest was gone. A title? A gift tag? It didn't make sense.

"I'm going to show this to your dad. I want to make sure I'm not taking something he cares about."

She lugged the canvas out of the room and into the kitchen, where Weldon was enjoying the bagels.

"Whatever you found," he said, without looking up, "I don't want it."

"This painting—" she began.

"I said I don't want it."

"Okay, but listen, Mr. Scott."

He looked up at that, his eyebrows raised, and she hastened to continue.

"This is a quality piece, but it's not identified, and I wonder if you have any idea where it came from."

"I know exactly where it came from," he said. "My wife brought it with her."

"Oh," Leila said. If that was the case, it should stay in the family. She could clean it up, frame it, and give it to Diana for Christmas.

"Always looked weird to me," he went on. "But Heather loved that thing."

"I wonder why she didn't take it with her," Leila mused. "There's a label on the back, but it's torn. It says 'For J,' but the rest is missing. Was this a gift for someone? Or did someone give it to her?"

"How should I know? I should have burned the whole kit and caboodle down years ago. Junk and bad memories . . . that's all I have left." The toaster popped up, and he fished the bagel onto a plate. "Can't even get proper cream cheese anymore. Oliver shoulda let me die."

Brade Oliver had found Weldon and gotten him to the hospital in time to survive his heart attack. There were rumors that the old man had been drunk and armed, possibly considering ending his own life.

"Diana is grateful that he didn't," Leila replied. "But at the moment, I'm not entirely sure why."

Weldon looked up and a faint smile appeared in his eyes. "You're pretty snippy, aren't you? Didn't you used to be the nice one?"

"We all used to be nicer." Of the three of them, Kendall had always been the most likely to speak her mind. "People change."

With a sigh, the old man went back to his bagel. "That they do, missy. That they do."

CHAPTER ELEVEN

Ten miles outside Helena, MT

J P HUNG BACK in the bunkhouse after the others left to begin the winter chores. Warily, he pulled out the stack of letters, checked the dates and opened the first envelope. The girl, Heather, had not forgotten him. If anything, she'd been thinking of him far too much. Last thing he needed was to be stalked by some clingy gal who'd created a one-sided relationship. Good thing he hadn't slept with her.

> *Dear JP,*
>
> *You must think I'm an idiot. I probably am. I don't even know if you'll get this or that you'll want to read it if you do. You probably barely remember me. I'm sure you meet so many girls more interesting than me.*
>
> *But I'm going to pretend that you remember me and that you liked me, at least a little bit.*
>
> *I sure remember you. You have the most beautiful eyes. We had to read* Wuthering Heights *in English class, and you remind me of the character named Heathcliff, a dark, tortured soul. I hope you don't have a tragic story like Heathcliff. But your eyes tell me that*

maybe you do.

The words made him remember the sound of her voice, and he relaxed a little. He imagined Heather writing this in a bedroom with white furniture and a pink bedspread. She seemed to be a sparkly girly-girl. Maybe she was lying on her stomach as she wrote, with her heels kicked up behind her.

Some jerk came into the diner today. When he was done eating and I handed him the check, he asked, "What time do you get off work, honey?" and he grabbed my butt.

That, JP could picture with no problem. His fist gripped the thin page hard enough that he had to shake out the paper to continue reading. Part of him wanted to throw it down and not know whatever she was going to tell him. Another part needed to know that she'd handled it, that she was okay.

I never know what to do when that happens. My dad says I'm asking for it, that my clothes are too tight or low-cut, or I'm doing something to make these guys think I'm easy. You're probably laughing as you read this because I know that's how I seemed with you. But I liked you. You were my choice. And I was right about you because look at how honorable you were. The handsy guys in the diner aren't my choice. It's just something I have to live with because I need the job, and my boss would probably fire me if I made a customer mad.

Anyway, I'm just wearing my ugly uniform and I treat all my customers the same, so I don't know. Oh well. I get to keep my tips. This last guy left me a quarter.

JP shoved the letters into his backpack. He had work to do, and he was running late. He didn't know this girl, he reminded himself. She didn't know him. They were telling each other stories.

There was no reason for him to feel angry about the way she was being treated. She was nothing to him.

Yet, as he slung alfalfa bales onto the back of the flatbed, he pictured her in the diner, her head bent to take an order, her expression that mixture of caution and excitement for the world, her innocence beneath the mask of worldly experience.

Maybe she was playing him. But for what? It's not like he was a rich landowner or an heir apparent cowboying before he took his rightful place on a huge ranch somewhere. He had nothing but the strength in his arms and the determination to prove himself worthwhile.

He didn't think of his mother often anymore; he barely had any memories of her, anyway. But his grandmother had told him about her.

"She was a firecracker," she'd said, her face soft with sadness. "She was going places. Until . . ."

Until she had me.

He'd been just a kid, but he recognized the subtext, anyway. But his grandmother must have sensed what he hadn't said, for she turned to him fiercely.

"Your mother loved you, darlin'," she said. "Don't you ever doubt that."

He nodded dutifully.

"I mean that," she insisted. She took his smooth chin in her lined hands and brought her face close to his and sighed. "You were unexpected, but not unwanted. Never unwanted. Do you understand?"

"Okay."

But he suspected that the aunt and uncle who'd taken him and his sister in didn't feel the same way. He'd been just a tyke when Ma died, with Lizzie just a baby. Adding them to an already large household had been the way it worked then, but that didn't mean it was easy or that they liked it. Other family members helped; he recalled staying with his cousins on weekends, summers in their grandmother's small apartment, which was too hot and boring.

In fact, it was his cousin Carlton who'd explained the truth to him a few years later.

"Your sister's not really your sister, you know," Carlton said, hands fisted on chubby hips. They were on the basketball court a few blocks away, the one with the broken asphalt that had weeds growing through the cracks, that the big kids didn't use. They never got a chance to play on the good court, but they didn't mind. They got bothered less here.

"What do you mean?" JP asked him.

Carlton curled his lip. "Uncle Liam wasn't your dad."

"Liar." This is the cousin who regularly told him he had

shit for brains. Over the years, he'd informed JP that the raisins in raisin buns were really flies; that if you touched the old man who slept on the park bench, you'd get cooties; that when you slept outside, worms could burrow into your ears and turn your brains to scrambled eggs. (Most of Carlton's stories were bug related.) And on and on. There was no reason to believe this.

"Not this time." The little shit said it with an evil grin and an undertone of malice. "Your ma was knocked up by someone else when she married your dad."

He hadn't been entirely sure of what that meant at the time, but he knew enough that it was a slur against his parents. Or his mother, at any rate. He had only one option, given the circumstances.

He ran at Carlton and threw him into the dust, pummeling the older boy. They rolled around, yelling and throwing clumsy blows, and by the time they were finished, they were both bloody and breathing hard.

"It's still true," Carlton said. "But I shouldn't have told you like that."

JP glared at him but felt tears welling in his eyes. His nose was bleeding like a stuck pig, and he pretended that was the reason.

Carlton wasn't bad. He was just sort of stupid. He also had three older brothers of his own and had learned the hard way about how shit rolls downhill, and felt duty bound to share that knowledge with JP, as the next on the family downslope.

"Lizzie's still my sister," JP said, his voice thick and nasal.

Carlton shrugged. "They say your ma got Liam to marry her because she was in trouble, and he'd always liked her, anyway, so he wouldn't mind a little cuckoo in the nest."

"Cuckoo?"

Carlton shrugged. "Don't ask me. But I know what in trouble means."

JP nodded. He wasn't sure of it himself, but it wouldn't do to admit that.

Later, he went to Aunt Maria. "Is Lizzie really my sister?"

She glowered at him. "What are you talking about? What makes you ask such a thing? Has Carlton been running his mouth again? I don't know what I'm going to do with that boy."

Which answered the question, but without giving him any more useful information.

"I mean, is she my real sister? Or . . . I dunno. He said that my mom was in trouble when she married my dad. Something about a bird in the nest."

Aunt Maria stared at him. "Huh?"

"A . . . cuckoo?"

She closed her eyes and heaved a sigh. "Oh, Jesus Murphy."

She sat down then and held out her hand. He took it and she drew him close. She wasn't an affectionate woman, being too busy for things that didn't accomplish anything in the way of cooking, cleaning, or earning a crust, but she wasn't mean, either. So, this uncharacteristically gentle gesture both soothed JP and set his heart thumping with dread.

"She loved you, little man." She looked deep into his eyes. "No matter how you came into her life, she loved you. All of that was in the past once you entered the world. She was a strong, brave young woman. I was so proud of her, my little sister. She was taken from us too soon."

JP was deeply uncomfortable with his aunt's tears. She remembered someone he only knew from pictures and stories, but he put on a solemn face and nodded gravely.

After she patted him on the head and sent him back out to play, he realized that she hadn't answered his question and that, in fact, he was more confused now than ever.

CHAPTER TWELVE

"Nice," Lou commented when Leila leaned the painting up against the hallway wall. "Not as nice as your work, but good composition and use of light."

Leila laughed. "My goodness. Look who's been paying attention. Thanks, Dad. I like it too. At first, I thought it was junk, but it keeps drawing me back in, which means something."

Diana had insisted that Leila take the painting, even though it had been her mother's. If it hadn't been important enough to her to bring along when she left, then it wasn't important enough to save now. Besides, Diana had found some of her mother's clothing and, better yet, photo albums containing pictures of the two of them when Diana was a baby. Those items were vastly more meaningful to her, she said. Leila was the artist, after all, not her.

Leila frowned at the image again. A faint buzzing had set up in the back of her mind, like she was on the verge of seeing something important. She couldn't shake the feeling that she'd seen those characteristic brushstrokes, or that strange, almost kaleidoscope-like texture of the water before somewhere.

Which probably meant she'd been studying too hard for too long. If only she could use her education to figure out why this painting had been important to Diana's mother, then maybe she'd feel less like she was wasting her time.

"Looks a little like that piece Sue Anne Nylund wanted to hang in the school," Lou commented. "Except this one makes sense. The board wouldn't let her, so she took it home. She likes to brag she's got an original Mel Brooks or whatever." He looked up. "Sorry, are you a fan?"

Mel Brooks? The buzzing got louder. "Do you mean . . . Mel *Brezo*?"

"Some Mel guy," he said, waving a hand. "I don't know. That stream looks a bit familiar, like it's made up of tiny pieces of tile. Only the stream is where it belongs in this one, not falling out of the sky."

Leila sifted through her mental files to recall what she knew of the painter, which wasn't much. The gallery in Forsyth had held a Brezo exhibit a few years ago. Julia St. James, the owner, said it hadn't done well, but it was hard to say whether that was because the notoriously reclusive artist had refused to attend the event, or because he pushed the boundaries of realism with his work. Leila had worked one day of the exhibit and the lack of customers allowed her to spend most of her time studying, something Julia was fine with. The purchase by Sue Anne Nylund represented the only sale for the event.

Since then, they'd stuck to showings by regional artists with more recognizable styles. Grizzly bears, mountains, and horses, beautifully done, but to Leila's eye, not as challenging or engaging.

Like this painting.

Her pulse thudded thickly inside her head. Could she have happened on an early Mel Brezo? Could she be so lucky? But what would Heather Hudson have been doing with an original Brezo? She knelt in front of the painting again and studied the bottom corner. Were those paint slashes the initials MB?

They could be. She'd have to consult an artist signature and monogram dictionary. If it was indeed a Brezo, she might be able to match it. If it didn't match that artist's signature, she'd be back to square one.

That was the probable scenario, because how on earth would Diana's mother have ended up with such a valuable painting? And why hadn't she taken it with her when she left? Perhaps she hadn't known the value of what she had.

"I need to go see Sue Anne Nylund," she said, her thoughts spinning. "I have to look at her painting. Sorry, Dad, can you manage for an hour without me? This can't wait!"

"I can never manage without you, darlin'," he replied. "But that's my cross to bear. You run along and solve your mystery. I'll be here when you get back."

She snapped a quick photo of the painting with her phone, then dashed out the door. If she was right—and she already knew in her bones that she was—then not only did she have a valuable piece of artwork in her possession, but the forensics required for provenance would serve as the perfect final project for her degree.

This was what she'd been looking for. An original idea, interesting enough to get her across the finish line.

Not all mysteries can be solved, Mom. But this one can.

And she was going to prove it.

✪

"IT'S BEAUTIFUL," LEILA said.

Sue Anne Nylund had the painting displayed prominently above her couch in the front room of her house. In the mostly white room, accent pillows and vases drew attention to the vivid cadmium orange and phthalo blue used by the artist, and the effect was stunning.

"It's called *Under the Same Sky*," Sue Anne said, visibly pleased at Leila's reaction.

Unfortunately, the signature was no help. It was a pair of clearly stylized initials that she recognized from the monogram dictionary she'd already consulted. If Weldon's painting was an early Brezo, it was from before the artist had fully realized his style. It probably had not even been recorded.

"Can I see the back?" she asked.

Sue Anne grumbled but allowed her to lift it off the wall. "Don't put it back crooked, you hear?"

A business card of an art agency was stapled to the back, but nothing more.

"Thank you, Ms. Nylund," she said, replacing the painting.

Sue Anne shifted it, eyed it, then moved it back. "I sincerely doubt that Weldon Scott had a piece of artwork of this caliber. Good luck with your search."

Disappointed, Leila returned to the pub and was hanging clean glassware when Lou came out of his office and stood before her. He'd been balancing the ledger from the night before. He always insisted the cash be balanced to the penny from one day to the next.

"You have something you want to tell me about?"

Leila looked up at him while rubbing a water mark off a beer stein. His brow was more furrowed than normal, and his posture was rigid.

"What do you mean?"

He placed a small padded mailer on the bar, then slid it over to Leila. She caught it and her stomach plummeted. It was the DNA test kit she'd ordered.

"I was going to tell you."

"I'm sure."

"The look on your face is why I didn't. Honesty's not always the best policy, is it?"

"Since when do you keep from me, lass? If you want to find your birth parents, I'll support you, Leila, but it was a closed adoption. You know that." He paused. "However, if you're getting involved with that boy again—"

"Sawyer?" Her cheeks warmed. "First of all, he's a man, not a boy. And second, I'm all grown up now, too, in case you hadn't noticed. I can look after myself."

"Oh, Leila," he said, shaking his head. "You're still getting over Gary."

"Gary? I hardly think about him," she said, realizing it was the truth. "Things were over for a long time before I called it. I just didn't want to see it."

"But you see Lafferty clearly now, do you?"

She tipped her head and fought to keep her voice steady. "There's nothing going on between us. We had something special once, and then it ended."

"Because he ruined it."

She was quiet for a moment. "I played a role too."

Lou snorted.

"Look, Dad, I've never felt for anyone what I felt for Sawyer. If we're going to live in the same town, we have to find a way to deal with the past."

He was silent for a long moment. Then he nodded. "I understand. But you can't blame me for being protective of my best girl."

She leaned over and gave him a hug. "Thanks, Dad."

"Now." He extricated himself and pointed to the envelope. "Tell me how this works."

"It's a DNA test, the same one that Brade Oliver and Diana took that showed that they're related. I send in a spit sample, and I get a report that I can use to compare with anyone else who shows up on the databases of people who are seeking blood relatives. Brade was lucky to find Diana. I might never find someone else who matches."

"Then again," Lou said, "you could."

"I could."

"And when did you decide to go ahead with this, dar-lin'?" he asked, not looking at her.

Lou wasn't a top-down, heavy-handed parent. If any-thing, he'd probably been too lenient with her, though she hadn't exactly given him cause to be concerned. She'd always been a good girl. She had to be. Team Monahan. Lou and his best girl, the two of them against the world.

"I've been thinking about it since Diana did it," she ad-mitted. "But I didn't want to talk to you about it because I knew it would upset you."

"Has it been a good thing for Diana?" Lou asked.

"Of course it has. She loves having a big brother. And he seems thrilled to have a sister. You should see the kids with their uncle Brade. So, I couldn't help but think, what if I had siblings or half-siblings or cousins or whatever out there somewhere too?"

Lou sniffed.

Brade had stirred up some anger in the community when he'd arrived there looking for clues to his birth parents. He'd focused on Weldon Scott, who he all but accused of being his deadbeat biological father.

Instead, his digging revealed that Heather Scott, Wel-don's wife, had given up a child for adoption—Brade—before she married Weldon and had Diana. Weldon knew about it, but never told Diana about her half brother.

"He nearly killed Weldon with all of it," Lou said.

The complicated truth, and Brade's behavior being nothing short of heroic through it all, had softened most people toward him.

But apparently not Leila's father.

"Brade saved Weldon's life! You know this, Dad. What's this really about?"

Lou stapled yesterday's printed receipts together, then closed his laptop and shoved it away from him. "It's nothing, lass," he said, more softly. "It's just . . . after all these years, you've never felt it necessary to look for your . . . your . . . birth parents. I guess I got used to having you all to myself. You can't blame an old man for feeling a little insecure."

Leila's throat grew hot. She reached out and took her father's hand. "You're not an old man. And you should know better than to be insecure. I'll always be your daughter."

His eyes shone and he smiled but said nothing.

"But surely you can understand that I have to seek out any information I can, right? There is technology that we didn't have a few decades ago. There's no need for secrecy, is there?"

He swallowed. "Of course not. It just seems a bit impulsive. Have you considered that you might not like what you find? What if you discover connections you'd rather not have?"

"It's bound to be messy, but how is that different from anyone else? Look at Kendall and her messy family. At least they know who they are."

Lou tipped his head in acknowledgement, but his expression was troubled.

"And," Leila went on, "I want to have children."

"Of course, darlin'," he said, "but maybe you should have stuck it out with Gary, then."

Instantly, her jaw tightened. "Dad. For three years, I was ready to get married and start a family. He's the one who wouldn't commit."

"You were engaged."

"Yes, and when I pressed him to set a date, he led with, and I quote, 'Um, about that.'"

"Doesn't mean he didn't love you, darlin'."

"If he loved me," she began, then stopped, old memories crowding her throat. "If he loved me, he should have been dying to be with me. Did you know he'd been married before?"

Lou's brows went up. "No. When did you learn that?"

"About two seconds before I dumped him."

Lou didn't respond, but the tight line of his mouth expressed his opinion eloquently.

"I did not overreact, Dad. I reacted exactly appropriately."

She didn't regret her actions, but now she wondered if Gary's admission had touched the nerve still raw from Sawyer's marriage?

Why was love so hard for her? All she wanted was for someone to love her first and best and forever. Instead, she was . . . temporary. Convenient. Until she wasn't.

She took a breath. He was already upset, so might as well tell him the rest. "You should probably know that I'm considering a sperm bank."

Lou made a pained sound in the back of his throat.

"I want to have children and I'm tired of waiting. With my own genetic history a blank, getting pregnant by a syringe means my future children will know almost nothing."

Lou looked like he was herniating a spleen, but she ignored him.

"I have no idea what health conditions I might be prone to, what my ethnic or religious background might be, what part of the world my relatives live in. If I use donor sperm, I'll know a few things, but still, only on one side. My children deserve better, Dad. The DNA test is for them too."

"These theoretical children," he said, his voice tight, "deserve a father in their life."

"Believe me, that's my first choice, but I'd rather have an anonymous donor than someone who doesn't love me."

A vision of Sawyer with Piper flashed into her brain, startling her.

Lou's expression darkened. Then he sighed and all the fight seemed to go out of him. "I wish your mother were here."

He looked older suddenly. Older and sadder. Perhaps all adoptive parents felt this way when their children went seeking knowledge. Perhaps it had nothing to do with adoption and everything to do with children growing up and away.

"Me too, Dad," she said, taking his hand again. "Nothing between us will change."

"Like nothing changed between Weldon and Diana?" He smiled sadly. "Of course things will change, darlin'."

"He lied to her," she said. "You and Mom were always honest with me. You don't have anything to worry about. Okay?"

He heaved a great sigh, leaned over, and kissed her forehead. "You'll always be my best girl. No matter what, of that, there can never be any doubt."

Chapter Thirteen

THE NEXT MORNING, Sawyer followed Bayleigh through the main barn at Belle Vista, imagining the stalls all occupied with horses. So far, they had three, including Turtle. She wanted at least ten more, some specifically for clients with physical issues such as mobility, others that would be used for clients with mental health challenges or behavioral issues.

"I was thinking that a couple of draft horses would be good," she commented. "They're gentle and calm. Helping with things like grooming and feeding will encourage clients to develop emotional regulation and build self-confidence. For an anxious young person, being in charge of such a big animal is tremendously empowering." She smiled. "Of course, they'll always be under supervision."

"You're the psychologist," Sawyer replied.

She had a masters in clinical counseling and had a tendency to get carried away with shop talk, but her excitement was contagious, and Sawyer found himself enjoying it. He'd learned a lot from his time at the ranch where Turtle was boarded and was eager to build on that knowledge, even though his focus was caring for the horses and managing the business.

"I'll be contracting with a few other mental health professionals," she added. "Obviously, we need physical and occupational therapists, but I want Belle Vista to be a one-stop shop for equine-assisted therapeutic modalities. For example, interaction with horses can be very helpful for people dealing with post-traumatic stress disorder. Some of them feel separated from others by their anxiety and depression. They're terribly lonely, but they don't know how to go about making connections again. But when they work with a horse, they rediscover that connection. Often, they're able to take that home with them, to translate it into their human relationships." She gave a self-conscious laugh. "Sorry. I guess I'm just excited. Anyway, I've got the space; I might as well use it."

Sawyer wondered what personal experience might have informed this excitement. Whatever challenges she'd been through in her life had made her strong and compassionate.

Kind of like Leila. He winced inwardly, hating that he'd been part of the refining fire that had forged her character.

He looked away from Bayleigh. "I've spoken with a carpenter about installing wheelchair ramps. I think we can improve accessibility to tack and grooming equipment too."

"Good." Bayleigh nodded. "How about the website? What I have now is too basic."

Sawyer told her about the designer he'd talked to and her recommendations on host provision and general layout, as well as the information he thought was important to include.

"I'm not a tech expert by any means," he added.

Bayleigh laughed. "Well, I'm a Luddite by comparison, so I appreciate everything you're doing to keep us twenty-first-century compliant. But getting our horses here and ready for clients is the first priority."

Sawyer tipped an imaginary hat, glad to be back on less emotional ground. "Message received. I'm heading out to another ranch shortly to pick up a couple, hopefully. Owner says they're sound, mature animals, American quarter qorse mostly, I think. If all goes well, a few more stalls will be occupied by tonight."

"Excellent news! Thank you, Sawyer." She patted his arm and left the barn.

After setting a few dates with the carpenter, he secured the horse trailer and hit the road.

While driving, he initiated a hands-free call to his mother to check in on Piper. She had a playdate with a little friend she'd met at school, and everything had gone well, but something about his mother's voice didn't sound quite right.

"What aren't you telling me, Mom?" he asked.

"I didn't want to worry you," she began.

"Then don't ever begin a sentence like that, okay? Just tell me."

"I just found out for sure this morning. My surgery date has been moved up, honey. I'm getting my new knee next week! But that means I won't be able to do before- and after-school care for Piper. I'm so sorry, Sawyer."

He congratulated her and got a bit more information,

then ended the call, his mind whirling. He was glad his mother would be free of the pain that had plagued her for so long, but where would he find childcare on such short notice?

⭐

AT HOME THAT night, while he did the dishes, Piper chattered cheerfully to him about the imaginary game she'd created, how she'd helped Grandma bake oatmeal cookies, and how she wanted a puppy like the one her friend had.

"And when Grandma's getting her operation," she said, "I'm going to visit the pine-uh-pull lady."

Sawyer turned the tap off. "What?"

She turned innocent eyes on him. "Daddy, you don't listen very good."

"Sorry, honey. What did you say about Grandma's operation?"

"I'm going to visit the pine-uh-pull lady while Grandma gets a new leg in place of her old leg. How come her old leg doesn't work anymore? Is that what happens to legs?"

Sawyer dried his hands. "Degenerative joint disease . . . uh, never mind. Sometimes knees wear out. Are you talking about Leila?"

"Yeah." She nodded firmly. "I like her."

"Yes, I know, sweetheart. But what makes you think that Leila will look after you?"

"I asked Grandma, and she said Daddy would find a

friend to take care of me." She blinked up at him. "Do you have another friend?"

He rubbed his face. He didn't really have any friends, especially not Leila.

"She was at the park with another lady and that lady had two dogs, Daddy! A mommy dog and a baby dog. And they were so cute, and you said when we moved that we would get a puppy, and I'm so 'spon-sah-bull now. Can we get a puppy soon? Tomorrow?"

Sawyer squatted beside his little girl, the one who held his heart and made him crazy. "We'll talk about a puppy later, okay? Now, you say you saw Leila? At the park?"

He had a bad feeling about where this was going.

Piper nodded, then jumped up and down. "Grandma was resting, so I went to see the puppy. And I told Leila about her taking care of me, and she said she'd talk to you and that also she knew about four puppies that need forever homes. Can we get them, Daddy? Can we? You promised!"

Sawyer sighed and went to run the bathtub. He'd get Piper into bed and then give Leila a call. She'd be waiting. As revenge went, he was getting off easy.

LEILA ANSWERED ON the first ring.

"Four puppies?" he asked. "I hope you enjoyed yourself. Now I have to break a little girl's heart."

She laughed, that tinkly sound that took him straight

back.

"Nah," she said. "One puppy will make you her hero forever."

"I'm not ready for a puppy."

"You'll make it work," she said. "What's this about volunteering me for child-care duties?"

"A misunderstanding. I'm sorry you got put on the spot like that."

"Not at all. It's nice to have someone so excited to see me."

"Ouch."

"Oh, relax, Sawyer," she said lightly. "I've pivoted. You're back in Grand. I'm fine. Your kid likes me, I like her. Maybe you and I will even end up friends."

Talking with her had always been so easy. That is, until it wasn't.

Their breakup had been so stupid, a spat between two dumb kids that had somehow knocked them off-kilter so badly that a relationship that should have lasted forever went flying off the rails.

Suddenly, he felt like that lonely first-year student again, with the phone pressed to his ear, wishing he was with her, missing her but having to be the strong one because she would have given up everything for him, and he couldn't let that happen.

"Sawyer?" Leila said. "Do you really need someone to help with Piper?"

He grimaced. "We're fine. I'll be fine. It's just . . . my

mom is having knee replacement surgery next week. It was supposed to be in a couple of months, but there was an opening and she grabbed it. I haven't had time to make a contingency plan yet, but I will. I'll sort it out."

"Oh, yeah?" He could hear the smile in her voice. "Piper said I was your only friend."

"That kid." He had to laugh. "Shows what she knows."

"I guess we're ending up friends sooner than we thought."

Her voice was soft and warm, and his heart rolled over. "I guess we are."

"Listen, Sawyer," she said, serious now. "If you're in a pinch, I can help out after school. Until you find someone else."

"You don't have to do this, Leila. You have a job—"

"Two jobs, actually. And an undergrad project to finish."

"Oh!" He was ridiculously happy to hear it. She'd always minimized her own goals, pushed them aside, for him and for Lou, putting them second to taking care of other people. "But then you really don't have time."

"I'll make it work."

She was someone who saw possibilities and believed in them, even when the practical challenges seemed insurmountable, even when everything seemed impossible.

"You always were better at that than me," he said.

She was quiet for a moment. "Something tells me you've learned to make a lot of things work."

It was a concession, and he appreciated it. "Leila," he

said. "Can we talk sometime? I'd like to explain—"

"You don't owe me anything, Sawyer," she said.

"I think I do."

"No." Her voice was firm. "We were kids. Idealistic, immature, thoughtless. We made mistakes. Both of us. Then we grew up."

"I never stopped loving you."

Whoa. He hadn't meant to say that.

"Sawyer, shut up." Her voice was tight. "Just because your marriage didn't work out doesn't mean you can come back here and expect me to fall into your arms. You broke my heart. Then I got over it. End of story. Now, if you need me to help with your kid, I'm willing. If you think you're getting another chance to break my heart, forget it. I'm not that stupid. I'm also not that desperate. Love is a fantasy. You, of all people, should know that. I've got my career, my friends, my dad. I'm happy. If I ever want more . . ." she paused, "I'll get it myself. Your priority is your daughter, as it should be."

He liked this new, tough Leila. He'd fallen in love with the girl who'd worn her heart on her sleeve, but her emotional neediness had led to their destruction. Now her heart was guarded, protected by a carapace as rigid as any turtle's shell. If he was to find the real Leila again, he'd have to work for it.

"Piper is always my priority," he replied. "She likes you. If you're okay looking after her for my mom—"

"I already said I was."

"Then you should know her history."

Leila was quiet for a moment. "I don't know, Sawyer," she said, eventually.

"Her history is my history, Leila," Sawyer said. "And that connects with our history. We ended so badly. Please let me tell you what happened. I'm not asking for your forgiveness. I just want you to listen."

CHAPTER FOURTEEN

A FTER CLOSING THE pub a few nights later, Leila went upstairs to the apartment to continue her research into Mel Brezo, grateful for anything that kept her mind off Sawyer. She'd agreed to have dinner with him and listen to whatever he had to say, but she wasn't looking forward to it.

She couldn't remember those last few weeks of their relationship without squirming.

She opened her laptop and pulled up the file containing her notes. There had to be a connection between the artist and Heather Scott. Perhaps he was Brade's biological father. If Heather had been in love with Brezo before she married Weldon, it might explain why she'd kept the painting.

She sighed. The genetic aspect was Brade's journey. Hers was artistic provenance.

She looked at the painting, standing against the wall near her closet door. Like the one hanging in Sue Anne's home, this one had surreal, Piccaso-esque elements, geometric angles and mirror images that worked together to create an oddly harmonious result. Unlike Sue Anne's, however, the colors in this one were softer, muted, as if the artist had been unwilling or unable to fully commit to the vibrancy he'd later embrace.

If it was, in fact, him.

She was building a story, but until she had more evidence, that's all it was—another wild goose chase by Leila Monahan.

She sat at her desk, her chin in her hand.

Story of her life.

Had she done the same thing with Sawyer? Built their romance into this magical, bigger-than-life love that had no connection to reality? How immature she'd been. Impatient. Insecure. If she'd just trusted him, they wouldn't have had that big fight. Without the big fight, maybe he wouldn't have ended up in Miranda's arms.

The story she clung to was that Sawyer had hurt her. He was the bad guy.

The truth was, Leila had tried to force his hand.

Why was marriage such a big deal to her? Was she really broken in some elemental way that she couldn't accept a future without a family of her own? She'd always assumed she was an adoption success story, that she was so stable, so beloved, that the early rejection wound other adoptees talked about didn't apply to her. But look at her, so desperate to nail down permanent love that she'd been ready to settle for Gary.

She left her desk and threw herself onto her bed. "What's wrong with me?" she whispered.

✪

"WHAT DO YOU think about getting married?" Leila asked—casually, as if his answer didn't matter much one way or the other.

They were in his dorm room at Montana State, it being Sawyer's weekend to have privacy. Buckley, his sophomore roommate, didn't have a girlfriend and lived in worshipful admiration of Sawyer's conjugal visits. Buckley's real name was Steve, but the kid was asthmatic and lived on cough syrup. He'd have to get that phlegm situation under control if he ever wanted to change his status.

Sawyer jerked upright on the narrow bed. "What? Why? Are you pregnant?"

He was paranoid about birth control. He insisted he wasn't having her end up like his mother, pregnant too young, having to put her dreams on hold. But this *was* her dream. Didn't he understand?

"No, I'm not pregnant, you idiot." She snuggled into his side. "I just wondered where you were at with the future planning stuff. I know where I'm at."

He exhaled deeply. "Don't scare me like that."

"What's the big deal? We'd make it work."

They had a plan, and so what if the timing didn't work to his exact specifications? They'd talked it through at the end of that first magical summer and agreed that they could handle a long-distance relationship. Yes, he had a heavy course load and student loans up the wazoo. Lots of couples started out that way. He was all about "a solid financial foundation," as if that was more important than love.

"Leila." Sawyer turned to her and the seriousness in his eyes scared her a little. "A baby now would be a disaster. Don't joke about this, okay?"

"A baby is never a disaster! How can you say that?"

"You know what I mean," he snapped. "Why are you twisting my words?"

Leila got up and grabbed her sweater. She regretted starting the whole conversation in the first place, but now that they were in it, she couldn't let it go. "Why are you avoiding the subject? Is this not working for you anymore? Have you changed your mind about me?"

"Why are you even asking me this?" He flung a hand out. "I wouldn't have you here if I didn't want you."

"Then why don't you want to get married?"

"I do." He spoke slowly and carefully, as if she was an idiot. "Just not now."

She glared at him. "When, then?"

"I don't know, Leila!" He began yanking on his jeans. "One day."

"Why should I believe you?"

Tears sprang to her eyes. He seemed like a different person. She missed him so much and yet he seemed to have gone on with his new life here without her just fine. She had to get out of there. Her bus didn't leave for another hour, but she couldn't let him see how much he'd hurt her.

He turned to her then, his face gentled, familiar again. "You know I love you. But I'm not ready. We're going to finish college, get our careers started, and then we'll talk about marriage. Okay?"

They'd had this conversation so many times, and she always acquiesced. But this time, whatever had triggered her refused to stop firing.

"Dad said a gentleman would have already given me a ring."

"A gentleman?" Sawyer scoffed. "Did we slip back into the fifties when I wasn't looking? And don't tell me that Lou is pressuring you to get married. I don't buy that for a second."

"Of course not. But he doesn't want to see me hurt and after all this time—"

"It's only been three years, Leila."

"Three years, three months and five days. To be exact."

"Yeah, and we haven't dated anyone else, have we?"

The way he said it sounded like an accusation. She stomped into her boots, her motions hard and fast, swept her hair away from her face and went to the door.

"If you want to date someone else, go right ahead," she said. "I'm not interested in anyone else, but apparently you need to play the field. Fine. Have a great time. Call me when you're ready to man up to your true feelings."

★

To Sawyer's shock, Leila didn't speak to him for a full two weeks. No phone calls, no text messages, nothing. It was a bit of a relief, to be honest. He was swamped with work, and he didn't have time for her drama. He missed her, but he was annoyed too. Why couldn't she be patient?

Then one evening, while he was working with a fellow student over dinner, Leila showed up.

The optics weren't great, he had to admit. Miranda, his study partner, was attractive and attentive and, naturally, Leila walked in right when they were laughing about a stupid comment their prof had made.

The look on her face . . .

"Leila!" He leaped out of his seat and ran to her side. She was pale, her eyes enormous, her arms clutched over her chest.

She shook him off and left the cafe. "Your roommate told me where to look," she said. "He might have mentioned you were on a date."

"It's not a date!"

Sawyer directed Leila to the student hub, where they found a group of padded chairs in a secluded corner. Everyone was out drinking or messing around or, like Buckley, studying, so the place was quiet. They'd be able to talk here.

He could always kick Buckley out, but he'd recently discovered that the kid slept on these padded benches when Leila was in town, without complaint, and he didn't feel like asking anything more of him. Hero worship was a heavy responsibility.

"There's nothing going on between me and Miranda," he assured her.

Miranda had just returned from a student exchange program, and since they shared some classes, he was helping her get up to speed. They'd been working on a business analysis project all day, the only ones on their team who were taking it seriously, in fact, and when at six o'clock, they still hadn't finished, she suggested they get something to eat.

"The Point was the only place with a table, and we were each paying for ourselves," he explained.

He had nothing to feel bad about. So why was she looking at him with those tragic eyes, as if she'd just caught him cheating?

"You might think there's nothing going on," Leila said, "but I guarantee you, that's not what she's thinking."

"You're being paranoid."

Okay, the way Miranda looked at him was a pretty clear indicator that she was open to more than just academic teamwork with him, if he was available. And while he hadn't bitten on any of her fairly obvious hints, he also hadn't shut her down as concretely as maybe he should have.

Because, yeah, he was lonely. And, let's face it, Leila had been his only real girlfriend, and they were living far away from each other now, and what guy stays with his high school sweetheart, anyway, as the guys said?

This guy.

It might not be cool, but he intended to be with Leila forever. But she'd gotten so possessive, and he was feeling a little choked by it. And yeah, it had been refreshing to be out with Miranda, talking with someone who was interested in the stuff he was interested in. Leila was brilliant in her own way, but talking about profit-loss ratios or return on investment made her eyes glaze over.

Kind of like him when she got talking about Monet or Manet or whatever painter was her latest obsession.

"I am not paranoid," she said, and there was a chill in her voice. "I wanted to see my boyfriend. In fact, I had a surprise planned for you."

Guilt assailed him. She was trying to do something nice for him. She'd probably bought some new lacy underwear, which was never, ever wrong. But it was awkward, given Buckley and all, and they had more between them than sex, didn't they?

"I wanted to do this a little nicer," Leila said. She suddenly looked awkward and sort of vulnerable. She slid to her knees in front of him and the hair on the back of his neck stood up.

He glanced around to see if anyone was looking. "Leila, what are you doing?"

She fumbled in her pocket and brought out a small box. "Sawyer—"

Panic filled him. "What are you doing?" He reached for her arm and tried to tug her back onto the seat, but she yanked it away. She was like a dog with a bone when she wanted to be.

"Shut it, Sawyer. Let me do this."

No, no, no, this can't be happening.

But it was happening, all right. Like a slow-motion car wreck, he saw her open the box, reach inside with trembling fingers, and pull out a ring. For a second, he was confused. He expected her to have gotten herself an engagement ring, which would have made him sick to his stomach. He'd get her a ring when he was ready, when he had the money to buy her the kind of diamond he would be proud to see on her finger, not the chip he'd have to buy on installments now.

Because yes, he'd looked at rings. He wasn't as blind as she thought he was. Them getting engaged was a reasonable idea.

Except . . . something still held him back. They were too young. He was barely discovering all the potential his future might hold, all the possibilities for jobs in the financial sector. It was exhilarating, learning of everything the world had to offer. Surely, she felt the same way. She had so much in front of her, too, even though she seemed to think that Grand was the best and the only place for her. She needed to get away, to see more of the world, to experience life before she committed herself to him, even though she didn't see it that way.

He wanted her, but he wanted all of her and he wanted her to come to him as a well-rounded person, fully aware that choosing him meant not choosing all these other things.

All these other people.

He was afraid that one day, she'd grow tired of him and

resent that she'd never been with anyone else. At least, he'd dated a few other people before he'd met her. She hadn't even done that.

She held the ring between her thumb and forefinger. It was brown and shiny. A man's ring.

What was worse than your girlfriend buying an engagement ring for herself?

Your girlfriend buying an engagement ring for you.

"Sawyer Dean Lafferty," she said in a husky voice, "will you do me the honor of one day becoming my husband?"

LEILA KNEW AS the words were coming out of her mouth that she should have listened to the instinct telling her that this was not her weekend.

The look on Sawyer's face could only be described as . . . horror.

"Get up, Leila," he said, his voice an angry hiss. "Don't do this. Not here, not now."

She caught movement in the corner of her eye as Miranda walked into the hub.

"Sawyer, you forgot your . . . oh." Miranda stopped in her tracks. "Oh dear."

Where was a good old earthquake when you needed one? Did you have to be in California? Surely there were cracks in the earth's crust out here in Montana too. Something just big enough to swallow up a medium-size, lovesick art history major with impulse control deficiencies and abandonment issues.

Sawyer dropped her hand, sidestepped her, and in that small movement, Leila knew that she'd lost. He went to this woman, this stranger, as a colleague, a co-worker, an equal, to whom he'd express apologies for being interrupted by an inconvenient blast from the past. He'd explain about this poor girl who couldn't move on and how he needed to be kind, to look after her for a while, until she was ready to accept the truth.

Leila shifted onto the seat again, her face burning, her chest thick and hot. Miranda cut sympathetic eyes at her, which made Leila want to rip those blond waves out by the roots, and left the building.

"Come on, honey," Sawyer said, holding out his hand. He sounded . . . tired. "Let's go back to my room. Buckley can sleep out here and keep someone else awake with that infernal snoring. He must have adenoids like soccer balls."

Leila let him lead her through the hub, across campus, and back to the dorm room, where Buckley took one look at them and fled.

Sawyer sat down on the bed and patted the side of it. "What's this all about, Leila?"

He sounded so tender again that she forgot about being mad. All the clever words she'd planned evaporated from her head.

"These past two weeks have been . . ." she faltered. Awful . . . lonely . . . terrifying . . .? She wasn't sure how to finish.

"Important," Sawyer said.

She flinched. "What?"

He nodded thoughtfully. "What we have is something special. Something not many people get to experience."

There, there it was. That's what she was looking for. Tears of relief rushed her eyes. Then he continued.

"You know the saying, 'absence makes the heart grow fonder'?"

She gave a little snort. "Yeah. 'So stay away a little longer.' Is that the one?"

"We've known each other since we were eighteen."

"Seventeen," she corrected. If he was going to break up with her, she wasn't going to let him off on a technicality.

"Point is," he said with a slight frown, "we were kids. We still are kids. You're barely twenty-one. You want to get married, but Leila, if we do that now, you know what the chances are that we'll stay married? Look it up. One-third of teenage marriages end in divorce within five years, and almost half wind up divorcing within ten years. Only thirty percent of teen mothers who marry after their child is born are still married by the time they're forty."

"We're not teenagers anymore and we don't have a baby," she pointed out.

"Yes," he said patiently, "but if it were up to you, we'd be married with at least one kid on the ground already. Why do you think I insist on condoms? I know you, Leila."

She cringed. She was on the pill, but she had to admit

she wasn't the most reliable at remembering to take it. A part of her had wished that the decision to marry would be taken out of their hands. They were going to get married, anyway, so what if it happened a little ahead of schedule?

She hadn't realized that he'd cottoned on to her.

"I'm not trying to trap you, Sawyer," she said quietly.

"I know, honey." His voice was unbearably tender. "But you have to stop thinking about me for a little while. I can't handle the pressure."

"Stop thinking about you?" she cried. "How can I do that when I miss you every moment of every day? You're all I think about. Isn't it the same way with you?"

He hesitated and she had her answer.

She jumped to her feet. "Never mind. I guess I know where I stand now. I thought these two weeks were about you coming to your senses and realizing how much you miss me, how much you love me. How wrong you were to cut me off like that." She gave a rough laugh. "I really am an idiot."

"Leila—"

"No. Don't you dare feel sorry for me. But answer me this: do you honestly not love me anymore?"

He sighed. "I'll always love you, Leila. It's not about that."

The last thing she could stand was some kind of pity love. She'd rather be dumped fair and square than have him hover on the edges of her life because he was worried that she'd collapse without him.

They needed each other. As long as it was mutual, it

stood. When one stepped aside, the structure crumbled.

It was really happening. They were breaking up. The thing she could never imagine, not in her worst nightmares, was coming true. The man she'd thought would hold her heart in his hands and protect her for the rest of his life had stopped loving her.

"This is for your own good—"

"Fuck you, Sawyer." She stalked to the door. "Don't pretend this is about you making some sacrifice. This allows you to play the field, like you probably always wanted. Fine. Go for it. Go date all the Mirandas and Tiffanys and Rebeccas you want. Have a great life, okay? And do not worry about me. I'll be fine."

Just before she slammed out the door, she remembered the reason she'd come. She still had it in her hand.

It hit him just under the eye and, though the edges were smooth, she threw it with such force that it left a mark.

CHAPTER FIFTEEN

"**H**EY, COWBOY. I hope the other guy looks worse."

Sawyer was in a bar off campus that catered to the student population by carrying cheap drafts on Thursdays, and the place was mobbed. It was a good place to go when you didn't want to feel alone. And Sawyer hadn't felt so alone since he'd left California. He remembered that first day in Grand, walking into the homeroom class, and how awful it felt to be the new kid when everyone else was already friends.

He looked up from his beer and winced to see Miranda standing in front of him. He touched the mark under his eye. Crazy that such a small thing could leave a shiner. The soft skin under the eye was very tender, he supposed.

"I bruise like a peach," he said. "The other guy walked away without a scratch."

She lifted her brows. "So, you're a gentleman, then. Because I have a feeling the other guy was a girl. Your girl. Mind if I sit? Or is she going to come after me next?"

Without waiting for a response, she slid her slender, denim-clad hips onto the stool next to him. They were in a bar off campus that catered to the student population by carrying cheap drafts on Thursdays, and the place was mobbed. It was a good place to be when you didn't want to feel alone.

Maybe Miranda was feeling weird to be back in Montana.

"She's gone." He lifted his almost empty glass. "But I'm about to head back. Big exam coming up. Gotta study."

She twinkled a smile at him. "We don't always have to talk about school, Sawyer, do we? It's barely seven o'clock. Have another beer with me." She lowered her voice. "To be honest, I'm avoiding someone. It would be great if you could play along. Do you mind?"

He looked around. "Who?"

She rolled her eyes, but something about the casual gesture seemed . . . off. "Nobody important. He's just a little intense. We broke up before I left, but he seems to think we're still together. I told him I was busy, but then my pals took off without me so . . ."

The bravado was a thin film over the vulnerability of a girl who preferred to appear that she had the world by the tail. She needed someone to be with. He was here.

"I understand intensity," he said, touching his face. Instantly, he felt guilty. What was he doing, throwing Leila under the bus? He was better than that.

"I thought you might."

Miranda had dimples in her cheeks and an attractive way of moving her head when she laughed. Graceful. Easygoing. Charming.

A charming woman who needed a little assistance and

chose him to be the one to give it. No pressure. No demands.

Casual. He could live with that.

So, he ordered another beer for himself and one for her. After that, they had another round and shared a plate of fries. It was fun to talk about something other than school. Turned out that Miranda was from California too. She missed the ocean, but she'd wanted to get away, try something new. She'd noticed him in their freshman year, she confessed shyly, and it didn't hurt him any to hear that.

"I don't mean to get in the way, if you're still attached . . .?" She let the question hang in the air.

"I'm not."

Her face brightened. "Okay, then."

He and Leila weren't over. They'd never be over. But they needed a break. He couldn't take the relentless pressure from her. He didn't especially want to date anyone else, but he was worried that they were both so inexperienced that they would come to resent each other if they didn't see other people, at least a little.

He didn't want to sleep with anyone else. But having a drink with someone else wasn't cheating. Going out for dinner with a nice girl, talking about ordinary things, learning about someone else's life—it would make him more well-rounded. Would make him appreciate Leila more.

He knew he hadn't treated her very well, but he didn't have the words to tell her how she made him feel like he was wearing a sweater that was two sizes too small, like he needed to rip it off so he could breathe. He loved her. That wasn't in question. But he was a kid! She wanted the whole happy-ever-after now, already, and he for damn sure couldn't give that to her yet. So where did that leave them?

She was mad. He kept waiting for her to call and apologize, but the longer it went on, the more he wondered if maybe she'd meant it. Maybe she was really done with him. If that was the case, he could date other girls with a clear conscience, right?

They would make their way back to each other. In time. He didn't doubt that for a second. But for now, he was entitled to be a normal college kid. He had a pretty girl across the table from him, a girl who liked him but had her own life that didn't revolve around him.

He wasn't drunk, by any means, but when Miranda asked him to walk her back to her room, not a single alarm bell went off.

When she asked him in, because her roommate was away for the weekend and she wanted to be certain the guy wasn't lying in wait for her, he felt like a hero. She needed a protector and even though she wasn't anyone special to him, it was tough to resist the opportunity to play the role.

When Miranda tugged him into the empty room and closed the door behind them, he didn't resist because . . . come on, he was a grown man and she was gorgeous and willing and he was lonely and, apparently, unattached.

It didn't occur to him at the time that he was being manipulated, because it seemed that women called all the shots when it came to relationships and the job of men was to react, mostly. He didn't like it, but he was stupid when it came to women, obviously. He'd tried the whole Big Love thing and it had gone so badly wrong that what did he know? Maybe a one-night stand was the way to go.

She was warm and inviting and fun and generous, and the sex was enthusiastic, if a little . . . clinical. Maybe that wasn't the right word, but somehow it felt as if she was running through a series of steps she'd read were necessary. Or required, perhaps. It didn't feel . . . spontaneous.

With Leila, it had always been deeply mutual, their desire perfectly matched, their need to connect far more than physical.

That was it. This girl wanted the physical connection, but there was nothing emotional behind it.

Maybe that was the whole point of casual hookups, he thought. No emotional baggage.

But after, when he was lying on his back, with her curled up into his side, running her manicured fingers up and down his arm, the little hairs lifted in their wake. The momentary relief of having a body next to his had left him yearning for what wasn't there. Worse, he didn't know this girl. This was a kind of fake intimacy that only highlighted what they didn't have and couldn't pretend to have, and left him with an urgent need to escape.

"I've gotta go," he told her, getting up.

"You could stay over," she said. "Kathy won't be back until tomorrow night. We could do it again."

But he'd already made a mistake and he wasn't about to compound it. She'd assured him she was on the pill, and he took her at her word, because by the time he realized he'd come unprepared, they were pretty far gone, and he was happy to believe her.

"I really need to study," he said, climbing over her. The student beds were so narrow, not meant for two people. Like that mattered. He threw on his clothes and walked down her hallway as fast as he could without running. Once he was outside, he bent over, braced his hands on his thighs and breathed in the chilly night air.

He couldn't believe he'd just had sex with someone who wasn't Leila. Check that box off the life lesson list. This wasn't like him.

He saw Miranda on campus the next day, and the next week, and she was nice, not too clingy, but obviously still interested in seeing him again. He claimed to be swamped, which wasn't a lie, and a little part of him wondered if maybe he'd overreacted that night. Maybe he ought to get to know her. She liked him.

But every time he thought about calling her, he remembered Leila and what it felt like to be with someone who was . . . real. Who fit him, who knew him. Who loved him.

Then, about five weeks after he'd slept with her, Miranda found him in the library and asked to speak with him.

Before she'd even said it, he knew what she was going to say.

She was pregnant.

LEILA REGRETTED HER actions almost as soon as she left Sawyer's dorm room. She was too embarrassed, though, to go back. Once more, she'd taken all the risks, and he'd been the passive recipient. But had she pushed him too hard?

Week after week she hoped that he'd call, that he'd show up and tell her it was all a mistake, that he'd realized how much he loved her and couldn't live without her and wanted to be with her for the rest of their lives.

And, week after week, he didn't call, he didn't show up. He didn't send a letter. Nothing.

She cringed, recalling the last words she'd thrown at him.

A childish tantrum, that's what she'd had. No wonder he was giving her so much time to cool off. Maybe they both needed to grow up a bit before they made such a big commitment. It hurt to think that he'd been right, but she had to face the truth.

What she couldn't believe, in her heart of hearts, was that they might truly be finished. That this wasn't just a break . . . but a breakup. That they might be over.

A million times she started to call him and a million times, she stopped herself. Had she given him the out he'd been waiting for? Was she actually the clingy high school sweetheart, too blind to see the truth staring her in the face?

She sifted through a thousand conversations, wondering if she'd imagined the love she felt from him, searching for clues that he'd been pulling away from her. She couldn't find any, but nor could she trust her recollection of their relationship.

Homesick, heartsick, and humiliated, she made it through finals, but her commitment showed in lackluster grades and a growing sense of having lost her way. When she came back to Grand that spring, she told Lou she was done. She could take online classes for many of her credits if she wanted, but she wasn't going back to Missoula.

He didn't push her. In fact, he treated her like one might treat someone who'd just announced they had a debilitating disease. He made her favorite foods for her. He spoke gently, and after their first conversation, didn't mention Sawyer at all. He didn't press her about getting a job, and when she said she wanted to get back on the floor at the pub, he just nodded and adjusted the shift schedule.

It was good to be home, but horrible at the same time. Was it only last year that she'd been overflowing with happiness, certain that the life unfolding before her was filled with everything she'd ever dreamed of? How could things have changed so drastically, so quickly?

Many of her friends were away, studying or traveling. The ones that were left were busy building their futures, pursuing careers, a few planning weddings. She could hardly bear to be around them.

Losing Sawyer opened something inside her, some wound that took her back to the dark days she spent hiding in her bedroom with Benji, trying not to hear her father weeping. At twelve, she'd been able to shove her mother's death into a closet in her mind and slam the door on it. Now, grief made her feel small again, helpless, and furious and so alone.

Sawyer understood her. He got her. He loved her, with all her anxieties and stubbornness. She was real with him. Maybe she'd been too real. She definitely hadn't listened to his point of view. She'd been selfish and she'd scared him.

But they were meant for each other. She still believed this with all her heart. She just had to be patient.

So, when she first heard that Sawyer had gotten married, she actually laughed.

Sue Anne Nylund, the high school secretary, was waiting for her pals on Thursday afternoon at the pub and waved Leila over. Sue Anne knew everything, it seemed, and loved to keep Grand informed.

"That boy you went around with," she said, shaking her head. "You dodged a bullet there. He was bad news."

"Sawyer?" Leila said, her heart thudding as it always did when someone mentioned him. "He's a great guy. Once he's done with school, we'll probably get back together, but if not, he's still a great guy."

She'd decided that was the best way to spin their breakup so as to keep her dignity.

Sue Anne sniffed. "Not likely, given that he's already married."

"Ha," she said. "You better check your sources, Ms. Nylund. You've got the wrong Sawyer."

"Oh, I've got the right one. Faith Lafferty told me herself." She shook her head, *tut-tutting*. "The way he treated you, keeping you dangling like that, then tying the knot with some rich girl from California. You two were a cute couple, but you're definitely better off without him."

"You . . ." Leila began, feeling faint. "You must be joking."

It was ludicrous. After all, she, the wife-to-be in question, was right here and definitely not married.

"It's not a joke at all, Leila." Sue Anne seemed to recognize suddenly how her audience was taking the news. "Oh dear. You should sit down. I'm so sorry. I shouldn't have said anything."

Some rich girl? From California?

Leila's face felt like it was made of wood. "I . . . I should get back to work. You want . . . um, a round of Prosecco?"

Sue Anne Nylund nodded, looking uncertain. "It's better that you know the truth, don't you think?"

The world turned to slow motion. The conversation, the rush and chatter of the bar customers faded away as her heart, so bruised and battered but still hopeful, finally split in two.

Sawyer, married. To someone else. In love with someone else. Sleeping with someone else. Building a life with someone else, someone who wasn't her. Sawyer, never returning to Grand to sweep her off her feet in a Hollywood movie-style ending to their stalemate and a beginning to the rest of their lives.

The future she'd planned, since the age of eighteen, crumbled to dust. The life she looked forward to, over.

She stumbled to Lou's little office at the back. "Did you know?" she managed to say. "About . . . Sawyer?"

Her father's face crumpled. He got to his feet and tried to pull her into his arms, but she pushed him away and stood on shaking legs, waiting for him to respond.

"I was going to tell you tonight," Lou said miserably. "I bumped into his mom at the grocery store this morning. Faith wasn't happy to be introduced to her only daughter-in-law at the wedding."

Daughter-in-law. The words drifted around her like clouds of mist. That was supposed to be her. Instead, it was someone else. Was it that Miranda girl? Had she followed him from California to Montana? Had she just been biding her time, waiting for Sawyer to get sick of his small-town sweetheart?

Bile rose in the back of her throat. She swallowed hard.

"Did . . . did she know the . . . the girl?"

"She didn't say. We didn't talk long. I think she's embarrassed, Leila. She asked me to apologize to you on Sawyer's behalf. I guess he hasn't been himself for a few months now and she'd been worried."

Sure. He wasn't himself because he'd been sneaking around with some other girl while the love of his life waited in Grand for him to come to his senses.

Married.

After all his *I'm not ready*, and *we need to have our careers established*, and *where will we live*, and *we're too young*. It turned out that Sawyer's objection wasn't so much to the timing of marriage, or to the institution itself . . . it was marriage to her.

And that hurt more than anything.

She searched the marriage announcements and found a small item in a local paper: Sawyer Lafferty of Grand, MT, to Miranda Price of Orange County, California.

Miranda. Just like she'd thought. And after all his protests that they were just classmates. What a liar! Leila felt like such a fool, such a cliché. Had he been dating her the whole time?

Of all the things she'd feared in her relationship with Sawyer, his cheating was never a true threat. How could it be? That was the ultimate scuzzy thing to do, and he was—there it was again, that word—a gentleman. He wasn't a cheater. He wouldn't do that to her.

But apparently, she was wrong. Sawyer wasn't the kind of person to act on a whim—she knew that better than anyone, didn't she?—so whatever happened must have started while they were still seeing each other.

Did he fall in love so fast and hard that he recognized it for something different from what he'd had with her? Was this new love brighter, better, more solid? Was this Miranda girl mature and patient and sensible?

This didn't seem like the actions of a mature, patient, sensible woman, but what did Leila know? She had no experience with such behavior.

Then another thought hit her. Had he gotten this girl pregnant? He was obsessive about birth control. She was certain he wouldn't have let something like that happen.

But if he had, if someone had set out to snag Sawyer Lafferty with a baby, he would do the honorable thing and stand by her. Leila was certain of that too.

Month after month, she waited to hear news of an impending birth. And finally, she saw it in the announcements section of the paper.

Piper Rain Lafferty, six pounds, eleven ounces, mother and child doing fine.

Whatever was left of Leila's heart turned to dust. Without a child, there was a chance he'd be able to get out of a disastrous mistake of a marriage and return to her. They could grow into better, smarter, more mature people, renew their love, and regain their future, the one they were supposed to have.

But now that there was a child in the picture, all hope of that disappeared. Leila's life was now Sawyer-less. She had to make the best of it.

CHAPTER SIXTEEN

THERE WAS NO honeymoon period for Sawyer and Miranda. They moved into married student housing as soon as they returned from city hall with the marriage certificate. Her family was furious, and his mom wasn't thrilled with him, either, but she gave grudging approval for him taking responsibility for this child he'd helped create.

They both planned to finish out the semester, and while Sawyer managed to get passing grades in everything, Miranda missed so many classes due to morning sickness, she finally quit. The feed company Sawyer worked for part-time agreed to take him on full-time, so they found a basement suite they could afford in Bozeman and settled into the rest of their lives.

Miranda's pregnancy was difficult, and she did not recover easily from the birth. After hours of awful labor, in which she couldn't get enough pain relief, she needed an emergency Caesarean section. The baby came out gray and limp. Sawyer's anguish was so great, he wondered how people survived having children.

The days in the hospital were filled with one crisis after another, from feeding problems, jaundice, to Miranda healing poorly and too uncomfortable to try breastfeeding.

Coming home didn't improve things. Miranda put on a good face. She told him she loved him all the time, called Piper their "precious angel," and posted regularly to her various social media platforms about how blessed she was. Unfortunately, she spent so much time arranging Piper's floss-like hair and secondhand clothing that by the time she had just the right image to share, she was too exhausted to actually do anything with the baby.

So, Sawyer took on more and more of the feeding, the diaper changes, the bathing, and the rocking. It seemed fair; he'd had all the fun and none of the pain, so the least he could do was ease Miranda's burden now.

Though, as the days went on, he began to wonder just what burden she was carrying. Linda, Miranda's mother, had come to stay with them to help for a couple of weeks, but she didn't seem to have much interest in her new granddaughter. She had even less interest in the guy who'd knocked up her own precious angel. Linda's "help" consisted of ordering takeout and wine and sitting in front of the television with Miranda, binge-watching crime dramas and situation comedies.

Sawyer felt like he was living in an endless episode of a comedy himself, only he was the butt of the joke, and nobody was laughing. He was glad when Linda went home. His own mother was sick and promised to come out when she could, but Sawyer wasn't holding his breath. No, this was his life and he had to make it work.

The only thing good about his hamster-wheel of responsibility, the endless list of tasks to complete, was that he never had time to think about how miserable he was. He wasn't sure how his life had gotten so badly off track, but somehow, in his determination not to let his love for Leila distract him from becoming successful and self-sufficient, he'd ended up without a college degree, working a low-end job, married to the wrong woman, and caring for an infant without any idea of what he was doing.

Piper mystified him when she wasn't terrifying him. How could so much noise come from such a small, delicate creature? Why was she so unhappy? What did she need? How could he fix this? He read books and followed parenting blogs, but many of them left him more confused than before. Most were aimed at mothers, not fathers, and he was left feeling inadequate and vaguely ashamed.

Yet, when he stood over the cradle in those random moments when his baby girl was sleeping, he found his heart swelling with something so much bigger than anything he'd felt before. He loved this child so much, he would die for her. He would kill for her. He would do whatever it took, make whatever sacrifices necessary to give her a good life. Miranda was right; Piper deserved the best. But since that was out of the question, he'd do his damndest to make sure she didn't suffer because of his ignorance.

As Sawyer's eight weeks of paid leave—a courtesy, given that he hadn't even worked a full year for the company—neared the end, he began to worry. Miranda had received an all-clear at her six-week postpartum check, but still complained of back pain, exhaustion, and headaches. She hadn't changed more than a handful of diapers and got teary when Sawyer instructed her on how to prepare bottles, saying he was treating her like a child.

"Not a child," he said. "But you've been on a lot of medication. I'm ahead of you on this stuff, that's all. But a week from now, you'll be looking after Piper full time, and I want you to feel confident in what you're doing."

"How can I feel confident when you do everything so well, so perfectly, and she doesn't even want me to hold her?"

He didn't tell her that it wasn't personal, that Piper was just being a baby and sometimes babies cried even when they were being held, and he couldn't argue that Miranda was awkward with her. Maybe the baby picked up on that. Whatever mothering instincts were supposed to kick in after birth seemed to have passed Miranda by. She looked at her daughter with a mixture of confusion, fear, and mild disgust.

"She doesn't like me," she complained to Sawyer, after a failed attempt to put the baby down for a nap. "She doesn't cuddle into me like she's supposed to."

He took wailing Piper from Miranda's stiff arms and caught an explanatory whiff.

"She needs a fresh diaper."

"But we just changed it an hour ago."

"Yes, but she pooped since then. Didn't you smell it?"

Miranda got a sulky look on her face. "Well, excuse me,

but I have a cold, and I guess it's messing with my sense of smell."

He hadn't noticed any coughing or sniffling.

"As of next week, I won't be here to do all this, Miranda."

"Diapers are expensive. I thought we weren't going to change her every single time."

He sighed. "You're right, but only when she pees. How would you like it if you had to sit in your poop for hours at a time?"

"Now you're just being mean."

Piper's cries had escalated by this time, and he was getting a headache.

"Can you just change the damn diaper, please?"

Miranda's face went stormy. "Fine."

She lifted the infant from the bassinet and moved to the bed, which they were using as a change table, since they had neither the money nor the room for any more furniture.

Piper's head flopped, and her cries turned to screams.

Sawyer jumped forward to cradle the infant. "Miranda! You have to support her head!"

"I was."

"No, you weren't. It's Parenting 101, Miranda. Even teenage babysitters know this!"

His head was pounding, but worse was the sense of dread growing in his belly. He had to leave his baby girl alone for eight hours with a woman who was ambivalent, at best, about her role as a mother.

"Okay, okay, I'll do better next time." Miranda backed away. "Can you make her stop screaming, Sawyer? She's giving me a migraine."

So, he changed Piper's dirty diaper and slathered a layer of zinc oxide on her little butt, which was red and angry-looking. "Make sure to use this until her rash is gone, okay, Miranda?"

"So what, three times a day?"

He sighed. "She'll probably need about eight diaper changes each day, though it depends. You'll have to watch her. Like I said, as soon as it's soiled, it needs to be changed, or this rash is going to get worse."

"Eight times! I won't get anything done."

"Tell me about it," he muttered, biting back what he really wanted to say.

Miranda crossed her arms, turned her back, and limped out of the bedroom. He heard the springs creak as she flopped onto the ratty couch in the living room.

"Who got almost split in half when this kid decided to come out the wrong way, huh, Sawyer?"

It was comments like that one that worried him the most. If Miranda blamed Sawyer for getting her into this world of maternal bliss, the second person in line for her ire was Piper. The baby cried too much. She didn't sleep long enough. She didn't like Miranda. She wasn't—and this one worried him the most—a "good" baby.

Grandma Linda had put this seed in Miranda's mind. "Good" babies slept. They were quiet. They fed easily and didn't spit up, they smiled and made eye contact, didn't grab hair, or arch their backs or shoot hosepipe shit when you were changing them.

By Linda's definition, and now Miranda's, Piper was not a good baby at all.

But surely this was a stage that would pass. Piper would settle down. Miranda would bond with her baby and discover things about her that she liked. Infancy was always hard, right? All parents went through this, didn't they?

The first day back at work, he was truly worried about how it would go in their awful little home. This, he thought, would have been the perfect time for Linda to come help her daughter. Not in those early weeks when Sawyer was there to do it all.

He called every time he had a break. The first time, he heard Piper wailing in the background.

"She's fine," Miranda said. "She's very stubborn, that's all. She needs to learn that she sleeps when I say she sleeps."

"She's a baby," he said, alarmed. "How long has she been crying?"

The sound had that frantic tone to it that suggested to him she'd been at it for a while.

"I don't know, not long. Anyway, can you remember to get beer on your way home? We're out."

But when he called at lunchtime, Miranda said everything was fine. The baby had gotten to sleep. She'd had her bottle and another diaper change. A few hours later, same thing, plus, Miranda was holding the baby while she talked to him, which was a good sign. He could tell because the baby's cry had a bounce to it that matched Miranda's.

When he got home that night, Miranda handed him the baby and went to the bathroom for a soak. But Piper seemed fine. Her rash wasn't improving, but it wasn't getting worse. The house was a disaster, but Sawyer didn't care about that as long as Piper's needs were met.

He prayed they would be okay.

He should have known better.

THE NEWS OF Sawyer's marriage hardened something inside Leila. The love of her life was gone. It was really over. The tiny, polished shards of hope she'd been holding tight to her heart shattered into dust and blew away with her exhaled breath.

It was time to grow up, to move on, and so she did. With the abscessed wound inside her drained, Leila finally began to heal, to look up and see the world around her once again. She wasn't a broken child any longer. She was a woman with heartache in her past, but who still believed in love.

Lou was beside himself with worry for her, so she forced herself to smile, threw herself into her painting, got a part-time job at the gallery and gift shop in Forsyth, and added a Spanish class to her schedule. Working at the bar kept her connected with people, and gradually, everyone saw that she was okay and stopped tiptoeing around her.

Her old high school friend Kendall McKinley had her own burdens to bear, having assumed responsibility for her younger sister and brother while their mother disappeared to parts unknown, and the bond they shared deepened. Kendall's friend Diana Scott, who had her own troubled family history, often joined them, and the three developed a friendship that turned into something that began to sustain Leila in ways she hadn't experienced. She'd been so focused on Sawyer that she'd lost sight of her women friends; now that he was gone, she realized that a person needs love of many kinds.

When Diana Scott married Randall O'Sullivan, Leila and Kendall stood up with her, weeping with joy and a little fear that they'd lose their pal. But, while Diana had less free time, especially once Marcus was born, the women seemed to all understand the priceless role they played in each other's lives.

Leila looked back on her time with Sawyer with bittersweet fondness, knowing that the love they shared was unlikely to be repeated in her lifetime. But she still believed that another version, a more mature version of love was out there for her. Growing up an only child, an adopted child, had left her with a deep desire for family, to have people who looked like her, sounded like her, acted like her. She wanted to have at least two children, so they'd never have to experience the pain of being alone. Or lonely. Because surely siblings changed all that, right?

She wanted a partner, someone to build a family with,

but going into a potential relationship with a list of prerequisites felt . . . predatory, somehow. Love would be great, but she knew too well that love was simply not enough. For too long, she'd been giving out vibes that said without a doubt that she was not on the market. But dating was awkward.

Her friends tried to help.

"What are you waiting for?" Kendall said, after bullying Leila into meeting a new guy during a group bowling date. "He was nice. He's clearly into you, yet you gave him the impression that you're one mass away from becoming the bride of Christ. At least go on a few dates. If you can remember how to do that."

She couldn't, in fact. She and Sawyer had been together during the time when those lessons were being learned and she'd only learned them with him. She knew how to behave with a man she was in love with. But what did you do in that endless beige landscape of meeting people who didn't light up the world around you? In time, would she feel something for one of them? Would that feeling turn into love? How did you make that all happen?

So, when Gary Hill rolled into town, a salesman or something, and sat down in front of her at the bar one night, she decided to give him a proper smile and make some conversation.

He was nice. A little older, closer to forty to her almost twenty-eight, she guessed. A little maturity might be a nice change. He didn't make a pass at her or make inappropriate remarks, or tried to cop a feel, like some of the roughnecks who came through. (They never tried it twice, by the way.)

He tipped well, was polite to Lou, even before he knew that he was Leila's dad.

And the following weekend, Gary was back, sitting in the same place. It became something of a habit, and she grew to look forward to his visits. He told her about the crazy people he met on the road, how important it was to be punctual, which she heartily agreed with, how much he enjoyed the burger combo at Lou's, and did she make it? And, if so, would she marry him?

It was a joke, that was clear.

But there was something in his eyes that told her he might be someone who could commit, given enough time.

He was nice.

He wasn't the sort of guy who would break her heart.

She wasn't looking for a great love anymore. She'd learned her lesson. She wanted someone solid, who treated her well, who would be a good father. Someone she could depend on.

A traveling salesman who understood punctuality was, by necessity, dependable, if he wanted to make a good living. And, apparently, Gary did.

He started to buy her presents. Just small things at first.

But then, a year into their relationship, when they'd been sleeping together for about six months, every time he was in town, he bought her a ring. He took her out to dinner in Forsyth, where they had steak and lobster, and the table was filled with red roses. After dessert, he went down on one knee and presented her with a beautiful ring, with a diamond the size of a Chihuahua, and asked if she'd do him the honor of agreeing to become his wife.

It was perfect. He did everything right, was a perfect gentleman, and checked off all the boxes, romance-wise.

Of course, she agreed. This was the story they were acting out, and this was her part. If it didn't seem entirely real to her, it wasn't Gary's fault. He understood she'd had a bad breakup in her past and still suffered occasional pangs of regret from that. But when she told him she loved him, she meant it.

There were different kinds of love, she guessed. She felt safe with Gary. Secure in her future. She knew they'd have a solid life together, and if he wasn't always around because of work, well, he always came back, didn't he? He'd provide a good life for her and their children. He supported her desire for a family.

After much cajoling, she finally met his parents. They were older than Lou, serious, buttoned-up people, polite, but distant. They didn't seem very interested in Leila, or even their son, for that matter. Wedding talk seemed to bore them. But Gary assured her that she'd made a great impression on them, that they "approved the match," an unenthusiastic response that made her feel like a brood mare.

Leila tried not to complain to her friends because they did not like Gary.

"Of course I like Gary," Kendall protested when Leila challenged her.

"You make a 'pruney' face every time you see us together."

"I do not!"

"There. You're doing it again."

They'd been at the Grand Master Brewery and Taproom, taste-testing Hannah's latest spring beers. Leila intended to ask Lou to start offering a rotating tap of Hannah's beer at the pub. Might be good for both establishments.

Kendall pushed her glass away. "It's not Gary. It's the beer. Why can't she keep a bottle of Chardonnay behind the counter for me? Just one? Is that too much to ask?"

"It's a brewery," Leila said. "So, yes, it's too much to ask."

Kendall insisted that she supported Leila in this relationship, and Leila appreciated it.

She and Gary didn't set a date immediately, which was okay with her. She'd learned patience the hard way, after all. She wasn't about to lose another man because she was more eager than he was to tie the knot. And this time, waiting seemed just fine. If Gary also seemed to lack urgency about sealing the deal, she put it off to him being too busy making money to buy a house for them, too busy climbing the corporate ladder that would see them through their life together. There was no rush. No rush at all.

But after the second year of their engagement, she began talking about it.

"Which do you think is better, spring weddings or fall weddings?" she asked. "Or maybe a winter wedding? A fur-lined dress for me and all."

They were eating at the pub, as usual. Gary knew what he liked there and didn't see any need to go pay money elsewhere for a potentially disappointing experience. He was a little set in his ways, but it wasn't worth fighting about.

"Uh, whatever you like," Gary said. "It doesn't matter to me."

"It should," she said, surprised. "It's your wedding too."

"Come on, babe," he said, dabbing a bit of pizza sauce off her cheek. "It's all about the bride. No one cares about the groom, so why should I care?"

She swatted his hand away. "I care about the groom!"

"Plus," he said, cutting his burger in half, "seems kind of redundant."

She put down her slice of pizza, ham and pineapple, a gift from the gods. "Excuse me. Redundant? How is a wedding redundant?"

"I mean, for me," he said. "After . . . you know."

He'd had a bad breakup that he didn't like to talk about, which she completely respected. But something about the way he'd said it made her neck prickle. "How does an ex-girlfriend make marriage redundant?"

He looked uncomfortable. "She was really an ex-wife. But it was so short, it barely counted."

For a moment, she couldn't find her voice. She glanced around the pub, hoping nobody was listening to their conversation.

"I asked you once why you'd never gotten married." She

spoke slowly and deliberately. "You said you'd never found anyone you wanted to be married to."

He shrugged. "I deluded myself for about six months, but otherwise, it's true."

"Then why didn't you say so at the time?" she whispered hotly. "Why did you lie?"

He flicked his hand dismissively. "It wasn't a big deal."

She gaped at him. "Not a big deal? What the hell are you saying to me?"

Suddenly she heard what he *wasn't* saying.

He wasn't saying: I never found anyone I wanted to be married to... until now.

He wasn't saying: everything changed when I met you.

He wasn't saying: you've shown me what love really is.

Finally, he looked up, mild surprise on his smooth face. "Lots of people have starter marriages. It barely counts."

"It counts to me, Gary." She was battling the urge to smash the remains of her pizza into his face. "I cannot believe that in all the time we've known each other, you haven't thought to mention this earlier." A little ping of memory sounded. "Is that why your parents weren't that interested in meeting me? Maybe they don't think I really count, either? Is that it?"

"They loved you, babe." He smiled. "You have nothing to worry about."

"You're missing the point, Gary." There was ice in her tone, but she felt hot tears in the back of her throat. Another man who lied to her. Who claimed to commit, but then pulled a massive, stinking one-eighty on a huge deal. Well, she wasn't going to be the idiot this time around. "I'm going home. Next time you come to town, don't bother calling me."

Chapter Seventeen

Idaho Falls, MT

A S THE CALENDAR turned over to a new year and the winter dragged on and the jobs were fewer and farther apart, JP Malone turned to Heather Hudson's letters over and over. They made him feel warm. He wrote her back, but his letters were never as long or as frequent as Heather's. He just didn't have the words.

> *I hate that those things happen to you at work. No one should treat you that way. Tell me about your house. I'd like to picture where you are when you're writing me.*
>
> *Tonight, the sky was so dark it looked like velvet above me. An owl roosted in the tree near our camp, and the sound was spooky and soothing at the same time. I wish you could be here, but I'm glad you're not. These men probably make your customers look like kindergarten teachers.*
>
> *Tell me about your family. Do you have brothers and sisters? What are your parents like?*

He knew that she might ask him the same questions

back, but he figured he could dodge them. This was, he knew, a fantasy they were both participating in. They might never actually see each other again, but for now, they served a purpose. What he was distracting her from, he didn't know and didn't really want to know. But she was a good distraction for him, and selfishly, he wanted it to continue.

She told him about her mother, how she'd passed away a few years ago, how she'd always called her "Honey" instead of Heather, because of the color of her hair. Her mom had been an artist, and Heather liked to draw and paint too. Said it reminded her of her mom.

> *Your mom was right about your hair. Would it be okay if I called you Honey too? What kind of things do you like to paint? Landscapes? I wish I had a camera so I could take pictures of this valley we're in right now. It's so beautiful. I think you could make a very pretty painting of this place.*

With each letter, she seemed more real, and it made him sad because he knew that this little fantasy was as much as they'd ever have. He ought to keep his guard up with her. He knew that. He ought to ignore her letters. He definitely shouldn't encourage her. But it felt so good to write what was on his heart, to believe that someone was going to read it and maybe even care about him and his life, that he kept it going.

> *Tomorrow we're picking up a few head that wandered past a gorge. If they spook, good chance some of*

*them will go over the edge, so we'll have to be careful.
No room for mistakes here. But Aramis is smart, smarter than any Hereford, so he'll keep me safe.*

He was a good horse. Good in the ring, good on the range. Without Aramis, JP wouldn't be able to earn anything.

We've got one guy on our crew who's young. Sixteen, I think. I worry about him. He's got no business being out here and I just hope he doesn't get himself killed. He should still be in school.

A lot of the guys on this crew had left school as soon as possible. Some of them were barely literate. JP knew he was lucky to have gotten the education he had, even if he'd sometimes wondered if the nuns at St. Mary's would be the death of him. He had options, even if they were limited. For these guys, there wasn't much else they could do, at least not that would bring them the kind of joy they got out on the range.

Can you send me one of your pictures? Something you drew? Or painted? Something small that would fit in an envelope? It would remind me of you and make me happy. Your letters make me happy too, Honey.

He put down his pen and closed his notepad. He ought to get some sleep. Tomorrow was going to be rough.

CHAPTER EIGHTEEN

S AWYER SAT ACROSS from Leila in a small Italian restaurant in Forsyth, where the chances of being observed by
someone they knew were slim.

It looked like a date. It felt like a date. But this wasn't a
date. Leila made sure he understood that.

Aside from his mom, who was looking after Piper, nobody knew that they were out together tonight. He wanted
to convince her that they could still be good together, that he
still loved her, that he was ready to have a life with her.

But first, before they went any further, he had to tell her
everything. No matter how badly he wanted her again, she
had to understand how messy his life was now. It was only
fair.

The server set their glasses in front of them, a California
cabernet sauvignon for him, New Zealand sauvignon blanc
for her.

"Cheers," she said, touching the rim of her glass to his.

She hadn't said much on the drive over. Nor had he.
Once, they'd never lacked for conversation, always eager to
tell each other about the latest event in their lives, sharing
everything in the desperate, you're-everything-to-me, I-can't-

live-without-you youthful enmeshment that was bound to burn out. Would they have gotten through that stage if they'd not been forced apart?

He took a deep breath. "I never intended to get involved with Miranda. She caught me when I was angry and lonely, but it's no excuse, Leila. I was stupid and wrong."

"We were broken up," Leila said quietly. "You did nothing wrong."

"If the tables were turned, I'd feel just as betrayed. But thank you."

She cleared her throat. "When I think about that . . . proposal . . . I can't believe I did that. I was stupid and wrong too."

"We were young, mostly."

Their eyes met across the table. Hers were shining and he suspected his were too.

"You were my first love." She swallowed. "It ended badly. But . . . Sawyer, I don't regret it."

His chest constricted. Whatever happened or didn't happen between them in the future, knowing this would sustain him.

"I have more to tell you. It's not a pretty story, so I'm just going to dive in, okay? Go ahead and eat your salad."

Her lips twisted. "I agreed to listen, didn't I?"

The lightheartedness in her words was underscored by her steely tone, and it bolstered his courage. He wanted Leila in his life, but his life was complicated If he was to have any hope, she had to know everything.

He took a slug of wine and began talking, starting with the birth. Memories of Miranda's screams, the organized urgency of the obstetric team, and Piper's tiny, gray body flooded back, and he forced himself to tell only what was necessary.

"A month after I went to work, when Piper was about three months old, I thought that maybe the worst was over, and we were settling into a routine."

He lifted his glass again. He hated revisiting that time. He'd had a decent job and his boss, Ezra Johnson, was an upstanding guy who seemed sympathetic to Sawyer's situation, so Sawyer worked his ass off, fixed mistakes when he found them, never talked smack about anyone, and always called the boss "Sir." It wasn't the life path he'd have chosen, but it was the one he'd been given, and he was going to make the best of it.

When Sawyer mentioned that the baby was fussy, Ezra had shown up the next day with an old rocking chair he said they didn't need. Miranda didn't say anything when he brought it home, but once he settled her in it with the baby and a bunch of pillows, they both seemed calmer. He hoped that if she could sit comfortably and watch TV during the day that she might let Piper sleep in her arms. They might start to bond.

Then one day, when he called home at lunchtime, Miranda didn't answer. They couldn't afford two cell phones, and the apartment had come with a landline, so they'd kept the ancient rotary device installed and he took the smart phone to work with him, since he was often out making deliveries to ranches. He added an answering machine to the house phone, though, so at least he could leave a message.

"Just checking in," he said. "You're probably rocking the baby and can't get up. Let me know if you need anything, okay? Love you."

He always told her he loved her, though it felt fake. He hoped that with enough repetition, it would become true.

Sawyer paused as the server arrived with their meals. Although his spaghetti carbonara smelled fantastic, he had little appetite. He motioned for Leila to eat her lasagna.

"I'm afraid to hear what comes next," she said.

"I hate talking about it," he admitted.

He'd gone back to work that afternoon, telling himself to ignore the nibble of concern in his gut. But when he called again an hour later, there was still no answer.

He left work early, with apologies and promises to his boss that he'd make it up to them. When he arrived home, the place was silent.

"Miranda?"

No answer. The apartment was empty. Okay, he'd overreacted. Miranda must have taken the baby outside for some air. That's why she hadn't answered the phone. That was a great step, as she hadn't gone out with the baby on her own, that he was aware of. That would build her confidence, help bond her to Piper, and she might even make some friends when people stopped to admire her beautiful baby.

But when he went to hang up his jacket, he noticed that

the rickety second-hand stroller he'd found at a thrift store was sitting inside the closet, untouched.

Alarm bells began to ring in his head.

"Miranda?" he called again, tiptoeing to the bedroom. Maybe they were both asleep.

The lights were off and the curtains closed, but his wife was not lying in the tangled, sour-smelling sheets. The bassinet, which usually lay on a low table at the foot of their bed, was empty.

Alarm bells shrieked.

Where was Piper?

That's when he heard it—a soft, pitiful cry, nearby, but muffled.

He whirled around, scanning the room.

"Piper! Where are you, baby girl?"

A second later, he found her. Miranda had wedged the soft-sided carrier between the wall and the edge of the bed, barely visible in the dim light. She'd probably intended to keep the baby safe, but instead, Piper had rolled into the padded side, her face up against the fabric. She was stuck, and who knows how long she'd been like this?

He picked her up, his breath coming fast and hot. "Oh, Pipes, baby, what's going on, huh?"

She could have suffocated in that corner. Once in his arms, she began whimpering.

Her diaper was sodden and smelly. His hands shook as he unsnapped her outfit. How long had his daughter been lying here alone and uncared for?

Her diaper rash had gone wild, the skin angry and red, but Piper barely cried. Her lips looked tacky, her eyes dull. When he had her cleaned up and changed, he grabbed one of the bottles he'd left for Miranda. He counted. She hadn't fed the baby at all. Nearly seven hours since he'd fed Piper before leaving for work, and she hadn't had anything since then.

Worse, Piper's suck was weak, and she didn't take much before turning her face away.

With shaking hands, he bundled her up, buckled her into her car seat and raced to the hospital. He didn't know how serious it was for an infant not to eat for this long, but he wasn't taking any chances.

Sawyer was frantic and furious, but he was also afraid for Miranda. Where was she? What had happened to her? Surely she wouldn't have left her child voluntarily, like this. Had she been in an accident? They only had one vehicle and he'd taken it to work, so she hadn't been driving. Maybe she'd stepped out to grab some groceries or pick up a prescription. She was still on painkillers, another thing they argued about. She insisted she could barely walk, the pain was so bad. He wasn't comfortable with her looking after the baby while under the influence of opiates. But what could he do? The doctor prescribed them. And, as she reminded him ever so frequently, he wasn't the one who'd given birth, so what did he know?

Had she been hit by a car crossing the street? Had she been abducted?

He'd ask at the ER, and then he'd call the cops.

But first, there was an alarming amount of red tape to go through.

The baby had gotten dehydrated enough that the emergency room pediatrician put her on fluids. Seeing the clear line taped to his daughter's arm made Sawyer feel like such a failure. The trauma of her birth—because despite what Miranda said, she wasn't the only one to have suffered in that experience—was now being complicated by a completely preventable medical intervention. If Miranda had only done what she was supposed to do, Piper wouldn't be here in the hospital.

"I need to ask you some questions," said a woman carrying a clipboard and a briefcase.

"Okay," Sawyer replied cautiously. He knew how this looked. He was young and he was alone, and the baby had obviously been neglected.

He didn't know where Piper's mother was or what had happened. He hadn't thought to check Miranda's belongings before rushing out of the apartment, to see if she'd actually left, but once the woman began asking her questions, he realized it was a true possibility.

Has the mother been suffering from depression?

He didn't know.

Has the mother been seen mistreating the child?

Of course not.

What was the mother's support system? Did they have family nearby who could help?

He'd been doing everything, but he was back to work now. His mother-in-law wasn't interested, and his own mother lived too far away. As the woman probed, Sawyer realized that he should have paid closer attention to Miranda's mental health. But how could he? The endless nights of broken sleep had left him barely able to focus on the baby.

"I thought they were going to take her away from me," he said quietly, not looking at Leila. "It was a nightmare, and none of it was Piper's fault."

✪

LEILA PUSHED HER lasagna away.

"Was the food not to your liking?" asked the server anxiously.

"Oh, no." She smiled at him, but Sawyer could tell it was forced. "We overestimated our appetites, but we'd love to take it home for lunch tomorrow, if you don't mind. And perhaps coffee?"

"Worst non-date ever," Sawyer said with a wry smile.

She reached across to touch his hand. The anger he'd seen in her had dissipated during his story. If she'd wanted him punished, life had taken care of that for her.

"Thank you for telling me," she said softly. "I'm so sorry you had to go through that."

It felt good to share this with Leila. He hadn't even told his mom the full extent of his early fatherhood experiences. He'd made his bed, as they said. He had to lie in it.

They'd kept Piper in the hospital overnight and he'd stayed next to her little bassinet the whole time. At half past six the next morning, Miranda called his cell phone, wondering where he was, with no apology and no query about Piper. When he demanded an explanation, she started crying, saying she had to get out, that she couldn't take it anymore, that the baby hadn't been alone that long, that he was overreacting, that he didn't understand, that it was all a mistake.

As he listened, the question he'd wrestled with during the long, horrible night was answered. He wanted a divorce and full custody of Piper. How he'd manage, he had no idea. But he knew that he couldn't live, knowing his child was in danger.

That's when the apologies came. Miranda made a mistake. She was restless, felt trapped, but she'd do better. She'd do anything, whatever he said. She needed him. She couldn't live without him and Piper. A baby needed her mother.

So, against his better judgement, unable to find a better alternative, he stayed married. But there were conditions. Miranda had to take parenting classes. She had to join a mom-and-tots group. She had to see a therapist. When the therapist suspected bipolar disorder, Miranda was sent to a psychiatrist, who put her on medication.

Sawyer drew up a detailed schedule of tasks to be completed each day. She had to call him twice a day and inform him of all outings.

And for a while, it worked. The medication dampened

the wild mood swings and Miranda finally seemed to wake up from the fugue she'd been in since Piper's birth. If she wasn't thrilled with motherhood, she at least went through the motions. Sawyer watched her like a hawk, had no life outside of work and Piper, and he refused to think of the life he might have had.

And then, when Piper was almost two and he'd started to relax a little, he came home to find the toddler sitting in front of the television, alone. She had a sippy cup of water and a plastic bowl of dry cereal with her, but her diaper needed changing, and her nose was runny. She didn't know how long Mama had been gone, but she did know which shows she'd watched, and according to that, Piper had been alone for well over an hour.

Miranda came home the next morning, full of tearful apologies again. But Sawyer had already spoken to a lawyer. They were done. The only thing to fight over was Piper, and he was prepared for that. Since that night in the pediatric emergency room, he'd kept careful records. If Miranda demanded custody, he told her, he'd present his case and she'd be lucky if she wasn't charged with child endangerment. He didn't know if that was true, but the threat worked.

Miranda moved back to California and for about six months, he didn't hear a thing from her. She'd always wanted to travel, and he suspected her parents had taken her on a trip. But when she finally contacted him again, she was more subdued, contrite even. He guessed she'd finally gotten more help.

She wanted to be a mother, but she understood that Sawyer didn't trust her, so she'd let him call the shots. He insisted that she come to them if she wanted. Her parents were supporting her now; they could pay for airfare for their daughter to visit the child they barely recognized as their granddaughter.

"She's popped in and out since then." He exhaled. "But suddenly, Miranda wants to get more involved in Piper's life."

Leila's eyes widened. "You've heard from her?"

"She called shortly after we arrived."

He'd had to let his ex-wife know about the move, obviously, and he half expected her to show up any day, claiming fresh sobriety, a good new man, a permanent job. But he knew not to believe it.

"But you have full custody, right?"

"Yes."

"So, she has no say."

"You're right. Officially, she has no say. But, practically speaking, she can make things easy for us, or she can make things difficult for us."

"How difficult?"

He hesitated. He owed Miranda no loyalty. Yet she was Piper's mother, and anything he said could get back to her. One day, his sweet, loving daughter would be fourteen and then, if urban legend and all the child development books were correct, it was possible that she'd turn on him like a rabid dog. Anything he'd ever said against her mother could come back to bite him and Piper might choose to live with Miranda, instead of him.

His gut turned to ice just at the thought of that.

"Piper loves her mother," he started.

"But it's not reciprocated."

"I think it is, but I don't care about how she feels. I care about what she does. In the past three years," he continued, aware that the restaurant was closing soon, "Miranda's visited Piper for her birthday, for Christmas, and a couple of times in the summer. She brings her presents and makes it a big event, and Piper's always happy to see her. Miranda was not excited about us moving to Grand and I expect she might want me to fly Piper back to California for a weekend or maybe a week or something, now that she's a little older."

"A week!"

"It's just a guess."

"But you don't have to agree."

He nodded. "You're right. But how do I say no to a little girl who wants to see her mother? Piper has no conscious memories of Miranda at her worst, and I won't tell her. But that makes me the big meanie, and Miranda becomes even more of a fantasy in her little mind. It's already like that. Miranda takes her to McDonald's for supper. I make her eat cauliflower. Mom is movies and popcorn. Daddy is wash your hands and brush your teeth. Mom is all fun and laughter. Dad is tired and grumpy and worried."

"I see what you mean," Leila said. "But for the record, I

don't think she sees you grumpy."

"That's what tired and worried is to a kid, though. They see the surface. Not what's underneath."

And worry was what lay underneath everything he did with Piper.

When she was a baby, he worried that he wasn't feeding her right, that she wasn't growing fast enough, that she was spitting up too much, or not pooping enough. He had no experience with babies, but boy, he'd gotten the full master class intensive, thrown in the deep end, up the river with no paddle.

Now that she was in school, he worried that she wasn't reading at her level, that she was being bullied, or maybe that she was a bully, that the kids laughed at her because her dad wasn't very good at braids yet or didn't bring the right snack to the after-school party. He never felt like he was doing a good job and then, just when he figured something out or got the hang of something, she'd change. Overnight, she'd grow out of her favorite outfit, or she'd come up with a different song she wanted him to sing, or she'd tell him he was the worst cook in the whole, entire world because she was sick of waffles and wanted only creamy scrambled eggs like Tiffany's mom made and why were his so gross and rubbery?

"Maybe," Leila said tentatively, "having me watch her over the next few weeks will help. Maybe if Piper has me for a . . . friend . . . you can be a little less tired and worried. She already likes me."

"True, but that's part of my concern. The more Piper likes you, the bigger a problem you will be for Miranda. She'll be jealous. I think she's been mostly compliant with me so far because she's had a clear, if minimal, role." And there was no other woman in Sawyer's life. "If she feels that Piper might see someone else as a mother figure, that our little limping family might become functional, with no place for her, she'll be hurt and angry. Hurt, anger, and jealousy is a dangerous mix."

Leila crossed her arms. "She should have thought of that before she walked out on her daughter. You shouldn't have to be constantly thinking about her."

Sawyer glanced at his phone, but there were no messages from his mother, so Piper must have gone to bed without a battle.

"Leila," he said, knowing she'd never truly understand. "Once you've feared for your child's life, it's hard to let your guard down."

How could he explain it? Piper'd been seventeen months when she'd come down with a wicked case of whooping cough. A person didn't know panic until they were sitting in a steamy bathroom, holding a toddler who was choking and gagging, unable to draw breath, and they'd left their phone in the other room and weren't sure if she'd die if they let her go long enough to call 911. Miranda complained that he was overreacting, but he'd pulled her crib into their bedroom until he was certain she was over the worst of it. Most nights, he'd fallen asleep exhausted, with her on his chest, a wall of pillows bracing her from falling off.

Then, afraid that Miranda would use it to build an unsavory narrative—a man sleeping in the same room, maybe the same bed, as his baby girl—he put her back in her own room, with the baby monitor turned up to max volume.

Leila looked at him with shock. "Diana and Rand have at least one kid in their bed with them every night. She says it's called co-sleeping and it's good for bonding, and the only way to survive the early years."

"Sure, if you've got a partner who's on board with the concept. But when you have an adversarial relationship with your co-parent, you have to always think about how your behavior might be misconstrued in a court of law."

"Oh."

"Yeah. You think it's done when you win the custody battle. In my case, it wasn't even a battle, so I thought it was going to be smooth sailing. But, gradually, I realized that I'll have to be constantly vigilant, until Piper is grown and probably even after that. But I also have to be as non-confrontational as possible." He looked down at the thin layer of scum floating on his untouched coffee. "If I alienate Miranda completely, I run the risk of losing Piper completely too. If not now, then later. Surely you can see that I won't let that happen."

"I guess," Leila said slowly. "So, what does that mean for me? Can I be friends with Piper? Can I be friends with . . . you?"

His heart soared at the possibility in her words. He

reached for her hand. It was cold, but she didn't pull away.

"There aren't many people I trust," he said, "but I trust you. That never changed."

Again, her eyes filled. "Sawyer," she whispered. "What are you saying?"

"I'm saying," he began. "I'm saying that I didn't expect this, Leila. I thought you'd be married. I came back here for Mom. But then . . . now . . . look at us."

She glanced down at their entwined fingers and nodded.

"I'm saying," he said again, "that I'm here, me and Piper and all this baggage. It's not your baggage. I understand if you want to stay . . . just friends . . . instead of something more."

Leila would never be just a friend, but if she wanted to try again with him, she had to do it with open eyes, fully aware of the challenges ahead of her.

His heart thudded heavily as she trapped his hand tightly between hers and leaned forward, her eyes shining.

"Sawyer," she said. "Everyone has baggage. Let's carry ours together."

CHAPTER NINETEEN

LEILA FOLLOWED SAWYER back to Grand that evening and parked her little car on the street outside his new house. Faith had Piper for the night, he'd told her. She was anxious for as much grandmother time as she could get before her surgery, so if Leila wanted . . .

She wanted.

He took her hand at the door and pulled her inside. When she walked into his arms, the first thing she thought was how natural it felt. Her body responded to his as if no time had passed, as if they recognized each other on a cellular level and were simply picking up where they'd left off.

His arms around her body brought a sense of peace to her that she hadn't felt in so long. When his lips met hers, a thrill zip-lined through her, a mystery finally resolved, and a treasure at last revealed.

"You're home," she whispered against his neck. "You actually came back."

She felt the low rumble of agreement in his chest. "I wish I'd never left."

Leila pulled away. "No. Don't say that. What happened was meant to happen. Our timing was wrong then."

He nodded, but his face was solemn. "What I really regret, Leila, with all my heart, is how I hurt you."

Her throat tightened. She'd yearned for this for so long, but now that the moment was here and the magical reunion she'd dreamed of had finally arrived, she didn't want to focus on the past. They'd both screwed up—his having more consequences—but that was all over now.

"The important thing," she said, "is that we're together now. We've been given a second chance. We're not going to ruin it this time, are we?"

He gave a little huff of laughter. "No, ma'am."

HOURS LATER, HER body sated like a cream-fed cat, she turned to snuggle closer into his chest. "Was it ever this good when we were kids?"

"No one in the history of the world," Sawyer said, "has ever had sex this good."

She kissed his shoulder. The faint tang of salt was deliciously familiar. "We're going to make this work, you know."

"I hope so," he said.

"We will. You'll see." She lifted herself up onto an elbow so she could look him in the face. "I wish I was Piper's mother. I wish I could adopt her."

"Leila." He shook his head.

"I know, I know." She flopped onto her back. "It just

seems so unfair. Her birth mother can't care for her. I'd love to be there for her."

"And you can be. You will be. And one day we'll give her a brother or a sister." He touched her nose. "We'll be a proper family, just like you always wanted."

"You know, I was ready to visit a sperm bank? You came back in the nick of time."

"Hold your horses, Leila," he said with a laugh. "I said one day."

One day.

How she hated those words.

But she had to trust him and be patient.

She had to trust him about Miranda, too, though that was harder.

Mothers and motherhood were complicated. Coralee McKinley's here-and-then-gone-again parenting had left Kendall with scars. She minimized it, but Leila could tell. Kendall's younger siblings, Ashley and Jason were affected too, of course, but Kendall had done her best to protect them, to be not just a big sister, but the mother that Coralee couldn't be.

For Piper's sake, Leila had to be as supportive of Miranda as possible. The child would have rocky territory ahead of her, and a good stepmother would do her best to help forge a safe pathway.

"A proper family." She ran a hand down her flat belly, wondering what it would be like to carry Sawyer's child. "I sent off a DNA test, by the way. I'd been thinking about it for a while and Diana's experience made me take the plunge. I want to learn about my birth family. It will be good information to have. You know, for one day when we have kids of our own."

Sawyer was quiet.

"Don't you think that's cool?"

He eased his arm out from beneath her head and got out of bed. "It's a big door to open, isn't it?"

Not exactly the enthusiasm she expected. "I might not like everything I find. But it's my information. Don't you think that's important?"

He began pulling his clothing on. "You never wanted it before. Why now?"

"If not now, then when? Don't you think our babies should know what their genetic heritage is, on both sides?"

He turned to look at her then. "Babies, plural? How many are we having?"

"Imagine," she murmured. "A little dark-haired brother or sister for Piper. That's why I'm doing the test. I mean, even if Piper never sees Miranda again, she knows why her hair curls the way it does. She knows where to find out what diseases run in the family. I want whatever children I give birth to, to have that same knowledge."

He sat down on the bed and pulled her over for a kiss. "You're already dealing with so much. Finishing your degree, me and Piper. Genealogy searches can take a long time and you might not like the answers you get."

"I know. I can handle it. And you and Piper are the best

part of my life right now, okay? Once I've finished my project, I'll close my laptop for a month and wallow in bed here with you. We can de-stress each other. How does that sound?"

"A month." He gave her a heated look that told her everything. "I better get my life organized then."

The way he said it softened her heart immediately. She trailed her hand down his still-naked torso. "De-stressing, a little baby-making practice time."

"Whoa there, girl. One step at a time," he said. "I've got to get to work, and I want to stop at Mom's so I can walk Piper to school. How does Lou feel about the DNA test?"

She swallowed her disappointment. He hadn't invited her to walk with them.

"He's being surprisingly unsupportive."

"Why is that surprising? You've been his daughter since you were born. He's afraid of losing you."

"And I've told him, over and over, that will never happen. He ought to know better."

"But Leila," Sawyer said, "you can't assure him of that. You don't know what you might find."

"I'll never find a better dad or a better mom than my own parents," she said. "That I'm certain of."

Sawyer nodded. "That's good. But surely you can see how he might feel threatened."

"He'll get over it. Why are you taking his side? I thought you'd be excited for me?"

"I am, Leila," he said. "But I'm a single father myself. I

can't imagine a world without Piper in it. No matter how much assurance you give him, he's still terrified. And not just of losing you. What if the people you find are not good for you? What if you find out that the story of your birth is full of heartache, or worse? You might end up wishing you'd never opened this Pandora's box."

"Or," she countered, "I might discover someone who is so grateful to my parents for giving me the life they couldn't. Maybe they've felt badly all their lives that they lost me and have always hoped I had a good life. This is my chance to let them see that they made the right decision, that I've turned out happy and healthy, and that I've been loved my whole life. This gives me a chance to give them closure. What about that outcome?"

He nodded. "That would be wonderful, wouldn't it?"

But there was a faraway look in his eye that told her he didn't believe this would be the case.

Then again, between the two of them, Sawyer had always been the pessimist.

LEILA SAT ON a bench at the edge of the dog park, letting the warm morning sunshine wash over her while she watched Piper and her friend Lily chasing four-legged Monty. The old dog, who lived next door to Faith, had more energy than anyone thought.

Faith was at the laboratory for her presurgical bloodwork, so Leila was getting a taste of childcare, to her delight. She and Sawyer were back together. He trusted her with his child, whom Leila also adored. All the clichés she'd ever heard were true and happening to her: the sky looked bluer, the air was sweeter, the birds sang just for them, and yesterday—honestly!—a tiny bunny crossed their path while they were walking with Piper.

She felt like Snow White and Cinderella and all the princesses in all the fairy tales. Her prince was back. The only man she'd ever felt had actually seen her and loved her. The Evil Witch had imprisoned him for a time, but that was over now. They were free to start their lives together.

"Leila," Piper said, tugging on her hand. "I have to go to the bathroom."

Zippity-doo-dah, back to earth.

"Okay, Pipes," she said. "I just have to grab Monty and then we'll walk back to Grandma's, okay?"

"But I have to go now," Piper said, doing a little dance. She darted her eyes sideways and leaned closer to Leila. "It's number two."

Well, shit, as they say.

The dog wasn't ready to leave, having not yet completed his "hump all your friends" ritual.

"Come on, boy," she cajoled, holding a treat in one hand and the leash in the other.

Two other dogs came racing up to her, fighting for the treat.

Monty ignored her.

"Leila!" Piper called. "I have to go!"

She heard the urgency in the child's voice.

Okay, change of plans.

She walked over to a young mother with a stroller. "Would you mind keeping an eye on Monty for a minute? We have to run to the washroom."

The woman smiled. "No problem."

Piper tugged on her hand, then let go and raced ahead of her.

Leila followed her inside, wrinkling her nose at the smell of bleach and humanity. The floor was both sandy and sticky, an unpleasant mix, and the row of sinks beneath the mirrorless wall bore faint brown stains. One stall bore an OUT OF ORDER sign, with a puddle of water visible beneath the door.

It was clean enough to meet health code standards, she imagined, but there are standards and there are standards. She'd spent her life in a restaurant. Nothing was ever clean enough for her.

"You need any help?"

"Go away," Piper muttered. "I need pie-va-see."

Privacy suited Leila just fine, but no way was she leaving a child, any child, alone in here.

"I'm waiting by the door," she called.

When they returned to the dog park, the young mother was packing up and a few other people had arrived. Leila collected Monty, tired now, but as she was walking through the page-wire gates, she sensed someone watching her.

Watching them.

Beneath a big tree at the far end of the park, a woman stood motionless, the direction of her gaze obscured by dark sunglasses. Beneath a wide-brimmed hat floated hair the same gossamer silk as Piper's.

Piper, chattering on about something Lily had told her, didn't notice the other woman, but instinctively, Leila tightened her grip on the little hand at her side.

Was that Miranda? Leila couldn't be sure. If she was in town, wouldn't Sawyer and Faith know? Should she say something? Was she overreacting?

"Have you heard from Miranda?" she asked later, once Sawyer got home and Piper was playing in the backyard, safely out of earshot.

Sawyer's head jolted up. "No. Why?"

She told him about the woman she'd seen at the dog park.

Sawyer got out his cell phone and punched in digits from memory. "I'll find out right now." His lips were tight, his tone firm.

But Miranda didn't pick up.

"Be careful," he said. "She's supposed to inform me every time she wants to see Piper."

"What do you think she'll do? She wouldn't hurt Piper, would she?"

Sawyer went to stand at the sliding doors framing a view of his daughter squatting in a patch of clover. "Not knowingly," he said finally, "but she makes bad decisions." He tipped his head and gave a wry smile. "For example, me."

★

THAT NIGHT, WHEN she and Sawyer lay in bed, limp from lovemaking, she asked, "Is this what happily-ever-after feels like?"

He was quiet for a long time. Finally, he said, "I don't know, Leila. I've never had it."

Joy and sadness twisted in her heart. He'd explained that he and Miranda had eloped, but a few weeks after, her parents had insisted on a big reception to show everyone that they were celebrating their wayward daughter despite the stumble that would become public knowledge in about six months.

The desperate show of happiness had not followed him into his marriage.

"But I think," he added, "my luck is changing."

She tucked her head closer against his shoulder. "Get used to it, buddy. Happy is going to be your default, from now on."

"Oh yeah?" he said, smiling.

"Absolutely. And it won't involve a big, fancy wedding, either."

She'd planned one of those with Gary. No need to revisit that.

He grew still. "Are you sure, Leila? You always wanted to get married."

"Oh, we'll get married," she amended. "But we'll keep it simple."

He didn't respond, and suddenly a chill fell over her.

Not again.

Her chest suddenly felt too small to take in the air she needed. If only she could reel the words back in. Had she learned nothing? Why couldn't she just enjoy what they had right now and trust that the future would work itself out? Was she that insecure?

What was wrong with her?

What was wrong with her that, once again, her desire for commitment wasn't reciprocated?

Then Sawyer tightened his arm around her shoulders. "Leila, whatever you're doing, stop it. We've found each other again. That's a miracle, okay?"

She nodded, unable to speak.

"You deserve everything," he continued. "You deserve the music, the flowers, the moment, the memories that you've always dreamed of. We're going to have that. When we start off this time, we're going to do it right."

When? She wanted to say. When will that be?

She'd spent the better part of a decade waiting, yearning to give her love to someone who loved her in return. She'd been fine until she'd met him all those years ago. Then, Sawyer had awakened something in her, a sleeping need that had been pacing restlessly ever since. She wanted to be his one and only, his most precious, the apple of his eye.

She wanted to be wanted. By him. Forever.

"Be patient, Leila," he whispered.

She squeezed her eyes shut. She had no choice but to try.

CHAPTER TWENTY

Big Timber, Montana

J P MALONE HAD created such a bubble around the letters between himself and Honey that next spring, when he saw her again, the flesh and blood version didn't compute with what he'd created in his mind. He felt a physical jolt when he looked up, his blood still up from nearly being gored by Furious Frank, to see that she'd followed him back to his rig.

"You feeling okay, cowboy?" she said. "That was a close one."

Her hair was different from what he remembered. She seemed like a stranger, with no relation to the gentle girl who'd written about sunsets and dreams.

"I'm fine. I don't have much time, Heather." He didn't want to hurt her. He didn't want to hurt anyone. He never did.

"It's Honey, to you, JP. Remember?" Her lashes dipped and lifted. Her lips curved up and she leaned in, just a little. She smelled clean and fresh, like strawberries. An arc of heat jumped between them.

She was sweet and soft, and he craved her warmth with every beat of his heart.

"Want me to write you a letter?" she asked softly. "To remind you who I am?"

"I liked your letters," he admitted.

"I liked yours too." She touched his arm. "I like you."

They liked each other. She wanted him. There was no doubt about that. It went against his upbringing, but Catholic or not, he was a lonely man desperate to sink himself into a sweet, soft, willing woman, and Honey was all that and more. This time, when she followed him into the trailer, he let her.

It didn't have to mean anything. He could disappear at any time. He'd given her a carefully curated view of himself, and he had no doubt she'd done the same. But for now, they could enjoy each other. Create some new memories to keep him warm.

⭐

WHEN JP BACKED his rig out of the arena lot the next morning, Heather walked alongside his open window.

"When will I see you again?" she asked. She looked younger today in the sunlight, with her cheeks flushed.

"Dunno," he said, peering into the rearview mirror, itchy to get away. "It's gonna be a busy summer."

"But you'll be around," she said, putting her hand on the door. "I've got a car. I can come find you. We've got something special, don't you think?"

He stopped the truck. "Don't talk like that."

Something about the look on his face, or the tone of his voice, made her take a step back.

"But the letters," she said, her voice faltering. "We've gotten to know each other. And now . . . this. Don't you think that's worth something?"

He put the truck in park, leaned over and caught her hand. How could he make her understand? "Honey, listen." He swallowed, thinking about all the ways he'd said this same thing to Lizzie, as clumsy as only a big brother filling the role of father could be, and all the times she'd ignored him. Figure out your life, he wanted to say. Don't hang around waiting for some guy. Make your own happiness. You're worth it.

"Forget about men for a few years," he settled on. "Forget about me, especially."

"I don't want to forget you." Tears welled up in her eyes. "I'm going to keep writing. Will you write me back?"

He kicked himself internally. He knew this would happen. He knew it, and he'd done it, anyway. And now, the only thing he could do was make a clean cut.

"I'll try," he said. Then he put the truck in gear and slowly turned toward the road.

He focused on the road, not wanting to see her shaking shoulders, her crumpled face, her defeated posture.

I will forget her, he promised himself. I will.

But he didn't.

CHAPTER TWENTY-ONE

L EILA GOT UP from her desk, stretched, and glanced at her watch. Getting back to her research was difficult and the day had dragged. Neither the artist's scrawl on the bottom of Weldon Scott's painting, nor the handwriting on the scrap tacked to the back was a clear match to anything recorded by the artist, Mel Brezo. It wasn't a match to any other artist, however, so she still had nothing to go on.

For her research project, the process was more important than the result, so whether she got the answers she was seeking, it would fulfill the last credit required for her degree. At least there was that.

Only now that her curiosity was piqued, she found herself unable to stop searching, however fruitlessly.

She was preoccupied with Sawyer, too, wondering when they'd go public with their relationship, when he might ask her to move in. Get married. Have a baby.

Not *if*. She refused to think about *if*.

It would happen. He asked her to be patient. She had to trust him.

She continued for another hour, poring through old issues of magazines and journals, and looking for Mel Brezo in periodical indexes. He didn't have a large body of work, but his most recent work was within the year, so it was likely he was still painting. None of the images she saw matched the one she'd found in Weldon Scott's storeroom, but they all shared a similarity in style. What was she missing?

Finally, it was time to quit. She and Kendall were having dinner at Diana's, and she was bringing pub food—and her DNA report. The results had arrived yesterday, but she wanted Diana's help to decipher them.

She had to tell them about her and Sawyer too. The memory of their nights together brought a smile to her lips. He tasted just as she remembered and the feel of him in her arms was like waking from a dark dream or recovering from a bad illness and recognizing that you were home and safe. Finally.

She gathered the package of food from the refrigerator where Boyd had left it, tossed a denim jacket onto the passenger seat, and headed for the O'Sullivan home, gathering her thoughts. Sawyer's concern about Miranda's potential reaction to their relationship was a little unsettling. Surely, he was being overly cautious. He had full custody. Piper liked her. Bringing her into their little family could only be a good thing.

As soon as she got to Diana and Rand's house, the comfortable chaos lifted her spirits. She held out a bag containing Lou's *carnitas* with all the fixings and exchanged it for the baby in Diana's arms. "Come to your favorite auntie, Reese."

"Hey," came a voice from inside. "I'm her favorite auntie. Don't make me fight you. You know I'll win."

"You're an aunt by marriage." She went inside and leaned down to give Kendall an air kiss. "I'm an aunt by long association and better food."

They went to the kitchen to divvy up their meal. Leila pulled the envelope out of her bag and dropped it on the table.

"I hope you can help me make more sense of it. I think the clustering indicates that I might have genetic relatives in this area, too, but I'm not sure. I don't have anyone to compare reports with, the way you did with Brade."

"Wouldn't that be cool if you and I ended up being related?" Kendall licked the taco drippings off her fingers. "Entirely possible, given what I know about my dad. Heck, Coralee could have had a baby on one of her junkets and given it to some commune. What am I saying? She'd have brought it home for me to raise." She shuddered.

Kendall was making cautious inroads toward a functional relationship with her mother, but the woman had a lot to make up for. Since Coralee's return to Grand, she'd moved back into the house, relieving Kendall of all responsibility for Ashley and Jason. Even though they were mostly independent—thanks to Kendall—they were thrilled to have their mother back, and Kendall was free to finally pursue her own dreams.

"Coralee seems better these days," Diana said. "I talked to her at the grocery store the other day. She asked after my kids, said how much she enjoyed you guys when you were little."

Kendall raised her eyebrows. "So, she liked the baby stage. Good for her."

"Has she said anything about her time away?" Leila asked. Kendall didn't seem to appreciate the fact that she still had a mother. Whatever had driven Coralee away from Grand, she'd come home. They still had a chance at a relationship.

"Not really," Kendall said. "Something probably happened with a man."

Reese was fussing, so Leila handed her back to her mother.

"Just like your father, always hungry." Diana nuzzled the baby, then turned to Leila. "I always knew you were adopted, but I sort of forgot about it. Now it seems like I'm seeing adopted people everywhere. Brade and I are talking with people every day, every single day, who are seeking birth parents."

"I mean," Leila said, "how many people were giving away babies around here thirty years ago? Who are these people?"

Diana settled onto the couch to nurse her daughter. Marcus was at a playdate, and Olivia was in the back with the babysitter, another thing Brade had arranged to help his beleaguered sister. In addition to grocery delivery and a cleaning service.

Kendall handed out the plates and lowered herself onto the floor. "We've heard some harsh stories. Life wasn't easy for women who got pregnant 'out of wedlock,' as they called it then. There was a lot of shame involved. The mothers were pressured to give up their babies. Sent away to give birth so no one would know."

"In a community that's supposed to be so God-fearing and close." Diana got up to take the now-sleeping infant to the nursery. "Pretty hypocritical, if you ask me."

She left the room, and Kendall glanced at Leila. "She's a little bitter about what she's learned about how her mother was treated. She doesn't go to church anymore, you know that?"

"I can't say I blame her." Leila had been raised Catholic, but not in a serious way. "Weldon was strict when she was dating Rand. She was a virgin on her wedding night, remember?"

"I know. Good for her, I guess."

"Maybe." Kendall shrugged. "I think they got lucky. She and Rand are good together, and he listens to her. He's not all patriarchal and shit."

"Yeah, because you'd kick his ass if he hurt Diana."

"Me, you, and half of Grand."

Leila laughed, then sobered. "But the other half would be telling her to be quiet and obey her husband."

"Okay, this got dark fast." Kendall shook her blond mane and blinked. "We're here to figure out the next step on your genetic journey. I've been through this with Brade, so maybe I can help a bit too. And if I can't, I know he can."

Leila got out the papers she'd received in the mail. She hadn't shown them to Lou, and she felt a little guilty showing her girlfriends before telling him. But they were one-hundred-percent supportive whereas he . . . he really wanted to be supportive, but there was so much at stake for him. She wanted to know what she was talking about before she had a conversation with him.

Kendall laid Brade's report out on the table in front of them, then put Diana's next to it. "Let's look at theirs first and I'll explain what I know. Then we'll compare the markers on your report."

Leila had deliberately used the same testing company that Brade and Diana had gone through, because she figured it would be easiest if they could compare apples to apples, so to speak. She was an art major, after all. Genetics was out of her wheelhouse. Brade had checked the box indicating his desire to connect with anyone whose test results indicated a genetic link, but both parties had to consent and until it was mutual, all identifying information was hidden. Unless other relatives were searching, a single test result didn't mean much. She wasn't ready to take that step, not until she understood the report a bit better.

But Leila hoped to learn something from Diana and Brade's experiences. It was the first step of many. What if it turned out that she had all sorts of biological relatives? What if she discovered a sister? Diana and Kendall were like sisters to her, but what if she found someone who looked like her? Had her laugh or her walk or her earlobes? It's not like she felt that her life with Lou was lacking; he'd given her everything. Above all, love. That was never in doubt.

But already she could see the resemblance between little Reese and her siblings, and every time Diana mentioned how Marcus was like a mini-Rand, or how Olivia came by her temper honestly, it was like a little speed bump in Leila's brain. She didn't know what she'd inherited from anyone. No woman had sat on a couch and fed her from her body. Even Lou, for all his love, looked mystified at her sometimes, as if he also wondered where her tendency to this or that came from.

Kendall pointed to a line of data marked by abbreviations that meant nothing to Leila. It reminded her of an old high school multiple-choice test her mom had once showed her, where they'd answer the questions by penciling in tiny circles on a rectangular card. Lines of data that reminded her of *The Matrix*.

"I think I need Morpheus to give me a red pill," she said.

Kendall looked at her blankly.

"How far does the rabbit hole go?" Leila tried again. "Free your mind? God. You're worse than Gary."

Her ex-fiancé had fallen asleep during the movie. Why had she ever thought they'd be a good match?

The Matrix had taken on cult status among a few of them in high school. She and Sawyer had watched the first and the last endlessly—the middle one a dog—and could quote at will.

"All she's offering," Diana said as she returned to the room, "is the truth. Nothing more."

"Yes!" Leila yelped.

"Shush!" Diana gave her a dirty look. "I just got her down!"

Leila slapped her hands over her mouth.

"If we could get down to business," Kendall said with a laugh, "some of us have work waiting for us."

"Says the woman engaged to a gazillionaire," Diana said. "Like you have to work."

Kendall gave a coy smile. "Someone's got to set a good example. I like what I do. What can I say?"

She was the top-selling real estate agent in their small town, but what she'd always wanted to do was restore old houses. Now, with Brade's backing, she'd gotten involved with the historical society, helping to save some of the wonderful buildings on the waterfront.

"This is weird," Diana said, frowning.

"What?" Leila said, peering at the pages.

"You'll have to get Brade to explain it," she said slowly. "I thought I'd be able to make sense of it, but yours looks kind of the same."

Kendall pulled out her phone and tapped a digit. "Brade? Can you drop by Diana's house? We need your brain."

He was there within fifteen minutes, and it took him less than two more to compare Leila's DNA report to his and Diana's.

"When did you send in your sample, Leila?" Brade reread the data, frowning.

She checked her phone calendar and gave him the date.

"And you provided the sample as instructed?"

"Yes. How do you screw up spitting into a tube?"

He made a face. "You should hear some of the stories from lab techs. Nothing, and I mean, nothing, can be assumed."

"Well, they also don't exactly put the instructions in the most user-friendly format." She was feeling a little attacked, and she didn't know Brade well enough to know if he was kidding.

"True," he said. "But some are cheek swabs, and some are saliva tests, and there are probably others out there now too."

"I asked Kendall and Diana which company to use. It was a saliva test. I spat in enough to get to the line on the plastic tube. I sealed it as instructed. I mailed it within the time frame, using the envelope provided. If there's a mistake, it's not mine."

"Hey," Brade said, finally looking up at her. "I'm not saying you did anything wrong. There might have been a mix-up at the lab. Those happen more often than you think. It's just that your report looks so similar to mine, I wonder if there was a mix-up."

"That brings the entire credibility of the company into question, doesn't it?" she asked. "How can we trust them if they'd make a mistake like this?"

"We can't," he said. "Contact them and get another test kit sent out. Repeating the test is the only way to know for sure."

She'd been looking forward to getting some answers;

starting the waiting game all over again was frustrating.

"Fine," she said. "Thanks, anyway. Sorry to waste your time."

"It's okay, Leila. I'm happy to do it. Adoptees need to support each other, after all, right?"

But he was looking at her strangely, and she wondered what he wasn't saying.

CHAPTER TWENTY-TWO

L EILA LEANED OVER the neck of her mount, glanced over her shoulder at Kendall, and urged the mare to go faster. Kendall, missing the rides she used to take with Diana, had convinced Leila to join her in exploring the rough land Brade had recently purchased. It was a beautiful day for it, and a great way to clear her head of her many frustrations.

Every lead on Mel Brezo led nowhere, and her advisor was pushing her to submit her project. Leila would rather get an answer, but to delay this project further would mean restarting the project next semester.

Also frustrating her was that none of the queries she, Diana, and Brade had sent out about Heather Hudson had garnered a single response. She still believed there was a connection between Heather Hudson and Mel Brezo, but whatever it was, it was buried deep. How would Heather have come to possess an original Brezo? Had she known the artist? Were they friends? Lovers? Maybe Brezo was the man who'd fathered Brade. Maybe that's why Heather had the painting. But then, why would she leave it behind?

It didn't make sense.

On top of all that, she and Sawyer were in a holding pattern while he dangled, willingly, on the end of Miranda's hook. His attitude drove her crazy. He had ammunition, he had power, he had the courts on his side. Yet, still, he vacillated between allowing Miranda to call the shots and insisting she was dangerous.

She squeezed her knees and urged the mare, Marty, to go faster.

It was hard to be mad at a guy who would sacrifice his own happiness for the sake of his child. But wouldn't Piper be better off if Miranda was out of her life entirely?

And that was the rub. Piper loved Miranda. Sawyer was, in fact, attempting to do the impossible, to keep Piper safe physically, while protecting that elemental bond between mother and child.

The wind rushing past her brought tears to Leila's eyes. There was no good way to lose a mother. She'd watched her adoptive mother, Angela, grow smaller and smaller, until she simply faded away. Some days, even now, the gutting grief still overcame her. Sooner or later, Piper would understand the truth about Miranda, and Leila could hardly blame Sawyer for wanting to spare the little girl that sorrow now.

But where did that leave her, the hopeful stepmother, waiting in the wings?

She would never, ever want Sawyer to feel he had to choose between her or Piper. Nevertheless, she couldn't help wishing that for once, she could come first with him.

"Hey, Dale Evans, slow down!"

Leila jumped as Kendall came alongside her, then reined in her horse to a trot.

"Sorry about that," she said, wiping her cheeks. "I guess I needed that."

"You okay?"

"Fine," Leila lied. "Brought back a lot of memories. I guess I missed this more than I realized."

Though she knew how to ride—every high school girl in her right mind learned to ride; how could you get a hot cowboy boyfriend otherwise?—Leila hadn't done much of it in the past few years. When her hot cowboy boyfriend married someone else, it had taken the shine off the activity.

After a few more minutes, they allowed the horses to slow to a walk. The conversation, naturally, turned to their love lives. Kendall and Brade were planning on getting married in a few months. It would be a casual event, given that Brade's adoptive parents had both passed away and he hadn't yet located his birth parents. Heather Hudson had taken pains to create a new life for herself that didn't have room for the children she'd left behind. Diana was taking it especially hard.

"And you and Sawyer?" Kendall prompted. "How's that going?"

"Good! Great. It's amazing, like a dream come true." She realized she was overselling it and made herself slow down. Kendall knew her too well. "I thought I'd been heartbroken when dipshit Gary turned out to be a loser, but in fact, once the disappointment was over, I felt relief. I'd never been in love with him the way I loved Sawyer."

All of that was true.

"Am I hearing a but?"

Leila glanced at her sharply. "You don't miss much, do you?"

"What are friends for?"

Leila sighed and nodded. "I love Piper, you know? I mean, I could be a mother to her, if Sawyer and I can make it work this time."

"But you're worried that maybe you won't?"

Trust Kendall to ask the hard questions. Hearing her doubts put into words made Leila feel even worse.

"I know he loves me. And I never stopped loving him. We were stupid kids who made stupid mistakes."

"And Piper is a reminder every day of that mistake."

"Ouch," Leila said. "Only a really small, really insecure person would blame a kid for a parent's mistake."

"Or," Kendall said gently, "someone who has been badly hurt and wants to make sure she's not pretending away any real issues. I think it's good that you're looking critically at your relationship, Leila. You tend to be a little . . ."

"What?"

"Well, you know. Gary was never the prince you thought he was. But you wanted him to be, so you saw what you wanted to see."

"Yeah. But honestly, Piper isn't the problem."

"Then what is?"

Leila sighed. "It's her mother. She didn't contest the divorce, or custody, but she wants to be able to visit whenever she wants, to take Piper to California or wherever, to basically have the option to be a mother whenever the mood hits and it's convenient. Miranda could waltz back into our life at any time and demand to be part of Piper's life again."

Kendall was quiet for a few moments. "That's got to be a scary thought."

"If we got married, and Miranda agreed, I could adopt Piper," Leila said quietly. "But Miranda would never agree. Sawyer thinks if he asks her, she'll freak out and take Piper away from him. And she's the mother. She could do that. I mean, of course there are all sorts of legal requirements and obligations and everything, but she's disappeared before. What's to say she wouldn't try it again, with Piper? Do you know the statistics on parental abductions? It happens all the time. Kids get used as weapons. I think it kills him to think that this might happen to Piper. It kills me, and I'm just getting to know her."

She hadn't thought of it exactly like that until the words left her mouth, but as soon as she said it, she knew she was right.

"Surely the law is on Sawyer's side," Kendall argued. "Miranda couldn't just take her away."

"Of course she's not allowed to and she'd be punished if she did," Leila said. "But they'd have to find her first, and what happens to Piper in the meantime? I'm a coward," she added. "I should be focused on making sure Piper knows how much she's loved, no matter what. It's our job to protect her. But I'm so afraid of setting myself up for another loss."

"That sounds like mother love to me," Kendall said. "But I have another perspective."

Leila braced herself. Kendall had a complicated relationship with her own mother and had spent some tough years as a young adult raising her two younger siblings. But Coralee was back now and seemed to be patching things up with her little family.

"What if," Kendall went on, "what if Miranda really does want the best for Piper, but she feels ashamed of what she did and doesn't know how to come back from that?"

"She should be ashamed," Leila said. "There is no coming back from abandoning an infant."

"True," Kendall said. "When Coralee left us, I was mature enough to pick up the slack, so I know it's not the same as leaving a baby. But my mother has had her own struggles, you know? I'm not making apologies for her, nor is she asking me to. And she's not trying to run Ashley's and Jason's lives or anything. She respects the life we built without her. But I see her sadness now. She's different. Whatever demons she was battling before, they seem to be gone. And I see how happy Ash and Jay are to have her back in their lives."

"But your brother and sister are almost grown. You don't have to worry about her abducting them, or abusing them, or neglecting them. You've already taught them to look after themselves."

"More or less," Kendall said with a wry smile. "Neither of them knows how to change a light bulb as far as I can tell, but you're right. The stakes are the same. But Piper isn't a baby anymore, either. She can tell you things, she can express her feelings, she has opinions."

Leila shuddered. "Still no match for an adult."

CHAPTER TWENTY-THREE

THE NEXT DAY, Leila stopped to pick up her mail on her way to pick Piper up from school. Faith Lafferty's surgery had been a success, but she'd be busy with post-op rehabilitation and unable to resume childcare for at least several weeks. Leila didn't mind. She enjoyed her time with the little girl. Often, she delivered her to Sawyer's house a little early and made a simple supper for them. It felt so natural, so domestic, to hear him come through the door calling, "I'm home!"

They felt like a family. But is that how he felt too?

Patience, she cautioned herself.

Be patient.

As she walked, she sorted the private pieces from the business bills. The DNA testing company had insisted that there had been no error in the results, but since they made no sense, she'd sent in a second sample.

This time the envelope with the report didn't feel quite as weighty as before, though it held the same information. Having already gone through the anticipation and disappointment once had removed some of the drama she was about to learn.

"Leila!"

She looked up to see Piper's small form racing toward her. She bent down just in time to have the little girl crash into her knees.

"Daddy's home early today! He says that means you can have the day off, but I said that we're fast friends and you would miss me and I'm hungry for pine-uh-pull pizza, so can we eat supper at Mr. Lou's, please?" She stopped to draw a breath. "What's fast friends?"

Leila laughed and gave the girl a hug. "I think it means stuck tight, like glue."

A grin wreathed Piper's face. "Then we're def-nit-ly fast friends." Her smile faded. "Grandma was wrong, though. She said I'd be fast friends with Lily, but Lily was mean."

Then Sawyer was there, swooping Piper into his arms. "Apparently, there was an incident." He raised his eyebrows and glanced down at Piper. "My girl is a bit of a crusader."

"She hurt Monty."

"No!" Leila said. "Why?"

"I dunno." Piper scowled. "But he was on the school playground, and she kicked him, so I kicked her. Then the principal came, and everyone got mad."

"Yes," Sawyer said. "The principal called Daddy, and here we are."

He met her eyes over the top of Piper's head and sighed.

"Would pineapple pizza help?" Leila asked. "I have to work later, but I can visit with you first."

"Yay!" Piper yelled.

"You and I are going to have a talk, young lady." Sawyer looked sternly at his daughter, then sighed. "But I guess it can wait. I was going to make sandwiches, so supper at Lou's sounds great."

Between his work and Piper, and her jobs and studies, Leila and Sawyer didn't get much time alone together. Good thing the kid was irresistible. Like father, like daughter.

Which reminded her of the envelope in her hand.

Sawyer's gaze followed hers and she saw the moment that he recognized the DNA company logo. He raised his eyebrows but said nothing.

"There are times for sandwiches," she said to Piper, "and there are times for pizza. I'd say protecting an old dog is worthy of pizza, wouldn't you?"

"Def-nit-ly."

Sawyer gave her a wry grin. Or maybe it was a tired grin. "That's one way of looking at it."

They walked back to the pub, listening to Piper chatter about the craft she'd done in art that morning and what other transgressions Lily had committed against various and sundry characters. The girl knew how to tell a story.

She put Sawyer and Piper on a four-top near the windows, a comfortable distance from the bar, and set the little girl up with milk, crayons, and coloring books while the pizza baked. She sipped her half-glass of mango wheat ale, while Sawyer had a small hazy IPA. They got a few glances, including a glare from Lou, but Leila just smiled blandly until they looked away. She visited with lots of customers like this. People could think whatever they wanted. It was none of their business.

She got caught up on Sawyer's work at Belle Vista and shared with him her frustrations at identifying Weldon Scott's painting. She didn't mention the DNA report, though it was burning a hole in her pocket. After they finished their meal, she excused herself to make sure Sam was ready for the supper rush.

Sam had the floor covered, and Lou was dealing with yesterday's receipts in his office, so Leila took a moment to open the envelope in relative privacy.

She pulled out the report and spread it out on the bar next to the first one she'd received. She looked at the columns of data in the new report, then looked at the columns and data in the first report.

The same.

She read the letter that came with the report, which contained an additional note on the bottom.

As per your request, we have evaluated your genetic information using the new sample you provided. Please find attached our report. Note that it is identical to the previous report, indicating that no error occurred in the first test. Please let us know if we can be of any assistance in interpreting these results.

No mistake, then.
She texted Diana.

Hey girl. Got my second test back. Same result as the first. When can we talk?

Then she texted Kendall.

I need to borrow your boyfriend again. My new DNA report is back, and I can't see any difference. Hopefully, he can make sense of it.

After sending in the second sample, she'd spent some time reading about genetic testing, mitochondria, alleles, and whatnot, and it seemed to her that it all came down to math. Percentages. Odds.

Geneticists apparently were hesitant to give hard answers. Instead, they interpreted the data and gave answers like: matches at certain places increased the likelihood of a sibling relationship. At other places, they likely indicated a cousin relationship. But it all had to be compared to another sample, and she had nothing to compare to.

Brade had started out on his search the same way, she recalled. He'd put his data into a genealogy site and from that, he was able to get information on the locations where he'd be most likely to find genetic relatives. That, plus information from his adoptive father, had led him to Grand, which had led him to Diana, which had led them to compare results.

Leila had nothing from Lou to go on. According to the adoption agency, her birth records were sealed, with her birth mother requesting no contact and she had no one with whom to compare results.

At least, that's what she'd assumed.

But even she'd been able to recognize that some of the patterns on her report looked like those on Brade's report.

If it wasn't a mistake, then there was only one other explanation.

"You avoiding us?"

She jumped as Sawyer sat down across from her.

"Where's the sprite?" she asked him.

"Over there, making friends and influencing people," he said. "As usual."

Indeed, the child was standing next to the table occupied by Father Patrick and a couple of parishioners, who were listening attentively to whatever she was saying.

"She's in good hands." Then she realized that Sawyer was looking at her. "Did you want to order some dessert?"

He looked down at the reports. "What's going on here?"

"Oh." She felt herself blush and gathered the pages together. "My report."

His eyebrows lifted. "Anything interesting?"

"No." She frowned. "It's weird. I'll have to get Brade to explain it to me. The reports all look the same to me, so obviously I don't know how to read them."

He touched her arm and leaned closer. "Think you can get away tonight?"

She felt his breath on her throat. Her flesh tingled. "I'm closing, so probably not."

"I miss you."

"Me too."

Dating with a kid in the background wasn't easy, but

Sawyer didn't want to confuse her and, reluctantly, Leila agreed. They'd only had one full night together, and she was aching for more.

"Daddy?" Piper called, pointing at the priest. "Is he really my father?"

Father Patrick smiled and waved. "Sorry, lad. I may be confusing the little one."

"That's my cue," Sawyer said.

Leila nodded. She understood. But one of these days, she was going to need more of him.

BRADE OLIVER SMOOTHED the reports out on Diana's kitchen table. Before coming over, Leila had gone out to the Grand Master brewery for a couple of growlers of Hannah's latest creations, a dark, substantial Belgian dubbel and a crisp corn lager. Hannah always had a rotating supply of interesting beverages on tap, and wow, the woman knew beer.

And wow, if ever an evening required the addition of alcohol, Leila suspected this one would be it. She wished Sawyer was here with her. She wished she'd told him of her suspicions, so he could have talked her down.

Brade took a long pull on his dark beer, then set down his glass and took a deep breath.

"Have you read this over for yourself, Leila?" he asked.

She took a sip of lager before answering. Her throat was dry, her pulse jumpy.

"I have," she answered. "And I've boned up on genetics about as much as an art history student can stand, via the internet."

A coincidence was one thing. But this was not a coincidence. She was scarcely able to admit to herself what she thought it might be. Surely, she was reading it wrong.

"Well, I've been busy changing diapers and cleaning spit-up," Diana said. "Anyone want to give me the Cliffs Notes?"

Kendall put her arm around Diana. "So impatient. Where's my sweet, loving, tolerant friend?"

"She was killed by the sleep-deprived maniac who now inhabits her body. You guys are exchanging more heavy looks than a roomful of moony teenagers on prom night." Diana glared at them each in turn. "What is the deal? Just tell me."

"It appears," Brade said, looking over at her, "that we have a complication. Can I see the first report again?"

"You've read it three times," Kendall said. "Just tell her, Brade."

"Tell her what?" Diana said.

"I think, Leila," Brade said slowly, "that you are my . . . sister."

Leila felt the muscles in her abdominal wall stutter as breathing and swallowing suddenly became very complicated. She couldn't speak. There was a hot mass of something blocking her throat. She'd suspected it, but to hear him say it out loud made it real.

"What?" Diana said.

Kendall now pulled Leila into a hug. "He made me promise not to say anything, but this has been killing me! Do you know what that means? You'll be my sister-in-law, for real! My two best friends are now actually related to me. I can't believe how lucky I am!"

Kendall's tears unlocked the blockage in Leila's throat. A rush of laughter and tears poured out.

"I suspected," she managed. "But it seemed like such a long shot. I couldn't believe it would be that easy. Look how much trouble it was for Brade to find relatives. Then I take the test and bingo, I find a brother right off the bat? Someone I already know? Someone who's engaged to one of my best friends?"

Kendall wiped the tears off Leila's face. "I know, right?"

"Are you serious?" Diana's voice had neither tears nor laughter, but only confusion.

"It's a lot to take in, Diana," Brade said.

"Use small words," Diana said. "I'm sure I can figure it out."

"The dates on our birth certificates are a couple of days apart," Brade said. "One or both is probably wrong, but it appears that we are twins."

"Twins," Diana echoed. "But shouldn't your reports be identical, then?"

"Only if we were identical twins," Brade said. "We're fraternal twins."

"Given that he's a man and I'm a woman," Leila said.

"Look at the giant brain on the art major," Kendall said

with a smile.

"Fraternal twins," Diana said. "Which is basically siblings, just born at the same time."

"That's right," Brade said. "Fraternal twins have as much overlap as any other siblings, which is to say, anywhere from 25-to-50 percent of their DNA will be the same."

"Whereas, half siblings, like us," Diana said, "can only have a maximum of 25 percent overlap."

"That's right," Brade confirmed.

"Wait." Diana turned to look at Leila. "Does that mean you're . . ."

"If she's a full sibling with me," Brade said, "which is what this report indicates, then she's also a half sibling with you, Diana."

"Surprise," Leila said with a weak smile. "I'm glad we're all sitting down."

"And I'm glad you brought beer," Diana said.

"Are you sure you're allowed to drink that? With the baby and all?" Leila asked.

Diana rolled her eyes at her. "One beer. Yes, it's fine. Just because you're my big sister doesn't mean you're the boss of me." Suddenly, she froze. Her eyes filled. "I can't believe it. You're my big sister."

Just then, Rand entered the kitchen. He'd been upstairs putting Marcus and Olivia to bed. "What? A big sister?"

Diana was full-on crying now. "Yes! Leila and Brade are twins! I have a big brother and a big sister. Can you believe it?"

"I'm happy for you, honey," he said. "But I just got the kids down. Unless your new family wants to take over caring for your old family, would you all keep it down? Please?"

Brade went into a bit more detail with them about how to interpret the various aspects of the report, but the gist of it was clear. She and Brade were siblings. Diana was their half sibling.

They shared . . .

"Wait," she said, interrupting them. "We're connected through your mother, Diana. Is that right?"

Brade and Diana both nodded.

"And she left . . . when you were about two or three?"

Diana took a deep breath. "I've tried to get more information out of Dad, but I don't think he knows what happened to her after that."

Weldon Scott wasn't the most cooperative man around, at the best of times. If he'd had an unhappy wife who disappeared, leaving him with a small child, Leila could totally see him preferring to let people believe she'd passed away. The pain of being a widower would have been far better than the shame of being such a bad husband that your wife abandoned both you and your child.

Leila looked at Brade. "And I suppose you're putting your vast resources to work on locating her?"

Her. Diana's mother. Brade's mother.

Her mother.

How bizarre.

She'd spent so much time grieving Angela, the only

mother she'd ever known and who'd been taken from them too soon, it was a big mental adjustment to consider that there was another person out there with a claim to that title.

"I am." He frowned. "We had a lot of false starts going into this until we realized that was who we were looking for. Her name was—"

"Is," Diana corrected.

"Is," Brade amended, "Heather Hudson Scott."

Heather Hudson. Not Angela Monahan. Or not only Angela Monahan. Also, Heather Hudson. Leila had been motherless for so long, but in fact, she had two mothers.

"She's gone to a lot of trouble to cover her tracks," Brade went on. "It seems that our mother, Heather Hudson, sometimes called Honey, is a woman who doesn't want to be found."

CHAPTER TWENTY-FOUR

Castle Ranch, southern slope of the Crazy Mountains

ON THE DAY of the big spring roundup, JP Malone knew before he'd finished his coffee that there was going to be trouble. Murphy, the kid with the least experience, had gotten a letter that had messed him up. His girl had dumped him for someone else. Big surprise. That happened all the time out here. Every letter he got from Honey was a gift, even though he told himself he didn't want them. Each one, he expected to be the last, as it should be. He, Murphy, all of them were nothing, nobodies. And Murphy was just a kid.

But, being just a kid, he'd taken it hard. He was angry, his thin shoulders hunched, his head down, his fists clenched. He was in no condition to sit a horse, let alone be part of a team leading a thousand head of prime beef over rough terrain where, in the upper reaches, they might still encounter snow. Even the clouds overhead were against them. Dust was bad enough, but if those clouds opened, the dry dust would turn to mud, slippery and oozing beneath heavy hooves. If the cattle got spooked at the wrong place, it could be bad.

But he wasn't in charge. Better minds than his had done this route before. They knew what they were doing, and if they weren't worried, then he shouldn't worry.

He curried Aramis carefully, checking for bug bites, scrapes, anything that might compromise the animal. He pried a rock from out of his left front hoof, surprised that he hadn't noticed a gait change. But Aramis was tough as nails and his feet were in great shape.

Let's hope it holds.

Then he loaded Aramis up with his lasso, his water, gloves, raincoat, and snacks, everything they'd need for some hard days of wrangling cattle that preferred to stay where they were.

He watched the horse's easy motion, checking to make sure the bob of his head was even because sometimes pain didn't show up right away. But so far, nothing to indicate a limp. Now that he'd taken the rock—really, it was a pebble—out of that hoof, the horse should be fine.

"JP," shouted the boss, "you take Murph and flank them up ahead."

He nudged Aramis into a lope and circled around to find the kid.

"Murph," he yelled.

The kid was riding at the back, his head down, not paying attention.

"Murphy! Get your ass up here," he called again.

The boy lifted his head at that and began moving closer.

Great. This is what he was partnered with today.

"Get your head in the game, Murph," he said.

"Fuck off," Murph muttered.

JP knew better than to expect enthusiasm, but he needed to elicit cooperation, at least. "I'm on your side, kid."

"What do you know?" Murphy lifted anguished eyes. "She left me for some guy named Anthony. He plays basketball and doesn't even know how to ride. What kind of a guy is that?"

"Sounds like she wasn't the one for you, kid," JP said.

"But she was!" Murphy cried. "She was the one. I'll never feel that way about anyone again. She tore out my heart. I hate her."

True love. Nothing like watching the idiotic agony of young love to make you appreciate getting older.

Not that JP felt old, exactly. But he was older in both years and experience than Heather.

Or Honey, as he preferred to call her. And this agonized love was what he suspected she felt for him. It was . . . too much, too big, and definitely way too soon for her.

But still, he couldn't resist her. She listened and eased his heart, somehow. After everything he'd been through in the past few years, her gentle innocence was a balm. Oh, she would try to seduce him again, he knew that, and that was pretty damn irresistible too. But he would do his best to stay strong, because she wasn't ready. Just like Lizzie.

He shook his head to dispel the memories of his sister the last time he'd seen her. He couldn't live with what had happened to her, but nor could he live with the shame of how he'd dealt with it. He knew she'd be missing him, but she didn't need an ex-con brother hanging around while she raised that poor child. She was a saint, Lizzie was, to keep the child. To love him, despite his origin. JP couldn't do it. Could hardly look at either of them. He wasn't ashamed of Lizzie. How could he be? And the child hadn't asked for any of this. Still, when he was in the room with them, he felt a kind of boiling pressure that made him want to run, and that is what he was ashamed of. That he couldn't be there for her the way she needed him to be.

So, he sent her money and made sure she couldn't find him. Maybe one day, he'd return. Once everything had faded. If it ever did.

But for now, they were all better off without him.

The cattle were cooperating, for now, and the lull of thousands of hoofbeats on grass sent his mind to an easier place. The air, the space, the regal rise of mountains, the rugged snowcapped ridges, all cooled the boil inside him.

Murphy cursing his mount did not.

"Knock it off, kid," he said, mildly. "She's just being a horse."

"She's not listening." Murphy reined the animal roughly away from a patch of grass.

"You're not paying attention," JP corrected. "She feels it."

Unlike Aramis, the horse Murphy was riding belonged to the outfitter and was more than happy to take advantage of a newbie. There was no bond there, no partnership. The mare had a job to do, but not for Murphy; for the feed she received at the end of the day. Anything she could gather along the way was a bonus.

The clouds that had lowered in the past half hour now began to open, sending hard shards of cold rain onto the herd, turning their dusty coats to brilliant cinnamon.

"Fine. Is this better?" Murphy yanked the reins and kicked the horse away from temptation.

The mare, who was probably too young and headstrong for an inexperienced rider like Murphy, did not appreciate the rough treatment and reared up a little, reaching back in an attempt to bite.

It was a small enough move, nothing that would alarm JP or any of the other riders. But Murphy was in no mood and had, at that moment, the foresight of a goldfish.

He yelled, yanked harder on the reins, and then punched the horse's neck.

The blow wouldn't have hurt the large animal much, but it certainly alarmed her. This time she reared up fully, sending Murphy flying backward into the now damp ground.

He scrambled up immediately, fury in every freckled line of his face. "You bitch!"

He threw himself at the horse, but she swung herself out of reach and then, to JP's horror, bolted into the herd.

"No!" He kicked Aramis, who was all ready to go after her, and the chase was on. The reins were just out of reach, but the mare was wily, on the way to being an excellent cutting horse, and the crazy bug had bitten hard. Her eyes rolled white as she dashed deeper into the herd.

The animals were lowing louder now, as concern spread like wildfire through them. She wasn't far enough away for him to use his lasso, and in a few strides, Aramis got him near enough for JP to grab the saddle. He leaped onto the wayward horse, leaning down to grasp the trailing reins.

There, he thought, panting. Disaster averted.

Then something that felt like a freight train plowed into him, and he felt himself falling. The last thing he heard before everything went black was the sound of horses, screaming.

CHAPTER TWENTY-FIVE

SAWYER SURVEYED THE last of the boxes he'd finally unpacked, then decided he'd earned a reward for his hard work. He grabbed a beer and went to sit on the back steps and admire the sunset. The bats would be coming out any minute now, and he loved to watch their darting swoops as they dove for mosquitoes.

He wished he was sitting out here with Leila, but she was working at the gallery in Forsyth. He was glad she was pursuing her career. She'd been too willing to set that aside when she was younger. Still, it would be nice when she had more time for them.

From the school playground came faint shouts, and the laughter of children wafted over the still air. Kendall had outdone herself, finding just the right house in just the right neighborhood. There was plenty of room for Leila to move in with them one day, too, when the time was right. She was probably waiting for him to suggest it.

He wanted to, but until he knew Miranda was stable, they had to lie low and maintain an image, at least, of keeping things casual between them. Miranda still hadn't answered any of his texts or emails; if the strange woman

Leila had seen was his ex-wife, she hadn't shown her face again. All he could do was hope she was getting healthy somewhere far, far away.

"Knock, knock," came a voice behind him.

Speak of the devil.

"Miranda!" He leaped to his feet so fast that the longneck went flying into the shrubbery. "What are you doing here?"

She stood in the shadows, her arms crossed over her chest. He couldn't see enough of her to know whether she was okay, and this terrified him. He moved between her and the door, just in case, and glanced up at Piper's window.

Thank goodness she was asleep.

"I told you I wanted to talk about seeing my daughter more," she said, as if he should know.

"Yes, and then you ghosted me."

"Talking in person is better."

"Then tell your lawyer to call mine."

Another bill he couldn't afford. But the advice had been clear: do not engage without legal representation.

She spoke in a small voice. "I'm tired of going through lawyers, aren't you? Couldn't we just . . . talk? Like human beings? We used to be able to do that, remember?"

Yes, until she'd flipped everything on its head, scared the ever-loving shit out of him, and traumatized Piper. Even if she hadn't meant to do it, he couldn't trust her. Would never trust her.

But tonight, when he was putting Piper to bed, she'd informed him that Grandma had taught her bedtime prayers.

She knelt at her bedside and asked God to bless Daddy and Grandma and Monty and Lily—they were friends again—and Leila, which had warmed his heart.

Then she'd added, "And God bless Mommy."

Forty pounds of sunshine and she could slay him with a word.

He looked at Miranda now. "You know you should have called first. I didn't even know you were in Montana, let alone Grand."

She could have been out of the country, for all he knew.

"Phones, FaceTime, Zoom," she said with a sniff. "It's not the same as a real visit. I want to see her. She's my daughter."

The words, the only ones that had true power over him, turned his insides to liquid. He had custody. The courts had sided with him. He didn't owe her anything.

Except, one day, Piper would grow up and ask questions. How he behaved now would affect their relationship later, when he had to defend his actions. What if Miranda had truly changed? What if she had cleaned up her act, gotten the help she needed, found some peace? Wouldn't it be taking the high road for him to allow her and Piper to have some kind of relationship? If he played hardball, it could antagonize Miranda further and trigger her to do something rash. Either way, he could lose Piper. He understood why some parents felt like they had no choice but to run away with their children and hide.

And what if Miranda felt the same way?

"She's asleep." Which she'd know if she'd called ahead.

"Right. I forget how early kids go to bed."

He suppressed a sigh. "How long are you in town?"

She shrugged and moved a step or two nearer. He planted himself on the porch, blocking her way to the house.

"Don't worry, Sawyer," she said, her voice low. "I'm not going to barge in."

"Whew." He kept his voice neutral. "That changes everything."

She was quiet, and suddenly, he felt like a bully. He ran a hand over his face. "Sorry. You startled me, is all."

She nodded, looking at the ground. "I get it. I haven't given you any reason to think well of me. But things are different now."

He waited. Part of him hoped she was right. The other part of him hoped she was lying, wished she'd do something so heinous that he could have her thrown in jail, out of Piper's life forever. No discussion, no obligation, no hope. She'd forever be the bad guy and he'd be the hero. Piper would understand.

Black and white was so much easier than gray.

"Travis's gone," Miranda said. "I ended it."

"Sorry." He wasn't. Piper was sleeping better now and didn't seem traumatized, but Sawyer couldn't believe there weren't psychological scars from whatever she'd witnessed.

"I never should have been with him in the first place." She hesitated, twisted a strand of hair around her finger. "He never hurt her, you know. I wouldn't let that happen."

"But he hurt you and she saw it, didn't she?"

She didn't answer. In the waning light, Sawyer thought he saw the shine of tears in her eyes. She wasn't one to manipulate him by crying. If anything, she tried too hard to hide her emotions from everyone, even herself. Perhaps if he'd have known more about what she was going through, they could have . . . what? Salvaged their marriage?

No. It never would have worked.

But Miranda had needed help, and he hadn't recognized how badly she was floundering. Nothing would excuse her for abandoning Piper the way she had . . . but desperate people do desperate things. Perhaps if she'd gotten the help she'd needed then, she wouldn't have been driven to do the things she had later.

"I'm sorry, Sawyer," she said. "I know nothing I can say will ever make up for the things I've done, but I want you to know that if I could go back and do it over again, I'd be better. I'd work harder. I'd be honest with you."

And just like that, all his inner kindness evaporated.

"I, I, I," he said. "This isn't about you, Miranda. This is about Piper. That's all I care about. And maybe what's-his-face is gone, but who's next? I'll never be able to trust that when Piper's with you, she won't be endangered by some dude who doesn't care about her or even want her around. You know she woke up crying every night for weeks after that visit? I won't let that happen ever again. Do you hear me?"

Miranda stiffened. She lifted her chin. "What about your

girlfriends? How do I know that *my daughter* is safe with whoever you bring around?"

Sawyer heard the unmistakable emphasis, and it filled him with dread.

"Talk to your lawyer, Miranda. And then go back to wherever it is you came from this time. I don't want you anywhere near Piper. I'll get a restraining order if I must. How will that look when you petition for more visitation?"

"Don't push me, Sawyer," she said softly. "I'm her mother. That will never change."

Icy fear ran down the back of his neck. He knew that look in Miranda's eye—sulky, pouting, but determined, the one that said she wanted something, and it didn't matter what anyone else said, she was going to get it.

"She's our daughter," he said, keeping his voice even. There was nothing to be gained by escalating things with her.

She narrowed her eyes. "And you've had her all this time."

"While you've been away and out of contact."

"I left so I could come back and be a better mother."

"Where were you, Miranda?"

"None of your business."

"Who were you with?"

She blinked slowly but didn't answer.

He took in a long, slow breath. "Is this someone going to be a part of Piper's life when she visits? If she visits?"

She lifted a thin, elegant shoulder. "Maybe next time I'll find someone who could be a good daddy to Pipes."

He wanted to slap his daughter's nickname off Miranda's lips. She hadn't earned the right to use that on Piper. The thought of some strange man holding her, having her call him Daddy . . . his gut churned.

"What's that supposed to mean?" His voice was too high, too loud. He swallowed. "I'm her father."

She shrugged. "You're on the birth certificate."

The words were both a threat and a lifeline. His status as Piper's father and main caregiver was his biggest weapon in the fight to keep his daughter safe.

Unfortunately, mother status often trumped father status.

"How is your health now, Miranda? You clean and sober? Taking your meds?"

She flinched but recovered quickly. "I am. You want to see a doctor's note?"

"Nothing will convince me that you won't crash again."

"I wasn't ready to be a mother then, but I am now. I've done everything you asked, taken the parenting classes, gotten help. I've got a place, a job I love."

Sawyer went to the gate and held it open. "We're done here. Have your lawyer send me a written request for visitation. Don't even think about approaching Piper without authorization."

Miranda looked at him for a long moment. Then she shoved her fists into her pockets, hunched her shoulders, and left without a word.

But any victory Sawyer might have felt was swallowed up in dread.

CHAPTER TWENTY-SIX

LEILA PRESSED SEND on yet another message, this time to a curator in Helena who was familiar with Mel Brezo's work. She was coming up empty everywhere, and she might have to face the fact that this was a mystery she couldn't solve.

At least not now.

She had to be patient.

And in the meantime, now that she'd done all she could, Sawyer had invited her to spend the afternoon with him at Belle Vista.

He pulled up in front of the pub, and she hopped into the cab. He leaned over and gave her a kiss, startling her. The boardwalk was a busy place.

"You know people can see us, right?" she murmured against his lips.

"Let them watch. Maybe they'll learn something." He reached a warm hand around the back of her head and pulled her closer.

This, she thought. This is what I've been waiting for.

Patience pays off, after all.

They drove leisurely, the late summer sun making her

feel languid and luxurious and lucky.

"Wow," she said as they approached Belle Vista. "It's beautiful. People are going to love coming here."

"I hope so."

He took her through the main training facility, then led her to the stalls to meet the horses he'd brought in as potential therapy animals. His preliminary examination indicated suitable temperament, but they required daily training and socialization before being added to the roster.

"This one is very gentle." He patted the small pony on her black-and-white neck. "Aren't you, Sally?"

The little mare nudged his pocket for a treat, and he complied.

"What kind of clients will you have?" Leila asked.

"Mostly children with mobility issues." He closed Sally's stall door and moved to the next one, where a big bay gelding waited. "Cerebral palsy, multiple sclerosis, brain injury, spinal cord injury . . . lots of conditions respond to therapeutic riding. Those clients will work with a physical therapist. But equine therapy also benefits people with autism, Down syndrome, learning disorders. Riding a thousand-pound animal is incredibly empowering to kids. Adults, too, for that matter."

Leila had watched Piper on Turtle. She could see the bond the two shared and could only guess at how much the horse had helped the little girl.

"Does it help people with mental illnesses too?"

Sawyer led the gelding into the breezeway and snapped

on the cross ties. "Leila."

"What? If Miranda does settle in Grand, this might be a good activity for her to do with Piper."

"Don't feel sorry for her," he warned. "There's no middle ground here."

"Is that the best way, though? Do you really think she's a psychopath? Beyond hope? Or is she ashamed and desperate, which might make her dangerous, but it might make her willing to compromise?"

Sawyer didn't look up from the horse he was grooming. "This isn't up for debate."

The tone of his voice tweaked her.

"Oh, really. Is that how this will be between us?"

"About Piper?" This time, he met her gaze. "Yes."

She took a step back, feeling it like a blow to the gut. "Wow. It's good to know where I stand."

"Don't blow this out of proportion, Leila."

Sawyer had a blind spot when it came to his daughter and, not having children of her own, she couldn't fight him on this. But what about once they were married and she was Piper's stepmother? Wouldn't she have a say then? What about when they had children of their own together? Would he treat Piper differently from them? Would he insist on being the boss man about them too?

"You know you're not being rational about this, right?" she said.

"Rational?" He dropped the currycomb and turned to face her. "One time, when Piper was about four, I flew out with her to California so she could have a weekend visit. Only Miranda and her boyfriend took her to San Diego. Without telling me. When I called to arrange pickup on Sunday evening, she said they'd be late. Car trouble or something. Then on Monday, when they still weren't back, I called my lawyer. I was told that Miranda was in communication, her delay was reasonable, and that Piper was safe with her mother, so I shouldn't worry. They could have hopped a plane to anywhere, Leila. She could have taken my daughter and disappeared and there was nothing I could do about it."

"Surely that's not allowed."

"Of course it's not allowed! But that doesn't mean it never happens. Until you've felt that panic, until you've faced a judge who could, with one swing of his gavel, let that happen, you can't possibly understand how I feel."

Leila's throat tightened. Hot tears pricked the back of her eyes. He'd never spoken to her like this. But underneath his words, she was certain she heard fear. He loved his daughter beyond measure, and he was terrified that he was going to lose her.

Leila didn't have to be a mother to understand this. He was in a situation he was unable to control, and he had no idea how to handle it.

"Sawyer," she said. "I'm so sorry. But I still don't understand. You're Piper's father. You have custody. She has a history of parental neglect and instability. Why can't you insist on supervised visits? Or no visits?"

His shoulders slumped and he bent his head against the

side of the bay gelding as if he couldn't bear the weight anymore.

"Piper's father," he said. "Yes, that's the problem."

"Sawyer?" She knelt beside him. "What's going on?"

He lifted his face and on his beloved features she saw a lifetime of ache, helplessness, and shame.

"I'm pretty sure," he started, then looked away, swallowed, and began again. His voice was low and flat. "Miranda tells everyone that Piper was, um, premature."

"Okay." She was mystified at the sudden change of subject.

"I mean . . . Miranda kept insisting Piper was premature, even though the doc said she was full term." He exhaled. "Miranda's parents were furious with me. No surprise. But I thought they'd come around. They did not. Miranda was a mess, but it wasn't until the divorce that she got mean."

"That's probably pretty common, don't you think?"

"She's never said it outright," Sawyer went on doggedly, "but I'm pretty sure . . . oh God. I can't believe I'm saying this out loud."

"What? For goodness' sake, Sawyer!"

Dust motes danced in the slanting sunshine of the barn, while Sawyer battled with the words that had clearly been festering inside him for a long, long time.

"I'm pretty sure," he said, "that, when Miranda came back from her student exchange trip to Sweden, she was already pregnant. Or she got pregnant by the stalker ex-boyfriend as soon as she came home."

Leila blinked. "What? You mean . . .?"

The full weight of his words landed, and suddenly, the pieces fell into place.

The only thing worse than the anguish in his eyes was the helplessness she saw behind it.

"I'm not her biological father," he said softly.

"Are you certain? Have you done a paternity test?"

"I should have done it early on." He shook his head. "But what did I know? Miranda was adamant about her dates. We'd been careless that night and I was feeling so stupid and guilty, so sure I'd ruined my life by cheating on you, I assumed this was my penance. It didn't even occur to me that she might not be mine until I heard this one nurse talking about 'premature babies' and rolling her eyes. By then it was too late. I couldn't give her up." He sighed heavily. "Now, I can't risk a paternity test because, because the second I find out for sure, I might lose my claim to Piper."

"That can't be true! You're on the birth certificate."

He tipped his head. "Sure. She needed a name. But genetics don't lie. You know that better than anyone. It opens a door that she could use to shut me out of Piper's life."

Wherever he stood as Piper's father legally, she understood the fear. What torture he must have gone through.

"Has Miranda admitted it?"

"Not in so many words, but it's just a matter of time. I was a better option than the other guys, so she made me believe it. I couldn't see past the guilt I was carrying about sleeping with her in the first place. She needed someone willing to raise Piper, and she chose me. She needed me to believe it and I did. But now, she doesn't care anymore. Maybe she's found someone more convenient, more accommodating, wealthier." He paused and pressed his fingers against his eyebrows. "If Miranda ever decides she wants to cut me out of Piper's life, all she has to do is demand a test. I will not let that happen, Leila. Do you understand?"

THAT NIGHT, ALONE in her apartment, Leila dreamed she was in an airport, about to check in. She had her passport and boarding pass in her hand, her purse over one shoulder, a backpack and tagged suitcase at her feet. She was with someone. Who? Dad? Kendall?

No.

It was Sawyer. And he had Piper with him.

Suddenly, she remembered that she hadn't packed her iPad or her earbuds. They were still on the night table next to her bed. Also, her allergy pills. Wait . . . had she packed any shoes?

Panic filled her. She had to go back. Sawyer and Piper had already gone through the wicket, but she had to go back. She wasn't ready.

She pushed through the crowd behind her and ran to the elevators. Her hotel was nearby, wasn't it? She could still make it. She wasn't ready . . . she couldn't leave yet . . . she hadn't prepared for anything. Was that even her passport in her hand? No. It was a parking slip.

With a jolt, Leila woke up. Her heart was pounding, and her forehead was slick with sweat. She rolled over, feeling a dull ache at the back of her neck.

Stupid dream. Her subconscious could at least do her the favor of being a tiny bit subtle, couldn't it?

She knew she wasn't going anywhere with Sawyer and Piper, and yeah, she knew it was her own damn fault.

She rolled out of bed and got to her feet. The plane had left without her, and she had no choice but to move forward.

Chapter Twenty-Seven

Niagara Falls, NY

JP Malone had indeed done his job, covered for the incompetence of his partner, and averted financial disaster for the rancher, not to mention protecting the animals from horrible injury and death. He'd seen what happened in a stampede.

The prison program that provided manpower to cowboy crews was very pleased with how he'd handled himself.

But JP himself didn't know anything about this for weeks. Cold winter turned to chilly spring before his broken skull allowed him to put information together. And even then, he learned it in bits and pieces.

He was lucky to be alive, no doubt about that. The head injury was minor compared to what happened to his leg. A couple of cows, running in tandem, had blindly crashed into him just as he was getting on the mare, sending them both flying. He was lucky he hadn't found the stirrups, or the mare's body weight might have killed him. As it was, his right leg had caught the bony bovine blow full-on, his already scarred shoulder had been dislocated . . . again, and his skull had bounced off a rock.

He remembered reaching for the mare, nothing more.

"Aramis," he mumbled. "Where's my horse?"

"Do you know where you are?" they asked repeatedly, as he drifted in and out of consciousness in those early days.

He'd never been able to answer appropriately, as the question confused him almost as much as their expressions did.

"Do you know today's date?" Another stupid question. It was . . . it was . . . but the answer evaded him.

"Step-tember," he said. They'd been taking a herd up to the high range, he was pretty sure. "Where's my horse?"

Some time later, he awoke from yet another nap and looked out the window, struggling to gather the thoughts that rollicked through his brain like a litter of kittens. After a long while, he noticed that the trees were different, smaller, the sky unblocked by mountains.

Where was he?

"Keep moving," the therapist urged him during his daily torture sessions. JP gathered, as hours or days or weeks passed, that he was in a government rehab center in Upstate New York, a perk he was receiving, they emphasized, due to his being a good citizen while a guest of the government.

His right thigh was encased in a variety of devices, none of which he had the attention span to remember, all of which induced pain at some point in his limb.

But apparently, if he didn't leap into action every time the sadists in white coats yelled "jump," he might be stuck with a cane for the rest of his life.

He lived for the moment when he could collapse back onto his hospital bed, receive the narcotic sacrament, and disappear back into oblivion.

He dreamed of Honey. He missed her so much, but she felt like something he'd imagined, in a world he'd never really visited. It all seemed so far away, so long ago. He was grateful he'd never told her his full legal name. Not that anyone wanted to know it. JP Malone was nobody, a broken, orphaned ex-con with no money, no education, no prospects, and a deep anger at the world. Part of him despised Honey for thinking that she loved him. All of him writhed with shame at how he'd succumbed to her in Big Timber. She would imagine their love was mutual now, and if it was—God help him, it was—she deserved so much better.

Months later, when he was finally as healed as the doctors decided he was ever going to be, they released him. He never contacted the feed store about any letters he might have received from her, and he never wrote to tell her what happened. It was better that she forget him as soon as possible. She shouldn't have her life tainted by the bad luck and misery that followed him around.

He wanted the best for his Honey. If he had any love for her at all, disappearing was the kindest thing he could do. This accident, painful as it was, was a message from God. JP would obey it.

CHAPTER TWENTY-EIGHT

L EILA SAT ON the playground bench with her laptop while Piper and Lily played tag. After the skirmish over the treatment of Monty, the girls were tighter than ever. The dog adored them, even Lily, and broke into Faith's yard whenever Piper was there.

Leila clicked on her email. She'd sent several messages through the contact form of the agency representing Mel Brezo, but all she'd received back were form responses saying the artist was unavailable for comment.

She still didn't know how the Brezo painting had come to be in Weldon Scott's possession. Or rather, Heather Hudson's possession.

Heather Hudson, sometimes called Honey. Her mother. The mysterious woman who'd given birth to twins, given them away, married Weldon Scott, had Diana, and then disappeared so thoroughly that no one could find her.

Something teased the back of her brain, something she couldn't put her finger on. How was Honey Hudson connected to this painting?

She pulled out her phone and dialed Diana's number.

"We must be missing something," she said. "I'm grateful

I found the painting, but why did your mom have it? What's the connection? She must have known the artist, but how? Was your mom interested in art? Maybe she wanted to be an artist herself."

"I have no idea. Dad's never mentioned it."

"Do you think Brezo is the man who got her pregnant with me and Brade?"

She couldn't use the word father. She could barely think of Heather Hudson as her mother.

Diana huffed into the phone. "My dad would never have let that picture onto the property, if that were the case."

"Sure," Leila said. "If he knew."

A few beats of silence followed, broken only by the sound of a children's television program in the background.

"Can you ask him again?" Leila suggested cautiously.

"The last time I asked," Diana said with a sigh, "he told me, and I quote, 'the longer Honey's gone, the less I knew her at all.' He doesn't want to think about her."

"I get that." Leila hung up, but her brain was buzzing again.

Heather, sometimes called Honey, had left a sticky mess behind her when she disappeared.

Honey.

Miel.

The buzzing crescendoed. What was she missing?

"Leila?"

She jumped as a shadow crossed in front of her. She shaded her eyes with her hand. "Yes? That's me."

A shriek sounded from the playground then, and Leila leaped to her feet, her heart in her throat. "Piper? What's wrong, honey?"

The child raced toward her, but she wasn't upset. There was no blood, no tears, not even dirt or torn clothing. In fact, Piper's face shone with delight.

And as she got closer, Leila realized Piper wasn't looking at her. That face-splitting grin was for the woman standing next to Leila.

"Mom!" Piper yelled and launched herself into the stranger's arms.

No! It couldn't be. But, yes, Piper obviously knew her mother, and the woman matched the photos Leila had seen of Miranda.

Did Sawyer know she was here?

"Piper," Leila said, reaching for her. "We're leaving."

Miranda kissed Piper, but helped her into Leila's grasp.

"But Mommy's here!" Piper looked at her with confusion.

"It's okay, baby," Miranda said. "I'll see you again."

Leila scrambled for an excuse that would lure Piper away. "Daddy says Turtle misses you."

At the mention of her beloved horse, the child's face changed. "Mommy, will you come visit tomorrow?"

Miranda nodded. "Sure, baby," she said lightly. "Give Turtle a kiss for me."

"You what?" Sawyer looked from Piper to Leila in disbelief.

He'd just gotten in the door after a long day on the road, bringing two more horses to Belle Vista. From the enticing aromas coming from the oven, Leila was keeping a plate of something delicious warm for him.

"I saw Mommy! She was at the playground." Piper's voice changed. "What's the matter, Daddy? Are you mad?"

Leila reached for him as if to calm him down. "Just listen, okay?"

He took a deep breath, but panic was accompanied by a spinning loss of control and, worse, a sense of betrayal. Whatever had happened, Leila knew about it and hadn't told him.

"I'm listening," he said through gritted teeth.

"Daddy?" Piper's lip was trembling. Tears clung to her lashes.

"Honey," Leila said, taking Piper's hand, "why don't I make you some cinnamon toast and you can eat it while you watch your favorite show, okay? Daddy and I need to talk while he eats his supper. I promise, he's not mad at you, are you, Daddy?"

She sent him a steely glare.

He bent and kissed Piper's head. "Of course not, sweetheart. Daddy's tired. And hungry."

"Hangry?" Piper said in a small voice.

"Hangry," he confirmed.

Such a copout. But Leila had some explaining to do.

Once Piper was settled comfortably on the couch with her toast, he sat down across from Leila at the kitchen table. A bowl of beef stroganoff sat in front of him, but he found he had no appetite.

"When were you going to tell me, Leila?"

She looked back at him evenly. "I wanted to wait until Piper was in bed. I should have known she'd blurt it out the second she saw you. Miranda came to the playground. I think she wanted to talk to me, but Piper saw her and of course came running."

"What did she want? What did she say?"

"Sawyer, hang on. Piper and I left right away. I took her to the ranch to see Turtle, which took her mind off things. Then we came home, now you're here, and we're all caught up."

"I have to call my lawyer. Next time, call me immediately. Do you understand?"

Leila frowned. "Don't you think you're overreacting a bit?"

A haze came over his vision. Overreacting. How many times had he heard that? "No, Leila," he said. "I am not overreacting. I am reacting exactly appropriately. I thought you understood what was at stake here."

"I do, Sawyer." Leila's face clouded. She glanced to make sure Piper was still immersed in her show, then leaned forward. "I think you've lost perspective here."

"Me?"

"Keep your voice down!"

He took a deep breath. "If anyone's lost perspective, it's you. You've been so preoccupied with finding your birth mother that somehow you've built a sympathetic narrative for Miranda."

"That's not true! I just think you should talk to her. Listen to her. There must be a better way than this constant push-pull. That's not good for Piper. I saw how excited she was to see her mother."

"Not everyone who gives birth is meant to raise children, Leila. Just because she's genetically related doesn't mean she's got Piper's best interests at heart. There's only one person in this entire universe who can claim that," he said, stabbing the table with this finger. "And that's me. The only one who's ever been there one hundred percent for this kid. That's how it is and that's how it's going to stay."

He saw when the words connected with Leila. First, hurt came over her face. Then, she wiped it away, got to her feet, and began clearing up the supper debris.

For a moment, she stood at the sink, her arms braced against the counter edge, her head low. Then she turned.

"I have work to do at home," she said. "Tell Piper good night for me, okay?"

And she left.

CHAPTER TWENTY-NINE

FAITH LAFFERTY WAS eager to resume caring for Piper, the walk to the school and back was still too much for her. Sawyer had been taking Piper every morning, and Leila had agreed to continue walking the child to her grandmother's every afternoon. Leila wasn't going to renege on her promise, no matter what.

She didn't ask Faith what her son had told her, and the older woman didn't seem to be aware of their spat.

If it was just a spat.

Maybe Faith didn't even know they were back together.

If they were back together.

Leila hadn't spoken to Sawyer for two days. She couldn't sleep, she mixed up orders at the bar, and she snapped at Lou, who just shook his head and muttered about "that Lafferty fellow." Lou was probably reeling from learning that Brade Oliver, the man he'd disparaged, was Leila's brother. He'd been oddly reticent, however, so she couldn't be sure, and she was far more concerned with Sawyer, anyway.

Men. Some days, they caused more trouble than they were worth.

She'd been spending all her spare time hunched over her

keyboard, trying every avenue she could think of to find a connection between Heather Hudson and Mel Brezo. So far, it was fruitless, but at least it kept her from spinning out.

This was just a fight.

They'd get over it.

She and Sawyer would be okay.

She couldn't think otherwise.

"I'll come get her right now," she told Faith.

Piper was as sunny and chatty as usual, Leila noted with relief. Whatever was going on between her and Sawyer, he hadn't let it affect his daughter.

Instead of taking Piper straight home, where Leila was no longer comfortable, they stopped at the playground. She pushed Piper on the swings, chased her around the big tree, and helped her on the climbing equipment. When Lily appeared, Piper ran off with her, and Leila retreated to the bench in the shade.

That's when she saw Miranda on the far side of the park, half-hidden by leafy shadows.

After a quick glance at Piper, Leila walked over to where Miranda was waiting patiently for her.

"You can't be here," Leila said.

"Just listen," Miranda said, holding her hands out in front of her.

She reached for her phone to let Sawyer know, but something about the woman's expression stopped her.

"What, Miranda? You can't keep doing this. Sawyer will get a restraining order."

Miranda looked down, nodding. "I know. That's why I'm appealing to you, not him."

"This is a mistake."

She turned to go before she gave Sawyer something more to hold against her, but Miranda stopped her.

"I'm moving to Grand," she said.

"What?! Does Sawyer know?"

"I wanted to tell him." Her lips twisted. "He's not exactly receptive to me. That's why I'm talking to you. Leila, I assume he's told you about my . . . breakdown? Or should I say 'breakdowns,' plural?"

She held herself tightly as she spoke, as if shoring herself up for battle, determined to tell her story to an audience that didn't want to hear it.

"You mean when you abandoned Piper as a baby?" Leila said. "Or when she was a toddler?"

"I did a lot of awful things, some of which I don't fully remember, but I remember those." Miranda nodded again, but her features were set, calm, resolute. "I have bipolar disorder."

"Oh." She assumed that was Sawyer's suspicion, rather than a fact. "Does Sawyer know?"

"I told him. Not sure he believes me. It took a while to be diagnosed, and in that time, I did a lot of bad things, hurt a lot of people. Sawyer and Piper are at the top of the list."

Leila shrugged. "So . . . what? You're not accountable for your actions because of that?"

"That's not what I'm saying." Miranda frowned. "I'm on

medication. I'm stable. I'm off drugs. I have a job. I had a place, but I'll have to find a new one here."

Leila didn't like where this was going. "So, you want custody now, is that it? You're ready to just start over?"

"Leila," Miranda said. "Can you please just listen?"

"You have nothing to say that I want to hear." She took a step closer, angry at herself for letting this woman appeal to her sympathy. "Miranda, I love Sawyer. I love Piper. He's already furious with me because I think he's—"

She stopped, not wanting to be disloyal to him in front of his ex.

"He's what?" Miranda's eyes lit up. "You see it, don't you? He's lost perspective. I'm not a bad person, Leila."

In her mind, Leila had built up a monstrous image of Piper's mother as a cold, selfish, unfeeling woman who cared for no one. Now, as Miranda took a moment to watch Piper across the park, Leila saw a glint of tears in her eyes and wondered if there was more to that story.

"He's done such a good job with her," Miranda said softly.

"He has," Leila said.

"Much better than I could have."

Leila didn't respond. This didn't sound like the sort of woman who would run away with her child. But now that she knew the source of Sawyer's fear, she understood that he, and therefore she, could never take that chance.

"I just want to see her grow up, you know?" Miranda said. "I want to know that she's living her best life."

"She is, as you can see."

Miranda nodded. Tears slipped down her cheeks.

Against her will, Leila felt a pang of understanding. Even sympathy. No matter what had happened in her life, Miranda was suffering now.

"I want her to be happy," Miranda added.

"She is."

"I know." Miranda gave her a quick, shy sideways glance. "And I'm glad you and Sawyer are back together."

Surprise made Leila stiffen. "Really."

"I should never have done what I did." She looked off into the distance again. "People love a love story. That's what you had." She gave a sad little laugh. "That is most definitely not what he and I had."

Leila didn't know what to say, so she just kept listening.

"Our marriage was doomed from the start," she went on. "But when Piper was born and I saw him with her, how he held her like she was the most precious thing he'd ever seen in his life, I knew I'd made one good decision. He was the right man to raise her."

It was an odd way to phrase it, and Leila wondered if it was an admission of sorts.

"He's an exceptional father," Leila said. "He'd do anything for her."

"I know and I'm grateful. I wish I could be that kind of mother."

"Miranda," Leila said. "Why are you here? Why aren't you working this out with Sawyer? If you're really moving to town, you have to tell him. But if you're planning to petition for custody, know that he'll fight you all the way."

"I know he will," Miranda said helplessly. "I don't want custody, Leila, but he's giving me no choice. I work for an airline. I'm starting as a flight attendant soon. It's what I've always wanted to do. All I want to do is visit her when I'm home. But if he refuses to let me see her, I'll take him to court. And Leila, I'll win."

Leila heard the threat. She also heard the desperation. Miranda didn't want to take Piper from Sawyer, but he'd pushed her into a corner. He thought he was being accommodating, but from Miranda's viewpoint, he was being anything but.

She thought about Honey Hudson and what she must have gone through, giving away two babies, and then leaving Diana behind. Those had to be the worst, hardest decisions of her life. Maybe it wasn't surprising that she chose not to be found.

But was that the only alternative?

She thought about her own parents. Angela and Lou Monahan had ached for a child and had been given her. If Leila could have known both mothers throughout her life, would that have been better? Or was it imperative that Heather—Honey—be cut out entirely?

Now that she was seeking unsuccessfully for her birth mother, she wondered what she'd missed, not knowing Honey growing up.

★

THAT NIGHT, LEILA tossed and turned until she gave up and went to the apartment kitchen for a glass of milk. She knew she had to tell Sawyer about her chat with Miranda, but she wasn't sure how to go about it, given his earlier reaction.

Lou's door opened.

"Leila?" he said, rubbing his eyes. "What's wrong?"

"Nothing, Dad. I just can't sleep."

"Okay, then. Good night, honey."

Honey. She liked that. It made her think of her other mother.

Honey.

Miel.

The buzzing blasted through her brain. She ran back to her bedroom, scrambling for her phone, but she already knew: the root word for honey in several languages was . . . *mel*.

Mel.

With trembling fingers, she keyed in the word *brezo*.

There it was. The answer she'd been looking for. It was there all along.

Brezo: the Spanish word for heather.

Honey Heather.

"I found her," she whispered. "Mel Brezo isn't my father. She's my mother."

First thing the next morning, she contacted Brade and

Diana with the news. This was the link they'd been looking for. Mel Brezo had to be Heather Hudson. The translation of the name, the fact that the artist never made public appearances . . . it all made sense.

Leila sent new messages to the art agency, all a variation on a theme:

My name is Leila Monahan. I have urgent information for the artist Mel Brezo, who I believe is also known as Heather Hudson Scott. I believe Ms. Hudson Scott is my birth mother. I have recently discovered a brother who is my biological twin, and a half sister. We are all eager to meet with your artist at her earliest convenience.

It was the only contact they had; surely, if Leila was correct, Heather would respond to them. Once again, they had to wait.

Story of her life.

CHAPTER THIRTY

S AWYER WAS OUT of town for a week on another horse-buying mission and Leila was glad for the respite. They were talking again, though both avoided any subjects that would lead to an argument, and neither had apologized. Faith had recovered sufficiently that she could have Piper with her for the duration, provided that Leila continued walking her to school and taking her on outings.

Whenever she and Piper went to the park after school now, she glanced around for Miranda, so she wasn't surprised that afternoon to see her standing beside the big tree. Once Piper and Lily were off playing, Leila waved Miranda over to the bench.

"What's this?" Miranda said. "Not calling the cavalry on me?"

"Listen, you're Piper's mother and you always will be. We have to find a way to make this work." She'd thought about this a lot over the past few days. "I can't stop you from being in the park when we're here. It's a public space. If you want to watch Piper, or even play with her—under my supervision—I won't stop you."

Miranda frowned. "Why are you doing this? Won't Sawyer be furious when he finds out?"

Yes, he would.

But Leila just shrugged. "I'll deal with him. But you can't mess this up, Miranda. Do you understand?"

Miranda joined Leila and Piper at the park the next two days. Diana and her kids joined them on the second day. On the third day, they had ice cream together. On the fourth day, they went to see Turtle at Belle Vista, where Leila introduced Miranda to Bayleigh Sutherland. The more people who knew Miranda, the better, Leila felt, if they were to have a cooperative relationship. Yes, there would be hell to pay with Sawyer, once he was home. But he'd see how happy Piper was, and that was the main thing, wasn't it?

They were at the playground on the fifth afternoon when Leila's phone chirped. It was Faith. She'd locked herself out of the house and wondered if Leila could come get the spare key from the hiding place for her, as it had fallen, and she couldn't bend enough to reach it.

Leila looked at Miranda, pushing Piper on the swing. They'd just gotten here, and Piper wouldn't be happy to leave. It would only take five minutes.

"I'll be right back, okay?" She gave Miranda a hard look. "Don't go anywhere. I'm trusting you. Lily's mom is watching, anyway."

"I'll stay right here," Miranda promised. "I'll look after her."

"We'll stay right here, Leila," Piper echoed. "You help Grandma and then come right back."

It took longer, of course, closer to forty-five minutes, to help Faith bring in and unpack her groceries. Although Leila had become increasingly comfortable with the interactions she'd witnessed between Miranda and Piper, she was anxious to get back to them.

But when she returned to the park, they were gone.

Her pulse spiked. She ran to Lily's mother.

"Have you seen Piper? She was here a minute ago. With her mother."

"Oh, yes, Miranda," the woman replied, looking around. "Piper fell and hurt her ankle. They went to sit on the bench, but Piper wanted to go home."

"To Sawyer's house? Or Faith's house?"

The woman shrugged apologetically.

Leila ran back to her car, keying Miranda's digits into her phone. Voicemail.

"Miranda, where are you? Call me back right away."

She raced back to Faith's house and screeched into the driveway.

"Is Piper here?"

"What? No. Oh, no, Leila, what happened?"

Faith approved of Leila's attempt to foster a relationship with Miranda, though she'd warned Leila that Sawyer wouldn't appreciate her going behind his back.

Panic lit up her insides like tongues of fire. Had this been a big setup all along? Had Miranda been playing her for a fool?

Her phone rang. Miranda.

"Thank God," Leila cried. "Where are you?"

"The hospital," Miranda said. "Piper's fine, but she twisted her ankle, and it was really hurting. I tried to call, but you didn't pick up, so I took her in. She's going to be fine."

Relief washed over her like a river. She glanced at her messages. Yes, she must have missed Miranda's call when she was helping Faith.

"I'll be right there," she said.

"I don't think they'll let you in," Miranda said. "Parents only. I'm sorry."

Parents only. And that wasn't her. Leila swallowed the hurt. "I'll meet you in the parking lot, then."

"And Leila," Miranda said. "The hospital contacted Sawyer."

⭐

IT HAD BEEN a bad scene and even now, Sawyer didn't know who he was most angry with: Miranda, for manipulating Leila; Faith, for not telling him what was going on; or Leila, for dismissing his fears.

He was sitting outside on the back step again, trying to get a grip on his emotions. It wasn't even anger he felt for Leila. It was something deeper, something frightening that bit down to an underlying conflict that might be unsurmountable.

He couldn't have a relationship without trust. If she

could violate his wishes as a father, if she could put his daughter at risk, if she could deceive him in such a way, could he ever trust her again?

Yet, it had been such a relief to share some of the weight of parenting with her. And she was so good at it. She loved Piper . . . he truly believed that. He was so tired of parenting alone.

He was so very tired of being alone, period.

He hadn't realized just how much he'd missed Leila's presence until he'd come back to Grand. Seeing her again, hearing her laugh, feeling her in his arms, loving her, it brought something in him back to life. He'd been a desiccated wraith of a human being; with her, he could breathe again, he could relax, he could smile.

And now what?

He'd never be able to stay in Grand if he and Leila weren't together. Not now. Not anymore.

But he couldn't let this stand. He had to be vigilant about Miranda, and if Leila couldn't abide by that, he had no choice.

Even his little wilderness garden brought no peace for him. The house was organized now, with no more boxes lining the hall, a few of Leila's framed paintings on the walls, and a general sense of permanence. She had offered to help him repaint the kitchen, but that was over now. Maybe for good.

He couldn't bear to think about it.

Piper was inside, asleep, her ankle bandaged, her hair

matted, her face red and tear-streaked. She'd cried when he told her that Leila wouldn't be visiting for a while. She turned her face away when he said Miranda couldn't visit her, either.

Even his mom had insisted that he listen to Leila, that Miranda had changed.

Was he wrong? He hung his head and raked his hands through his hair.

Years ago, he'd refused to listen to Leila, and his stubbornness had destroyed the future they'd both wanted. Now, he had a second chance and—idiot that he was—he was doing it all again.

But what choice did he have? He would not risk Piper's safety. He wiped his face, feeling moisture in his palm.

"Hey, Sawyer," came a small voice.

He jumped to his feet and whirled around.

Miranda, again. But this time, he had no fight left in him.

"What now? Haven't you done enough?"

She took a step inside the gate and closed it behind her. She stood for a moment next to the fence, rubbing the thumb of one hand. In the dim light, she looked young and small, not someone who had the power to destroy the most important thing in his life.

To his surprise, she gave a light laugh. "You're an idiot, Sawyer."

He took a step backward and watched her warily. "No argument."

Her face grew solemn. The tight, frantic energy he'd seen so often was gone.

"But I'm an idiot too. In fact, the only people who've shown any kind of sense are Piper . . . and Leila."

He felt his skin tighten. "You used her to get to me."

"Because you refused to talk. This doesn't have to be a zero-sum game, Sawyer! Not if we're both looking out for Piper's best interests."

"Don't talk to me about Piper's best interests! Where were you when she had to go to the hospital for ear infections?" Images flew through his head, times when he felt so out of his depth, so completely lost and alone, the only one caring for this child, knowing he had no idea what he was doing. "Where was all this concern when she was biting kids at daycare? Or when she was getting tested for a learning disability? Or ADHD? Or autism? Or when the child psychologist told me that all her problems were linked to attachment disorder because her mother fucking left her alone when she was a baby? Where were you then, huh?"

Miranda's head lowered. She nodded, and he thought he heard her sniff.

"You don't get to cry now, do you hear me?" He felt strangled, like all the fear and rage he'd been carrying for so long was filling his throat and soon he'd be unable to talk, unable to breathe, unable to keep putting one foot in front of the other because it was choking the life out of him.

"You don't get to tell me how to feel, Sawyer. And you don't know what I think."

"I'm afraid for Piper when she's with you. Which is why I can't let that happen."

"I looked after her just fine this afternoon."

"Sure, that's once. Piper must have been so scared."

"She was hurt," Miranda said, "but she wasn't scared. At least, not of me." There was no belligerence in her tone.

He didn't know how to respond.

"She's not afraid of me," Miranda repeated softly, "and that's because of you."

He hadn't been expecting that.

"You had every right to turn her against me, Sawyer, but you didn't. When I was at the park with her and Leila, she was happy to see me. She let me push her on the swings." She took a hitching breath. "She laughed at my dumb jokes and told me my hair was pretty."

She paused to collect herself, then continued, her voice so low Sawyer could hardly hear her.

"She likes me. I don't deserve that."

All the anger went out of him at her words, leaving him feeling empty, a shell echoing only with sadness at the years of unhappiness they'd both experienced.

"I'm sorry," she said. "I should never have made you go through all this."

"It's just a sprained ankle."

"No." She paused. "I mean, the pregnancy. It was my problem."

A bird in the tree above made a trilling sound that cut through the stillness of the evening. Soft wind soughed through the branches, and Sawyer wondered if this was the moment his life would change forever.

He chose his words carefully. "Piper never has and never will be a problem, Miranda."

She nodded quickly, her hair gleaming in the dusky light. "I know. But the guy I was with in Amsterdam was. He was a mistake. He was from Spain, I think. Messed up way worse than me."

The vice around his chest cinched tight, cutting off his breath. "I don't care about that."

"I shouldn't have dragged you into it," she went on.

"Miranda—"

"My parents would have lost their minds if they knew I got pregnant by some stranger in another country."

There it was, out loud, in front of him. His worst fear, the thing that he hadn't realized for far too long, the thing he'd chosen not to see, the one thing he couldn't live with.

"I'm Piper's father." His voice was thin.

"You're a good man, Sawyer. You're so good with her. I'm grateful."

Miranda leaned against the fence, hugging her arms over her body. It was growing cooler.

"Let's go inside," he offered, surprising himself. "You're cold."

But she shook her head. "I only have a few more things to say and I'm afraid if I don't say them now, I'll lose my courage."

"Okay."

There was a tensile quality to the air between them, a thin but powerful thread of connection, like a spider web glistening in the rain, unbroken by a thundering downpour but able to be ruined by a thoughtless hand.

"I knew you were a good guy, Sawyer." She swallowed. "You'd always treated me well and I saw you with other people. You treated everyone with courtesy. You were honest, reliable, but fun too. I was a little bit in love with you, you know."

He lifted his eyebrows. "Miranda."

She shrugged and gave a little laugh. "Enough, anyway, to believe I was doing the right thing. I liked you, so I took you to bed and let you believe it was your baby."

He was having a hard time breathing.

The words landed between them, but instead of the cannon ball he'd always expected, they landed softly, like a white flag.

"I'm so sorry, Sawyer." She was crying softly now. "I thought it wouldn't matter, that I just needed someone to own up, that we'd get a divorce, you'd support us, and we'd be okay. I never expected that you would . . . that you would love her. Especially since I couldn't."

Sawyer hadn't touched his ex-wife in years, but now he found himself standing next to her, pulling her into his arms, holding her as she shook.

Her voice was muffled against his chest. "You made it look so easy, and I hated you for that. She was my baby, not yours, yet the love that came so naturally to you was like a foreign language to me. I don't want to fight anymore, Sawyer. We have to work this out."

He made a soothing sound, but didn't speak, afraid that if he did, he'd stem the flow of honesty. They were on the brink of something huge, like their fraught, messy relationship was on the brink of a metamorphosis.

"I'm sorry for everything I put you through, Sawyer. And even more, I'm sorry for what I put Piper through."

At that, she broke into wracking sobs that brought tears to his own eyes.

"There's one thing you never have to apologize for, Miranda," he said, after a while, once she'd quieted at last.

"Really? What's that?"

He hesitated. Piper had claimed his heart from the moment she drew breath. Whether she stayed with him, or he lost her forever, he needed Miranda to know the depth of his love.

"Piper is the best thing that's ever happened to me. She wasn't what I was expecting at that point in my life, but I love her, Miranda. There's no father in the world who could love her more than I do." He swallowed around the huge lump in his throat. "Wherever we go from here, I'll always be grateful to you forever that you brought her into my life."

Miranda leaned away so she could look up into his face. "Oh, Sawyer. No wonder they love you."

CHAPTER THIRTY-ONE

S AWYER SAT IN his little kitchen, stunned, exhilarated, exhausted. Before Miranda left, she'd pressed an envelope into his hand. On the outside was scrawled the following: This is for Leila, but I want you to read it too. You belong together.

They did belong together.

Only one problem. The way he'd left things with Leila, he'd be lucky if she ever answered a call from him again. The things he'd said . . . yeah, he was filled with regret.

Just like last time.

Last time, he and Leila had been starry-eyed kids, full of themselves, believing they could overcome anything. And they'd been wrong. Love wasn't always enough. There also had to be honesty and trust and patience and maturity and humility . . . the list went on and on.

He'd hurt Leila twice. Badly. In the worst possible way. How could he ever earn her trust again?

Yet, she'd found a way to disarm his strongest opponent. Why?

He peeled the envelope open, pulled out the paper, and began reading.

Dear Leila,

You might not remember this, but I saw you way back when we were all freshmen. You came to visit one weekend and when you got off the bus and you saw Sawyer waiting for you, you ran into his arms and wrapped your legs around his waist. You were laughing, he was laughing, people around you were laughing. It was so clear that you were in love.

I was so jealous.

So later, when I was pregnant and you were broken up, I thought, here's my chance. I thought maybe Sawyer could love me like that too.

Obviously, I was wrong. The only person he loves like that is you. He loves you with his whole heart. He also loves Piper with his whole heart. And he's a good man. (An idiot at times, and I think now is one of them, but I hope you'll be smarter than him.)

So, listen. You've been so kind to me. You've made me believe that I can be a better person. But when I watch you with Piper, I see that I can never be that good. I take my meds. I talk to my counselor. I go to meetings. I'm stable and I hope to stay that way, but Sawyer's right not to trust me. I don't trust myself.

I do trust you.

Which brings me to my point. I never want to lose Piper, but I know I can't look after her the way you and Sawyer can. I see that. I doubt Piper's birth father will ever show up, but with DNA tests, it seems anything is possible these days. I want Piper protected.

I thought of having Sawyer formally adopt her, but because he's already on the birth certificate, it would raise a lot of messy questions I don't want Piper to have to deal with now. Later, when she's older, I trust Sawyer to give her the truth in a way she can handle. He will always be her father.

The best protection for Piper, Leila, is for you to adopt her. I'm asking this of you—or offering it to you, I'm not sure—because of how kindly you've treated me. I see that you love Piper already and you obviously still love Sawyer. This only works if you two are long term, which I hope you are.

But here's my condition: please let me stay in Piper's life. Please let me visit when I'm here. Please allow her to call me Mom, as she always has. I neglected her before, but I never intended to abandon her. I will relinquish my maternal rights if you agree to adopt her and let me stay in her life.

This is the hardest thing I've ever done in my life, but it feels like I'm finally doing something right. I'm going back to California to talk to my lawyer after this, but Sawyer knows how to contact me.

Whatever you decide, Leila, thank you for your kindness to me, to Piper, and to Sawyer.

Miranda

Sawyer's cheeks were wet when he folded the paper up

and put it back inside the envelope. He couldn't believe what he'd just read. He was being offered everything he ever wanted, just when he might have ruined it all.

✪

ON TUESDAY MORNING, he went straight to the pub. Leila wasn't answering his messages, and he couldn't wait around.

"You want Leila?"

Lou looked at Sawyer beneath brows bristling with suspicion.

"If she's around."

To his relief, she came from the back room to meet him at the bar.

"Is everything okay with Piper?" she asked immediately.

"Yes," he replied. He didn't know how to start. "Is there someplace we can go to talk?"

He couldn't read her face. She didn't look mad, nor did she look teary and hopeful, either. She looked . . . resolute. She was right, and she knew it, and she wasn't backing down.

"I want to apologize," he said, once they were seated at a corner table.

She nodded. "Go on."

He thought about the letter in his pocket. He couldn't give it to her the way things were between them right now. She'd immediately agree to Miranda's suggestion, but then he'd always wonder if she was with him for himself, or because it was a way to finally become a wife and mother.

"You were right, Leila. I overreacted."

Again, she nodded.

He rubbed his chin, wishing he had something to do with his hands, wishing he didn't see Lou watching from the bar. "I should have trusted you."

This time, she turned away, the wariness in her eyes replaced with pain. "Yes, you should have," she said quietly.

"And now you don't know if you can trust me."

She was fighting tears now and he hated that he'd done this.

But she held it together. The passionate girl who'd once thrown a ring at his face had turned into a woman who knew her own value and wasn't willing to compromise.

"I know you love your daughter," she said. "But I've come to love her too. You've been doing this alone for so long, you've forgotten that there are other people out there who can be counted on." She paused, took a breath, and continued, "I used to think I was broken, that I had to change to be whatever somebody wanted me to be, that I wasn't good enough as me. But I am enough, Sawyer. I have good instincts, and I took good care of Piper, but you tried to make me doubt myself."

She swallowed.

He reached across for her hand. "I'm so sorry, Leila. I love you. I want to marry you. We can get past this."

She gave him a moment, then withdrew her hand and stood up. "For what it's worth, I love you too. A decade ago, a year ago, even a month ago, those words would have sent me to the moon. But I've heard them before, Sawyer. Now, if you'll excuse me, I have a lot to do today."

★

AT WORK, BAYLEIGH Sutherland observed him for about ten minutes, then waylaid him and finally asked, "What's wrong?"

"What are you talking about?"

Her brows lifted. "I'm a trained therapist, you know. But also, you've been walking in circles."

She led him into the office, and he talked and talked and talked. She listened and asked a few questions.

Finally, he said, "I want to marry her. But I'm not sure she wants to marry me, now."

"Really?"

He made a face. "I think she doesn't believe me anymore."

"Then make her believe."

"How?"

Bayleigh smiled. "You know her best. Figure it out, cowboy. Let me know when congratulations are in order."

He thought about it all day, and on the way home, he realized the truth: the only way to make Leila believe that he wanted to marry her . . . was to marry her.

He called Kendall first.

"You apologize to Leila yet?" she asked.

"I've said the words," he said. "But it's not enough."

He explained what he wanted to do, and to his surprise, Kendall was speechless.

"You and Diana are her best friends," he said. "I can't do it without you."

After Kendall, he called the bakery and ordered a white sheet cake big enough to feed a crowd. Some roses and flourishes or whatever for decoration. He spelled out the words he wanted. It had to be ready by Friday at six. Yes, he'd pay for a rush job.

Then he called Lou. Three men were required for this event, all fathers. He was the first. Lou was the second.

"You're doing what?" Lou said.

"You heard me. I know you don't think much of me, but I love your daughter, and it's time I show her just how much."

Lou was quiet for a few minutes. Then he gave a gruff, deep laugh. "Good for you, son. You're a brave man. If you can pull this off, then you deserve her."

Then he called the third essential man: the priest, Father Patrick, who advised him on getting a marriage license and other necessary paperwork, and what he might want to include in a ceremony.

On Wednesday, he met up with Diana and Kendall at the Wayside Cafe.

"What's next?" Diana asked. "The kids are with my mother-in-law."

They bought their coffees and muffins and settled at a

seat overlooking the boardwalk.

He gave a quick recap of his conversation with Kendall.

"You guys know this," he said, shaking his head. "Leila wanted to get married years ago. We were too young, but I handled it all wrong. Then, you know . . . Miranda. Piper."

"All wrong times a million." Kendall eyed him over her mug. "Except you got a great kid out of it, so fate smiled on you."

"Then when I came back, and we got back together." He hesitated. The feelings were too precious, too intimate, too raw to share, even if he could put them into words. "It was good. Except I was afraid Miranda would challenge custody if I got involved with anyone."

"That's what you thought, anyway," Kendall scoffed.

He tipped his head. "For Piper's sake, I couldn't take the risk." He wasn't about to tell her the ugly truth. "But Leila has worked some kind of magic on Miranda."

Until it was signed, sealed, and delivered, he was afraid to put that magic into words, but he knew deep down it was solid.

"That's fantastic, right?" Diana said, smiling.

"Yes," Sawyer said. "Except for Leila. Between me and—"

"Asshat Gary," Kendall supplied.

"Yeah, him. The two of us have done some damage. I need her to know that I truly want to marry her. That I will marry her."

"Ha," Kendall said. "She's heard that before."

"I know. That's why I'm doing it without telling her. On

Friday."

He waited for his words to sink in.

Diana's reaction was even better than Kendall's; she squealed and clasped her hands in front of her mouth. "A surprise wedding!"

He nodded. "Do you think we can pull it off?"

Diana reached for Kendall's hand. "An actual half sister and a future sister-in-law? Of course we can."

"She's so lucky to have you in her life. And if I'm to have any chance of winning her back, I need you on my side. What do you say?"

Kendall pulled out her tablet. "Fortunately for you, I'm currently immersed in the world of wedding planning."

"Way ahead of you," Sawyer said, taking satisfaction in the surprise on both their faces. "Lou's Pub, white sheet cake, Lou, and Father Patrick."

"You've already arranged all that?" Diana said.

He nodded.

"You assumed we'd give you the green light," Kendall said.

"I was willing to fall on whatever sword was necessary to enlist your help," he admitted. "This is happening. But if she's to have a dress, flowers, and decorations, that's up to you."

They got to their feet. Kendall extended a hand to Sawyer, shook it, then sighed and pulled him into a hug.

"Well done, buddy," she whispered. "Leila's going to love this."

If he wasn't completely mistaken, he saw a tear in her eye.

★

IT WAS ONE of those days, Leila thought as she got ready to head to the gallery on Friday to end her week with an afternoon of talking to tourists. Or not talking to anyone, as the case might be. The season was mostly over, and she'd probably be alone most of the day.

Great. An afternoon of thinking about all the things in her life that had gone wrong lately. Her final project was safely with her advisor, but it had taken several tries to get it off. First, she'd had to reformat her images. Then the email program balked at the size, so she'd had to put them all into a zip file. Then the battery on her laptop died just as she was searching for the power cord, and she'd had to start all over. She'd made the deadline, but only just. The triumph she'd expected to feel was merely relief that the whole thing was done.

She'd successfully identified an early, previously un-known Mel Brezo painting. The artist in question was almost certainly her birth mother, Heather Hudson, though the artist had not yet replied to her queries. Maybe she never would.

Leila had a full brother in Brade Oliver, a twin, in fact, and a younger half sister in Diana, and while they were over the moon at the discovery, all she felt was disappointment in her birth mother.

Heather Hudson had abandoned her, then gone on to live in the same state, without any attempt to contact her.

It hurt. This is what her father had been trying to protect her from. More pain. More rejection.

Rejection that had started with Sawyer, continued with Gary, and then, just in case she'd forgotten how it felt, had come full circle with a too-little-too-late "I love you" from Sawyer.

And where did that leave them? How could she live in Grand, knowing Sawyer and Piper were here, but she couldn't be with them? How could she survive that? He'd apologized, but she could tell that his focus was on how he and Miranda were going to manage whatever new cooperative relationship they were building. He was grateful to her for helping him see a better way. He still loved her and hoped she could forgive him for reacting the way he had.

No *I can't live without you, Leila.*

She could accept taking second place to Piper, but she felt excluded from the little family unit they had with Miranda, and that she couldn't live with. Even though she'd played a role in engineering the détente.

When she got to the gallery, Julia St. James gave her a strange look.

"Leila, honey," she said. "You've been working so hard lately. I'm giving you the day off."

Julia was a wealthy woman and generous, but it would be wasted on Leila right now.

"Thanks, Julia," Leila said. "But it'll be good for me to get back to work, now that I'm finished with my project."

"Well, not off, exactly." She gave Leila an oddly conspiratorial grin. "I'm closing early, and you and I are spending the afternoon at the spa. You completed your degree. That's worthy of celebration, don't you think? We're going to be queens for the day. The full-meal deal. Massage, manis, pedis, facials, hair, the works. And after that, a surprise."

Leila frowned. "What do you mean?"

Julia wrinkled her nose. "Don't tell them I told you, but your friends want to take you out tonight. I think they're worried about you. They asked if I would make sure you were ready at around six."

Leila was touched. "Kendall and Diana?"

Julia nodded. "They really care about you, Leila."

Her heart lifted at the thought of spending time with her pals. Just the three musketeers, together again for a night on the town. Between life, kids, husbands, fiancés, it had been a while since they'd been able to do that.

Leila felt a pang that those weren't her problems. But maybe she was destined to be the favorite aunt, like Kendall.

But Kenny had never wanted to have kids.

Leila always had. Always. A husband, kids. A home and family to look after.

Oh well. What was that old Rolling Stones song? "You Can't Always Get What You Want."

Stupid song.

And so Leila found herself sitting in a comfortable massage recliner, having her feet pampered. It felt pretty good, she had to admit. Someone brought her a glass of iced cucumber water, someone else brought a small plate of dried fruit and nuts.

"Okay," she murmured, closing her eyes. "Queen for the day feels pretty good."

"I told you," Julia responded. "You deserve a day like this."

When they went to the front desk at the end, Julia waved away Leila's attempt to pay for her portion.

"I think your friends are waiting by the fountain," she said. "Have fun tonight, okay?"

And there they were, Kendall and Diana, all dressed to the nines.

"What's this all about?" Leila asked when they handed her a garment bag.

"Girls' night out," Diana said. "We've all earned it, but especially you, sister. It's time to celebrate."

Tears filled her eyes.

"No," Kendall said, giving her a light punch on the shoulder. "No crying. That makeup job is fantastic. We're going to get some great pictures of the three of us and you're not going to wash yours off with tears. Not yet, anyway."

She took the bag back to the changing room and opened it up. To her shock, she found a beautiful, shimmery silver dress that landed just above her knee and clung to her in all the right places. They'd included her best sexy underwear— trust Kendall to sweet-talk Lou into letting her raid Leila's wardrobe before a night like this—that worked perfectly under the dress, and they'd even found her favorite heels.

It was a great outfit and, yes, she had to admit, getting spoiled and dolled up was improving her mood. She wished, just for a moment, that Sawyer could see her.

Then she sighed. She would be happy, anyway, even without him. She'd find a way. Her life was filled with good things and wonderful people, including friends who were also family. Think of that. She had love. And she'd have more love, one day. Maybe even with Sawyer. She just had to trust and let go.

"Well?" she said at the doorway. She gave a twirl.

Diana sucked in a breath and pressed her knuckles to her mouth. "Leila, you look gorgeous!"

"A total babe," Kendall said, giving her a once-over. "Wow, girl, you clean up nice."

"And where are we going for this spectacular, fabulous night on the town?" Leila said, as they walked to Diana's car.

"That," Kendall said, bringing out a scarf, "is a surprise. Turn around."

"What?" Leila said, taking a step back. "What's this all about?"

"Stop arguing and just do what you're told, okay?" Kendall secured the scarf lightly over her eyes. "Don't fight it, or you'll wreck your lashes."

She felt the vehicle begin moving and tried to count the stops, starts, and turns, like you were supposed to do if you were kidnapped. But it soon became apparent that Diana had watched the same *Dateline* episode she had.

"You're going in circles, aren't you?" Leila accused.

Diana laughed. "Wouldn't you like to know?"

Something was up, but Leila had no idea what it was. This was more than a night out to celebrate her completing her program. Why the secrecy?

They lurched to a stop, and suddenly, Kendall was guiding her out of the car.

"Come on," Leila complained. "Surely you can take the blindfold off now."

"Nope. Step lightly, missy," Kendall said.

When they entered the building, Leila was immediately enveloped in the familiar smells of her father's pub.

"Here?" she said, faintly disappointed. She ate here most nights of her life. She'd been looking forward to something new and exciting.

"What do you mean?" Diana said.

"We're at Lou's," Leila said. "Give it up, ladies."

"Not yet," Kendall said. She led Leila inside until they were at what Leila figured was the center of the bar. Then she untied the blindfold.

"Congratulations," Kendall whispered, giving her a hug. Her eyes were shining.

"Love you, sis," Diana added softly on the other side. She was sniffing already.

In mounting confusion, Leila looked around. She wasn't sure what she was seeing.

Lou came to her side. He was wearing a suit. His hair

was smoothed back, and his eyes were shining.

"You look lovely, darlin' daughter." He took her hand. "Walk with me."

Her pulse started thudding in her ears. "What's going on, Daddy?" she whispered.

He began weaving through the crowded bar toward a table by the window on which lay a bouquet of flowers. Outside, she saw more people gathered on the boardwalk. A thought so outrageous as to be insane percolated through her mind. It looked like . . . like . . . like someone was getting married.

"What's happening? Why are all these people looking at me?"

Lou leaned down. "He's finally made good, darlin'. I'm happy for you."

"What—"

"Shush," he said, touching his finger to her nose. "The music's starting."

And it was. "Unforgettable," by Nat King Cole.

Then a man standing near the table turned around.

Sawyer.

In a tux.

Holding his hand out to her. His eyes were shining too.

Behind him, bouncing with delight and clutching at Faith's hand, was Piper, beaming.

CHAPTER THIRTY-TWO

FATHER PATRICK JOINED him next to the table, and Sawyer saw the moment that Leila understood exactly what was happening.

"Welcome everyone," said the minister. "Thank you for joining us this evening to witness the love of these two extraordinary people. This won't take long, by design, and the groom has asked to preface the event with a few words."

He nodded to Sawyer.

This was it. This was his chance to make it all right, finally.

"Leila," he began. His voice was hoarse, so he cleared his throat and began again. "Leila, I've loved you since I was eighteen years old. I've made so many mistakes in between then and now."

That got a small smile from her.

He cleared his throat again. "I'm terrified and winging it, so if I say something stupid, please don't hold it over my head for the rest of my life, okay? Because that's what this is about. You were always meant to be my bride. I lost you once. I won't lose you again. I want to marry you. Right here, right now. I want to spend the rest of my life with you and this time, I'm putting my money where my mouth is."

The people around them disappeared. For the moment, it was only him and Leila, her dark eyes looking into his, with wonder and fear and maybe hope and, hopefully, love.

"Leila," he said. "Time has never been on our side. We've lost too much already, so I'm not about to waste a single minute more. Father Patrick will take care of the rest, but first, I have to ask: Will you marry me? Right now?"

She blinked hard. Something was happening to her throat, like she was trying to swallow but couldn't. Was she going to turn him down? He'd gambled everything on this one last chance. Had he gambled wrong? Was this unexpected audacity, this completely out-of-character spontaneity, wrong?

It was too late now, though.

She was saying something. At least her mouth was moving and then everyone around them was cheering and jumping.

"What?" Panic filled him. Damn it, he'd missed it. What had she said?

"She said yes, Daddy!" Piper yelled. The crowd laughed.

Leila slipped her arms around his neck and kissed him. "Overthinking again, Sawyer?" she murmured. "I said yes."

Then she pulled back and turned to Father Patrick. "Let's get this thing started, shall we?"

★

AFTER THE FINAL toasts were made and the crowd settled into the jovial post-ceremony mood, Sawyer took her aside, an envelope in his hand.

"What's this?" she asked. "I don't know how many more surprises I can take."

"Open it," he said.

The note was from Miranda. Leila scanned the lines with disbelief, then reread them.

She looked up at Sawyer. "Is this for real?"

Sawyer's smile was crooked, and his eyes shone. "You did this, Leila."

"I didn't do anything."

"But you did. You were kind. You saw the elegant solution. You found a way to create a family for Piper that works for all of us."

She shook her head, as more tears sprang to her eyes. "How is this possible? This day is a miracle."

"Miranda trusts you, Leila. In such a short time, she realized that you are the perfect person to help raise Piper. You might not know this," Sawyer continued, "but Miranda knew you were searching for your birth parents. It made a big impression on her. I think she trusts that you'll value the open adoption concept."

"And you're okay with this?" It seemed too good to be true.

"To be honest," he said, "open adoption never crossed my mind until I read Miranda's letter. I'm skeptical about how it'll work, but if she'll agree to let you adopt Piper, how can I argue? And she's promised me that, when the time comes for Piper to learn about her biological father, we will approach it together, you, me, and Miranda. But I will always be Piper's father. And you will be one of her mothers."

Leila thought of Heather Hudson and Angela Monahan. She hoped she'd meet Heather Hudson one day, but even if she didn't, she'd already had one wonderful mother. She still had one wonderful father. And now, she had a husband, a brother, and a sister she never imagined. Soon, she would have a daughter too. She'd always wanted a family, and now she was blessed beyond her wildest dreams.

All she had to do was be patient.

He kissed her, hard, and who knows how long they'd have stood there, if not for a little voice calling them back to reality.

"Daddy?" Piper said, jumping up and down. "Leila's friend Kendall said she's getting me a wedding present! You know what it is? Do you?"

"Uh-oh," Leila said, biting back a smile.

"Leila." He glanced at his new wife. "What did you do?"

"We were visiting Kendall's old house. Piper saw them and fell in love." She grinned innocently. "What was I supposed to do?"

"Oh no," Sawyer said, but his stern tone was ruined by the smile tugging at his mouth.

"I'm getting a puppy, Daddy! It's the best day ever! I'm going to call it Banana Pie and it will be my best friend forever!"

She whirled back to the party.

"A puppy?" Sawyer murmured, pulling her close.

"Every kid needs a dog," Leila said. "Hey, she wanted all four. Be happy we settled on just one."

"You are a force to be reckoned with, Leila Monahan. I'm glad you're on my side."

"Always," she said. "And that's Leila Monahan Lafferty, I'll have you know."

"Come on, Leila Monahan Lafferty," Sawyer said, taking her hand. "We have a lot of friends and family ready to celebrate with us. We finally got our happy ending."

"No," she said, pulling him close for one more quick kiss before they rejoined everyone else. "What we have here, Sawyer, my love, is a happy beginning."

The End

If you enjoyed *The Rancher's Lost Bride*,
you'll love the next books in the...

The Malones of Grand, Montana Series

Book 1: *The Cowboy's Lost Family*

Book 2: *The Rancher's Lost Bride*

Book 3: *The Maverick's Surprise Family*
Coming soon!

Book 4: *The Wrangler's Christmas Gift*
Coming soon!

Available now at your favorite online retailer!

More Books by Roxanne Snopek

The Montana Home series

Book 1: Her Montana Hero

Book 2: A Sweet Montana Christmas

Book 3: The Cowboy Next Door

Book 4: Cinderella's Cowboy

Other titles

A Dog Called Valentine

Love at the Chocolate Shop Series

Book 4: *The Chocolate Cure*

Book 7: *The Chocolate Comeback*

Sweetheart Hunters Series

Book 1: *Shameless Sweetheart*

Book 2: *Forever Yours, Sweetheart*

Available now at your favorite online retailer!

Other Montana Romances by Roxanne Snopek

Wild Sky series

Book 1: *Montana Dawn*

Book 2: *Wild Sky Redemption*

Book 3: *Wild Sky Treasure*

Book 4: *Wild Sky Healing*

Available now at your favorite online retailer!

About the Author

USA TODAY bestselling author Roxanne Snopek writes contemporary romance both sexy and sweet, in small towns, big cities and secluded islands, with families and communities that will warm your heart. Her fictional heroes (like her own real-life hero) are swoon-worthy, uber-responsible, secretly vulnerable and occasionally dough-headed, but animals love them, which makes everything okay. Roxanne writes from British Columbia, Canada, where she is surrounded by wild flowers, wildlife and animals that require regular feeding. She does yoga to stay sane.
It works, mostly.

Thank you for reading

The Rancher's Lost Bride

If you enjoyed this book, you can find more from all our great authors at TulePublishing.com, or from your favorite online retailer.

TULE
PUBLISHING

Made in the USA
Columbia, SC
07 December 2024